I0616043

To Sam and Lucy for putting up with me for this long...

PROLOGUE

"Become a werewolf," they said.

"It'll be fun," they said.

Well, screw them. Because let me tell you, being a werewolf isn't all it's cracked up to be. The drooling and the howling... Not to mention, the itching, the sneezing, the watery eyes—thanks allergies. *Oh yeah*, then there's the whole being *stabbed* part! I mean, not every werewolf gets stabbed. It's not like there's some sort of hazing that requires someone shank you. But it *did* happen to me. And boy does it suck. Especially when your attacker uses a silver blade, which we're deathly allergic to. Chocolate, too. But that's a whole other can of worms that chaps my furry little ass.

Two years ago, I hadn't even known werewolves

existed, let alone suspected I'd soon become one. And now... Now I turn into a wolf who's allergic to herself. Because that's super fun.

Even worse, there's a lunatic out there attacking and turning innocent human-borns. And guess what? It's all because of me. All because I was the first human-born to be changed, showing others it's possible. So, now it's my responsibility to help clean up this little fiasco.

At least I don't have to handle any of this alone. I have Sam at my side. Together, we can do this. Put Corbin down like the dirty dog he is, and save the other human-borns from sharing my fate. Of course, I've been wrong before, so what do I know?

I'll tell you what I *do* know.

Reggie is dead—*vive le sperm donor*—and I'm now the alpha of the Mississippi Pack. Thanks, Reggie, you dick. Even in death, he's screwing me over. I never asked to be made alpha, but according to werewolf law, I have no choice, since I was Reggie's heir. That I'd refused the role means nothing to the pack, seeing as how Reggie never told them. Again, thank you, you dillweed. Yeah, yeah, I shouldn't speak ill of the dead. But you know what, he was a douche. Dying doesn't change that.

I also know that Sam's father—the New Orleans

alpha—wants me to choose a replacement. I just need to actually pick someone. Someone smart, capable, and strong. So, that's what we're doing. All while chasing down Corbin and shoving a spiked stick up his ass. Yeah, Vlad might have rubbed off on me a little. But hey, whatever gets results.

After all this, Sam and I can go home and finally start living our happily-ever-after.

Yeah, right. And pigs can fly.

CHAPTER
ONE

"High kick!" Anna shouted at me, arms crossed over her chest as she surveyed my technique with a keen eye.

I executed the movement with... well, about as much precision as I could muster after only five weeks of practice. I mean, it took a hell of a lot longer than that to master any form of martial arts. But hey, I was trying. Trying and only semi-failing, which I considered a win. Gotta look on the positive side of things, right?

"Front kick!" she ordered, her head cocking to the side as she studied my transition.

I snapped out my leg, wholly unprepared when Anna grabbed my ankle and twisted, throwing me off balance. Gasping, I rotated with her, then wrenched my leg back and returned to the ready stance—arms held in front of my body, fists clenched, legs straight, and feet shoulder-width apart.

Her mouth briefly curled upward, clearly impressed I'd managed to maintain balance.

"Side kick," she pressed.

Hardly missing a beat, I leaned to the side and implemented the attack with as much force as I could muster. My muscles practically begged for release, my brow beaded with sweat. We'd been at it for a few hours. But time truly meant nothing to immortals. I, however, was far from immortal, and my battered body begged for a break. Not that Anna would give me one.

"Good, Lucy," she praised, her face smoothing into a pleased grin. "You've improved so much."

I beamed at her, then righted my position.

It'd been nearly two months since that douchenozzle Corbin had stabbed me. The first two weeks had been the absolute worst. Helpless and slow, I hadn't been able to do anything for myself. Thank god for Sam and Anna. They'd pampered me like a princess, offering only kind words, even when I did nothing but whine about how the painkillers weren't working. Apparently, we werewolves metabolize drugs too quickly for them to be effective. So... yeah. Loads of fun.

Once I'd finally healed, Anna had taken it upon herself to teach me all the lessons Camilla had imparted upon her—with moderation, of course. Since I wasn't a vampire, I didn't heal quite the same. Camilla had been a brutal teacher, repetitively breaking every bone in Anna's body until she learned how to fight back. Luckily for me, Anna had adopted a far gentler approach. One that didn't leave me a weeping, broken mess.

"I know we've been working on the roundhouse, but you haven't been very successful with that one," Anna said, distracting me from my thoughts.

My mind jumped to the last time we'd attempted that particular move. I'd nearly broken my foot on Sam's chest. Anna had wanted me to land the kick just a smidgen higher—i.e. his head. But my mate was a brute of a man. A giant. A lumberjack, as Anna oft called him. We'd quickly learned I couldn't even get my leg that high, yoga be damned.

"Do you want to give it another shot?" she asked.

"Yes, Sensei," I said with a wink.

I steadied my body and focused. Usually Sam helped me train in some capacity, but he was currently in New Orleans, assisting his father with some pack business.

Anna assumed a defensive position, her eyes narrowing on me. "I'll buy you Starbucks for the next month if you nail this kick."

Oh, motivation! I certainly loved me some Starbucks.

With a creamy, vanilla Frappuccino now consuming my thoughts, I drew my knee into the chamber position, then struck.

Anna's arms blocked the blow, as they were supposed to, but she was grinning ear to ear as we both straightened. "Great job!"

Laughing, I shook out my whole body, then stripped off my shirt and used it to mop up the sweat beading my skin. I adjusted the straps of my sports bra, then moved into some fluid stretches. My muscles slackened, and I nearly moaned.

"Guess I'm buying your coffees for the next month."

"Darn straight! I would have taken you out if that kick had connected."

Anna chuckled. "Don't get too ahead of yourself. Real fights are nothing like this. But you really are doing amazing. In fact, you might need to find an actual class soon since I don't think I have anything more to teach you."

I perked up. "Really?"

"Well, I didn't get much training from Camilla before she passed," Anna said, the light in her eyes dimming. "Just the basics, really. Which I've now taught you. But if you're hoping to truly get good at this, you need a more experienced instructor."

My mouth pursed. "I don't think that's gonna be an option." Young werewolves weren't even allowed to partake in school sports due to our increased speed, strength, and healing. I couldn't imagine taking a martial arts class with a bunch of humans. How would I explain my abilities?

"Yeah..." Anna rubbed her mouth and nodded. "And we can't ask your pack for help. You can't look weak in front of them."

This time, I nodded. Werewolves were a judgy sorta bunch. They *knew* I was untrained and unfit to be their alpha. But if I paraded it around in front of them, they would challenge me for control of the pack. Werewolves *loved* fighting for dominance, if only to prove who had the bigger teeth. I was already at a disadvantage, seeing as how I was technically human-born and completely unprepared for this role. But I needed to present a strong persona. In the meantime, I also needed to prepare for the inevitable challenges I knew would come my way.

The only reason that hadn't happened yet was because of *The Code*—something I'd only recently learned about. *The Code* stated that any gravely injured alpha must be given two moon cycles to heal before any other pack member could challenge them. It was the only way to protect alphas from being slaughtered while in a vulnerable state. Prior to this law's creation, less powerful werewolves would challenge an injured alpha in order to take over the pack. That, in turn, had led to utter chaos. A weak alpha had no idea how to hold a pack together.

I only had seven days left until *The Code* no longer protected me. And I had no doubts someone from the pack would challenge me. Quite a few had expressed their animosity toward me. Which meant I needed to perfect my fighting skills—and *fast*—seeing as how all dominance fights were to the death. Why it couldn't be a submission-based fight, I had no idea. But all this only left me with one course of action: choose a successor and step down, all within the next week. A nice, practical, *safe* way of doing things.

Sadly, I hadn't found a suitable successor yet. So, here I stood. Trapped in a role I didn't want, learning to fight for my life, in case I failed to find a replacement.

"What about Sam's pack?" Anna asked, drawing me back into the conversation. "Maybe his father could help? Adrien sounds like a really good alpha."

I bit the inside of my lip and contemplated her suggestion. Adrien was a fantastic alpha. He cared about his people, adored his family, and had welcomed me with open arms. But now wasn't the time to burden him—or his family—further. The last two months had been hard on them too, considering one of Sam's little sisters had recently been murdered. They also had two new human-born-turned-werewolf pack members to train. Much like me, Sam's family had their hands full.

It went deeper than that, though. *I* was the Mississippi alpha now. I couldn't run to Adrien for help anymore. I needed to be able to stand on my own two feet—at least until I stepped down.

"No," I said, shaking my head. "I need to do this. I can't hide behind another alpha."

"What about Sam?"

A smile spread across my face when I thought of my mate. "He's been helping me as much as he can, teaching me how to be an alpha. But he's afraid to fight me." I chuckled. "Afraid he'll hurt me."

Anna snickered. "Okay. Then either you attend a human class and figure out how to pull your punches, or..." A wicked grin lit her face. A grin I didn't trust. I'd known this woman my whole life. She was my ride or die. That grin spelled trouble, and usually, I paid the price.

Giggling to herself, Anna practically skipped to the side of the room and grabbed her phone from the nearest table. She quickly punched in a number, then lifted the phone to her ear, still grinning. Oh yeah, I was completely screwed. Whatever plan she had brewing in that head of hers, it wouldn't be good.

When Vlad's voice rumbled across the line, I sighed. Anna immediately insisted he head to Jackson tonight. According to her, I needed to face a real challenge, one that came in the form of a five-hundred-year-old vampire. Like I said, I always paid the price for her little schemes. Vlad wouldn't go gentle on me either, not like he would if he was teaching Anna. I predicted torn muscles and a few broken bones.

With a small whimper, I wiped the sweat from my brow, then slipped out of the room, leaving Anna and Vlad to their conversation. It'd taken a sickeningly sweet turn, one that made me miss Sam. I didn't begrudge them, though. After Sam told her

I'd been stabbed, Anna had returned from her honeymoon and set out for Jackson. She'd officially named herself my protector and set up camp outside my bedroom door while I healed. Every night, she played the role of my personal bodyguard. She hadn't left Jackson since. I had to imagine she and Vlad were missing each other something fierce right now.

I hoofed it upstairs, then jerked to a stop.

Standing in the middle of the living room was Cole—my second in command.

"What the hell!" I shouted. "Don't you knock?"

He shrugged. "Never used to with Reginald."

"Well, I'm not Reggie," I growled. "And this is my home now." Compliments of Reggie's will. He'd not only left me the pack, but all his earthly possessions too. Including this house.

Cole ignored me and instead strode into the kitchen. Clenching my jaw, I counted to ten in my head, then jolted when I caught the sound of running water. What the hell was he doing in there? Maybe I could convince him to do my dishes while he was in there. Call it a perk of being the alpha.

When he finally popped back into the living room, he had a glass of water in hand. At first, I wondered if he intended to drink it in front of me but instead, he handed the glass to me.

"You looked thirsty," he said, his gaze locked on the bridge of my nose.

Ugh. I hated that. Somewhere, someone had written that those ranked lower than the alpha weren't allowed to stare into the alpha's eyes. *Why* someone had found that important enough to make it into a rule, I had no idea. As humans, we're taught that eye contact is pivotal. Polite, even. Ever had someone stare at your forehead while speaking to you? Pure awkwardness.

"Thanks," I said, reaching for the glass.

I had to admit, I was a bit parched, thanks to Anna's *Buns of Bronze* workout upstairs. I lifted the glass to my lips and slurped down a few gulps, all the while pondering Cole's intentions. While he hadn't been outwardly rude to me during my time here, he also hadn't welcomed me openly into the pack. Yet, here he stood, hydrating me.

These sorts of questions was why I was always exhausted. It sucked having to constantly wonder about people's objectives.

I placed the half-empty glass down on the dining room table, then made my way into the living room and sat on the couch. Only when I was comfortable did I gesture for him to have a seat.

He eased into the rocking chair across from me, his hands gripping the armrests.

"Alright. What do you want?" I demanded.

Cole's mouth crooked up at the sides. He leaned back in the rocking chair and studied me. After an uncomfortably long silence, he lifted one leg and rested his ankle against his knee.

"Comfortable?" I asked with a raised brow.

"Quite. Thanks."

My mouth quirked. The man enjoyed pushing buttons, and part of the fun, I suspected, was sussing out which actions pushed *mine*. It'd take more than crossing his damn legs to set me off. Instead, I leaned back and mimicked his position. "Care to tell me what this little visit of yours is about?"

"I've recently learned that Marcus and Bryn both intend to challenge you this upcoming moon."

And there it was. *Kaboom*. The bomb I'd been waiting to drop.

My hand instinctively moved to my bare, sweaty stomach, and my fingers brushed the three-inch scar marring my skin. Thankfully, the wound had long since healed, but in moments like these, I could still feel the blade embedded in my flesh—a sensation I'd never forget.

"Thank you for the warning," I said, my fingers reflexively twitching against my stomach. "But why bother?"

"Bother?" His brows slowly rose.

"Why bother telling me?"

"I'm your second. It's my job."

I considered his response with a wry stare. Cole *was* my second, yes, but I didn't get the feeling he was happy with my presence here. Interestingly, he hadn't mentioned challenging me himself. Did he not intend to? He was second in command, after all. Surely, the pack would gladly accept him as their new alpha. What sort of game was he playing?

For many werewolves—Reggie included—legacy meant everything. When he'd learned that one of his many, *many* abandoned human-born children had become a werewolf, he'd leaped at the opportunity to claim me. He'd even gone so far as to name me his heir without informing me. When I found out, I demanded he demote me, but he'd conveniently forgotten. Then Corbin had murdered him, and bingo, bango, boom, here I was. The Alpha of the Mississippi Pack. I hadn't earned the position, so many in the pack were slightly bitter about it.

"Well, thanks for the warning," I said. I'd been expecting a few challenges, but Marcus and Bryn hadn't registered in my mind. Truthfully, I couldn't even remember who they were. Even though I'd spent a year with the pack, I hadn't involved myself with them. I'd been more concerned with mourning the loss of my human life than integrating myself into Reggie's pack.

Cole rumbled out a deep laugh. "You don't even know who they are, do you?"

Shit. Was I that easy to read? Probably something I needed to work on.

"Bryn was your father's latest..." He waved a hand in the air.

"Piece of ass? Side piece? Paramour?" I finished. "And he isn't—wasn't—my *father*."

Cole only shook his head. "I would say girlfriend, but Reginald didn't do girlfriends."

No, he certainly didn't. He'd been more about lying to women to bed them, knocking them up, then bailing when the child was born fully human. A real piece of work. Believe me, there was a reason I wasn't mourning his loss.

"Anyway, she's been a bit riled up since the will reading," Cole continued.

Aha. Now I remembered her. The one who'd

lashed out at me, claiming I didn't deserve anything Reggie had left me. I hadn't realized she was his girlfriend. I'd just assumed she was a disgruntled pack member.

"And Marcus is just a prick," Cole finished. "He thinks he's strong enough to hold the pack together, but he isn't."

That made me blink. Insulting his own pack member? Interesting. It also brought up an intriguing thought. Was Cole trying to side with me? Possibly vying for the role of successor? I'd considered him at first. He seemed capable enough. But when a squabble had broken out among a couple pack members at Reggie's funeral, Cole hadn't done anything to take control of the situation. He'd shown no leadership skills whatsoever. I was looking for someone strong and capable. Someone like Adrien, with wonderful ideals and methods. That moment at the funeral had shown me Cole wasn't right for the job.

"Don't concern yourself with Marcus too much," Cole stated. "But Bryn is a beast, and she'll take your head clean off the first chance she gets."

Wonderful.

Did I mention how much I hated being the alpha? A part of me just wanted to pick a random wolf and name him the successor. But then I remembered what Adrien had told me. That I had to pick someone worthy, so that the Mississippi Pack never became a threat to the New Orleans one.

"Thanks for the advice. I'll take it under consideration."

A sly smile tugged at Cole's lips. Maybe he *could* read me that easily. If so, I needed develop a poker face or something.

"If you'll excuse me." I rose and waited for Cole to do the same.

He didn't so much as twitch. I lifted a brow and stared down at him. Did he have something more to say?

Eventually, he flattened his palms on the armrests and slowly pushed to his feet.

"If you really want to win these fights, you'll need more training than what your vampire friend has taught you."

I jerked, my eyes narrowing. "Excuse me?"

Cole shrugged, then picked a bit of lint off his shirt. "Your friend might be strong, but Bryn and Marcus are stronger. You need to learn how to fight like a werewolf. It's not as simple as throwing a few punches." He stepped forward. "I can help you with that."

I almost burst out laughing. Cole didn't know anything if he thought Bryn and Marcus were stronger than Anna. I'd been there in England with Anna and Vlad. I'd seen what those two bloodsuckers could do. Seen the things they'd faced and survived.

But that didn't mean I couldn't take Cole's offer seriously.

Because he was right about one thing—I *did* need to learn how to fight like a werewolf. Before returning to Jackson, I'd witnessed the nastiest brawl between Corbin and Sam. It'd been brutal and deadly. Nothing like the controlled spars Anna and I had engaged in. I'd known that since the beginning, but hadn't been able to find a solution to the problem. It wasn't like I knew of anyone here who would be willing to train me.

Until now.

Cole's offer raised questions, though.

"Why?" I demanded. "Why help me?"

His expression flickered. "Bryn and Marcus are useless. She's ranked seventh in the pack, he's ranked ninth. Given that you never spent any time with us before all this, we have no idea where you would have naturally fallen. However, I believe you'd make a better alpha than either of them. The pack is my family. I would hate to have one of them in charge. They'd ruin us."

That he didn't think *I'd* ruin the pack spoke volumes.

"If you're interested, meet me at my place tomorrow at nine a.m." And on that note, Cole left, leaving me to mull over everything he'd said.

Anna herself had suggested I find a more experienced trainer. I certainly couldn't rely on a human instructor. Which left me few choices. Only one, in fact.

Welp, guess this was happening. Lucky me?

CHAPTER
TWO

"What did Wolf Boy want?" Anna asked.

I turned at the sound of her voice, in time to watch her pocket her phone. She came to a stop beside me, her gaze locked on the door as though she expected Cole to burst through and start throwing punches.

"He came to warn me that two of my pack members are planning on challenging me at the next full moon."

Anna's eyes widened, and she swung toward me, alarm flashing across her face. "And that's when?"

"In a week," I reminded her. Vampires weren't as connected to the moon as we were.

She gave a low whistle, the skin at the corners of her eyes crinkling with worry. "Okay. A week. We

23

can handle that, right? You ready to kick a little werewolf ass?"

I considered her question. Thanks to Cole's assessment, I didn't feel remotely ready anymore.

When I didn't respond, Anna's frown deepened. "What's wrong? You've been working hard at this. You've *got* this."

My teeth scraped across my bottom lip. The more I thought about it, the more I realized Cole was right. I would remember that fight between Sam and Corbin for the rest of my life. The terror I'd felt wouldn't let me forget. If that was what awaited me... I released a slow breath and tried to calm my nerves.

Bryn and Marcus were werewolf-born. Meaning, they were experts in all things werewolf, including fighting. I'd been training for five weeks. That wasn't enough time. Sure, I could probably defend myself, but to go on the offensive? To kill someone? Was I strong enough—or even *ready*—for that?

I was still figuring all that out. I'd only shifted maybe half a dozen times since I'd been turned. It was no wonder the pack didn't want me as their alpha—I was a pup compared to them. Literally.

And I was someone their former alpha had forced upon them. They hadn't chosen me—hell, they didn't even know me. They likely felt like they were doing their pack a service by challenging me for control. I was an outsider. Perhaps if I named a successor before next week, they wouldn't feel the need to challenge me?

"Luce?" Anna waved a hand in front of my face. "Earth to Luce."

I blinked, my focus returning to the present.

"You spaced out there," she said. "Wanna share with the class what's going on in that head of yours?"

I flopped back onto the couch and slumped against the cushions, cursing my existence. "Cole claims that what you've taught me won't be enough. He wants to take over training me and asked me to meet with him tomorrow morning."

It wasn't often I saw Anna flabbergasted, but there she stood, as silent as the grave, her mouth gaping open. It almost made me laugh. If I could still take pictures of her, this would be one I framed.

After a few moments, Anna collected herself and gave her head a slight shake, her blonde hair spilling around her shoulders. "You said no, right?"

I didn't answer. Wasn't she the one that had urged me to seek additional training?

Anna blinked at me, then unleashed a condescending laugh. Her fangs flashed in the dim living room light—another stark reminder of how much our lives had changed. To think that two years ago, we'd been little more than struggling humans trying to find their way in life. Now, Anna was a rich socialite vampire married to Dracula himself, and I was a mated alpha werewolf. In a million years, I never would have thought this would become our lives.

"Luce, no. You can*not* agree to this. Call Cole up and tell him there's no way in hell you're meeting with him tomorrow," Anna said.

"Why not?"

"Why not?" she repeated, her voice jumping an octave. "Gee, let me list the reasons. We don't *know* him. We don't *trust* him. He's part of the *same* pack that wants you dead. Are those enough reasons?"

I lifted my hand and started flicked up a finger. "One, I *do* know him. Sort of. I spent a year here, remember?" I lifted a second finger. "Two, I *do* trust him. Sort of. He made some good points." And then a third finger. "Three, I don't think the *entire* wants me dead, per se. Just two."

An animalistic growl tore free of Anna. "You can't be serious. You barely got to know anyone in the pack while you were here. You don't actually know the first thing about him!"

True. "Anna, he's right. I need help. As much as

I can get. And if he can teach me how to fight werewolves, then I need to go. Don't forget, I'm protected by *The Code* for another week. Technically, Cole can't kill me, not without facing repercussions."

Anna slowly crossed the room, then dropped into the rocking chair across from me, her expression inscrutable. "And you believe him? That he wants to help you?" she asked, her voice quiet and contemplative.

"I do," I said.

She nodded, then leaned back in the chair and scrubbed a hand down her face. "I don't know what to make of any of this. But I will say, I don't understand werewolf politics and rules. Now vampires, I get."

I laughed. "Because every vampire's number one rule is look out for themselves."

She cracked a smile. "True. We're a bit of a selfish breed. It's me and Vlad against the world. But you guys..." She shook her head. "So many rules and mind games." Then her expression twisted. "Sam is gonna shit a brick when he finds out about all this."

I winced. "Yeah, most likely." He'd been a bit protective since my stabbing. When his father asked him to come home to help train their two new pack members, Sam had adamantly refused. But refusing an alpha was bad news bears. It just didn't happen. I'd insisted he go, so as to not create any problems with his pack and family, but he hadn't easily relented. It'd taken a lot of promises on my end to be careful and keep Anna at my side at all times before he'd finally agreed to leave. I didn't begrudge him, though. If he'd been the one stabbed, I would have reacted similarly.

"You're going to do this then?" Anna asked. "Meet with Cole tomorrow morning?"

I leaned forward on the couch and braced my elbows against my knees, considering her question. I hadn't been given much time to weigh all my options yet, but I was leaning heavily toward yes. "Here's the thing. Bryn and Marcus aren't my only problems."

Anna groaned. "Corbin."

"Corbin," I confirmed, my gut clenching the instant I spoke his name. "The night he stabbed me..." I shook my head. "He and Sam were like two rabid wolves, ripping and tearing into each other. I saw their fight. Saw how brutal and bloody it was. If that's what awaits me..."

Anna paled—a neat trick for a vampire.

"Do you remember when Sam killed Petrik?"

Her face twisted with disgust, an expression I

was intimately familiar with. She had her demons and I had mine. Petrik had been a thousand-year-old vampire who'd tried to kill Anna more than once.

"How could I forget?" she said.

That'd been a horrific day. When Sam and I stormed the mausoleum to find Anna nearly burned alive... The memory still played a horrible role in my nightmares.

I pushed away the images and focused on the most important part. "Do you remember how easily Sam took Petrik down? Sam stabbed him with a stake, and poof, he was dead."

"Yeah, so?"

"So, Petrik was a thousand years old. Corbin is a baby compared to that. And Sam wasn't able to take Corbin out. He nearly lost the fight."

Anna winced. "Corbin's that strong?"

"Guess so. And if that's what awaits me..." I sighed.

"Jesus," Anna whispered, collapsing back into her chair. "If that's the case—"

"Then I need to learn how to fight werewolf-style," I said, "and I only have a week to do it. Even if I find a way to keep Marcus and Bryn from challenging me, I still have the whole Corbin mess to deal with. And that bastard needs to pay for everything he's done. Preferably by my own hand."

Anna gave a slow nod, her gaze distant as she considered everything. I really didn't have any other options. It didn't seem wise to reject *anyone's* offer of help at this point. No matter how it made me look. I couldn't be so prideful as to handicap myself.

"I need to prepare," I told her. "And if Cole can help, then maybe he's someone I need in my corner. It sounds like he believes I could be a good alpha."

"But you don't want to be alpha," Anna reminded me.

"No, I don't. I want to go home with you and Sam. To New Orleans. But to do that, I need to name a successor."

"Then just choose one so we can go home already," Anna said. "It sounds like naming a successor would solve all your problems."

"It would, except for one big problem."

"Corbin," she muttered again.

I nodded. "If I name a successor, then I have to step down. And if I step down, I have to go home. If I go home..."

"You can't deal with Corbin."

I nodded again. "Territories are serious business among packs. You weren't there when Cole and a few members came to collect me in New Orleans. Adrien was pissed. They take breaches in territory almost personal. The second I step down, everything will change. The new alpha will cast me out of Mississippi. Not only would I be a threat to their image within the pack, but they'd likely refuse me permission to handle Corbin. That'd become their job. Handing it to me wouldn't strengthen their position with the pack. I can't let that happen. I can't just hand Corbin over to someone else. He's my responsibility. After everything he's done, I owe him pain."

Anna groaned and flopped back in the chair. "This is insane. You're talking fighting these two werewolves *to the death* all so you can stay in Mississippi and track Corbin down. You realize that won't even be possible if Marcus or Bryn win the fight?"

I winced at her bluntness. "I'm hoping I can convince them not to challenge me."

She frowned. "What? How?"

"I don't know yet." I gave a weak laugh. "But I'll think of something. Maybe just reassuring them that I plan to choose a successor after Corbin is handled will be enough to keep them from challenging me."

"Or maybe they won't give a shit about any of that."

"Maybe. I have to try though."

"Why?" Anna asked. "Why can't you just let this go? Let someone else handle Corbin. It doesn't *have* to be you."

Yes, it did. After everything—yes. It did.

"I get it now," I told her. "Why *you* had to be the one to go after Petrik after he tried killing you."

"Yeah, and look where it got me," she groused. "Charged with murder, and imprisoned in the Vampire Queen's dungeon for six months. I don't want that happening to you."

"There's no Werewolf Queen to imprison me," I teased.

Anna rolled her eyes. "Ha, ha. You know what I mean." After a moment's pause, she straightened in the chair, her intense stare boring into me. "Luce, you know I'm here for you. You're my *bish*. I would never abandon you. I just want you to be careful. Okay?"

"I know," I said. "Trust me. I don't want anything to happen to me either."

Her mouth curled into a small smile. "So you'll train with Cole then, instead of Vlad?"

I nodded.

"Fine. But you're missing out. Vlad makes for one sexy warrior. I'm not sure which I prefer more. Warrior mode or when he's naked. Or both..." Her gaze turned dreamy. "Definitely both. A naked warrior."

"Ew, Anna," I said, laughing. "Keep your grody fantasies to yourself. I don't want to know about your guys' creepy little sex games."

Anna scoffed, then chucked a pillow at my face. A year ago, that might have taken me out, my human reflexes too slow to counter the attack. Now? I snatched that fluffy bad boy out of the air and whipped it back at her, laughing when it smacked her right in the nose.

Grumbling, Anna stuffed the pillow under her thigh, then glanced at the clock, her expression brightening. I bit back a laugh. Clearly, someone was anxious for Vlad's arrival. Not that I blamed her. Sam had been back and forth to New Orleans over the past five weeks, and each time he left was harder than the last. He'd only been gone a week so far this time, and I desperately missed him. I couldn't imagine being parted from him for as long as Vlad and Anna had been. I wanted him *here* where he belonged. With me.

"I'm going to go for a bath," Anna said.

I almost snickered. Trust her to take a bath after thinking about her naked husband. "Okay. I'm gonna call it a night. If Cole's whooping my ass tomorrow, I'll need all the rest I can get."

"Good idea." Anna pushed to her feet but paused to stare down at me. "You sure you'll be okay tomorrow? I won't be able to go with you."

I nodded. It would be our first time apart in seven weeks. If anything, I was looking forward to it. I wasn't used to spending every minute with her anymore. And since she woke earlier than the sun set, we were often trapped together in the house until it was safe for her to go out.

"I'll be fine. And say hi to Vlad for me when he arrives. I guess I'll see him tomorrow night."

"If you're still alive tomorrow night," she teased.

"Thank you so much." I chuckled.

"Just keeping things real," she said, laughing. "Don't let Cole kick your ass too badly."

After blowing me a kiss, Anna disappeared in the house, though I quickly heard the water running. I stood in the middle of the living room and took stock of everything. It still felt like Reggie's place, not mine. In all the excitement, I hadn't found the time— nor energy—to redecorate.

I enjoyed the silence for a few more minutes,

then dialed Sam's number. My pulse jumped every time it rang, but sadly, he never picked up. My heart dropped like a stone as I disconnected the call. Man, I missed him, and would give anything to see him walk through that door right this second. It didn't budge. Because of course not. He was in New Orleans, with his family and his pack. And I was here, in Jackson.

Sighing, I pocketed my phone, then headed to bed. My body yearned to relax, and my brain needed a good night's sleep. Tonight, I intended to turn everything off and just rest. For one night, I didn't want to think of dominance fights, pack business, or Corbin. I just wanted to bundle myself up and float in a sea of blankets. And that was exactly what I did.

CHAPTER
THREE

THE NEXT MORNING, I STOOD IN FRONT OF Cole's antebellum house and steeled my nerves. I couldn't show how anxious this all made me, couldn't let him see my half-bitten nails and frayed hair, so I needed to button it all down right now.

It didn't help that I'd barely slept last night. I'd been determined to shut off my brain and rest, but my mind had refused to focus on anything other than the developing situation. *Seven days* had kept flashing in my mind's eye, like a bomb ticking down.

Now, it was six. Six days to learn how to fight werewolves. I was so screwed.

Anna and Vlad's reunion also hadn't helped me sleep. They'd assumed I was asleep and had indulged in a little fun of their own. The sort that continued to echo in my head even this morning. I'd let them be, knowing it'd been nearly two months since the newlywed couple had seen each other, but I'd heard things last night. Things I'd never forget. Things that even right now, made me shudder and curse my werewolf hearing.

The front door swung open, and an imposing figure stood in the doorway.

I gulped and stared up at him, wondering if this was the morning I died.

Under *The Code*, Cole couldn't kill me. I just had to keep reminding myself of that. But lots of people did illegal things, so... where did that leave us?

"You coming in or what?" he asked, his voice gruff.

Guess he wasn't a morning person. That made two of us.

"Just debating my options," I called up to him.

Cole sighed, a deep sound that rattled my bones, then he turned and strode inside, leaving his door wide open. The message was clear. *Stay or go, but don't expect me to hold your hand.* Good. I didn't want him holding my hand. I didn't want him—or anyone else—coddling me. I needed to be able to stand on my own two feet, needed to be able to defend myself. If that meant letting him beat the snot out of me, so be it. Not that I *wanted* that.

Maybe I should have said no to this. Maybe I should have tried harder to reach Sam. I could have called again. Could have kept trying. It wasn't that I enjoyed keeping secrets from him. I just didn't know how he'd handle all this. Or rather, I did, and didn't want to face his reaction. He didn't even know I was here. Man, he was going to lose his mind when he found out. But this hadn't felt like something I should text him. No, this felt more like a face-to-face conversation.

Or so I kept telling myself.

All right. Time to do this. Just suck it up and get in there. Take the beating, learn from it, then use those lessons to beat submission into Bryn and Marcus. And Corbin too. Couldn't forget him in all this.

I climbed the first step, then the second, my breath quickening with each passing second. If I wasn't mistaken, I was heading right toward a panic attack, and I refused to let that happen. Alphas didn't have panic attacks. We caused them.

Yeah, right.

At the top of the stairs, I drew a deep breath and squared my shoulders.

You can do this. You can do this. You can—

"Hurry up and get in here. You're letting the air out."

I entered his air-conditioned house and slowly closed the door behind me. The cool air enveloped me, and I released a long sigh. It was only spring, but it was quickly growing uncomfortably warm. Another month and it'd be stifling.

"Leave your shoes on," Cole called out.

I turned in the direction of his voice and found him standing in his kitchen, preparing a mug of tea. The sight reassured me and brought a smile to my lips. If he meant for us to drink tea, he couldn't be planning to whoop my ass too badly. Right?

Once he'd finished pouring the tea, he turned and pointed toward a staircase. "Everything's upstairs and ready for us."

I nodded, then ascended, wondering what could possibly be up here. From the looks of it, I wasn't getting a tour, so clearly he had a destination in mind.

When I reached the top, I froze.

The entire upper floor had been revamped into what looked like an indoor gym. A treadmill, elliptical, and row machine graced the back of the room. In the middle hung a punching bag, and next to it one of those rubber dudes people liked to smack the heck out of. I couldn't remember the name. Then, closest to the stairs, was a small boxing ring.

My heart plummeted at the sight. Somehow, I just knew I'd end up in there today.

Who was the tea for then? Or was it just to taunt me with pleasantries?

Cole brushed past me and stepped into his man-gym, placing the tea down on a small table near the back window.

I followed him and came to a stop by the punching bag. "So... this looks fun."

Cole shot me a look over his shoulder and grinned. "This is where you'll learn to fight properly."

Yeah, I kinda figured. And damn, I so wasn't prepared. My body ached just thinking about all this, and we hadn't even done anything yet. I groaned, already anticipating tomorrow's aches and pains.

"We're going to start by reviewing what your vamp friend taught you."

"Her name is Anna," I bit out. If he was going to beat the ever-loving hell out of me, the least he could do was learn her name.

"Fine. Anna." He shrugged. I had a feeling he didn't care much for vamps. "We'll review what she taught you and go from there." Cole picked up his tea, then turned to face me and leaned against the wall. He lifted the mug to his lips and took a long sip. "So, let's get started."

I lifted a brow.

"Show me what she taught you. You were doing some kicks yesterday when I dropped by."

Heat flushed my cheeks when I realized he wanted me to demonstrate everything. How embarrassing. With Anna, it'd felt natural because she'd been the one teaching me. But with Cole, it felt more like a performance, and he was here to grade me.

"Come on," Cole barked. "Do you want to learn to fight or not?"

My lip curled up, disliking the tone of his voice. He might be teaching me something, but I was still his alpha.

He waved a hand in my direction. "Proceed."

Proceed. I sneered again. As though he was giving me permission.

He was right, though. I was here to learn. And he couldn't teach me without seeing how much I already knew.

Closing my eyes, I drifted back into Anna's lessons and let my body do the rest. Five weeks wasn't a lot of time, but my body had developed some muscle memory. Enough so that I hoped I didn't look like a fool.

I went through the movements one at a time. Even I could admit my kicks felt a little clumsy, but I'd never been a good performer. The thought of doing anything for an audience had always frightened me. That was why Anna had become the entertainer and me, the manager. I preferred to remain behind the scenes.

After the final kick, I lowered my leg and opened my eyes to find Cole standing a few feet away, his eyes narrowed in assessment.

"Not bad," he finally said, his head bobbing. "Your form could do with a little improvement, but all in all, you have a good foundation."

I released a relieved breath.

"But."

My mouth slid to the side. I hated *buts*.

"This won't be enough to protect you. And it certainly won't be enough to win. If you want to win your upcoming challenges, you'll need to know how to truly fight. It's nothing like this. You don't stand in front of the pack and practice little kicks and punches. Dominance fights are brutal, almost savage. Sometimes they're in wolf form. Sometimes human.

The challenger gets to choose. So you need to be ready. The entire pack knows you're weakest in wolf form. You haven't had enough practice."

I felt sick, my stomach roiling at the thought of fighting in wolf form. I wasn't nearly as confident in that form.

"How many times have you shifted?" Cole asked.

"Less than half a dozen," I admitted. I didn't know the exact count anymore, but it wasn't many. "Sam and I had just started working on it when Corbin stabbed me. The pack doctor advised me not to shift for two weeks after that. Then I spent the last five learning to fight."

Cole frowned. "Reginald did a piss poor job when it came to your training."

I bit my lip to keep from speaking my mind on that particular subject.

"We'll start with fighting in human form," Cole said. "I think it's important to understand those basics first. The knowledge will apply to fighting in wolf form too. Like understanding when to defend and when to attack."

"Okay, so how do we start?"

Cole pointed to the small boxing ring behind us.

I groaned, closed my eyes, and focused on

breathing. *No panic attacks*. I wouldn't allow it. I needed to be strong and ready to learn.

"We'll get warmed up, and then I'll start teaching you how to fight. With only a week, I'm not sure how much I can impart upon you, but anything is better than nothing."

"Why are you doing this?" I demanded suddenly.

Cole grew quiet.

I opened my eyes and pinned him with a glare. "And don't tell me it's because you don't want Brynn or Marcus in charge. That isn't enough. You could have let one win, then challenged them yourself. Heck, you could challenge me and take over. So, why are you truly doing this?"

Cole sighed, then strode to the boxing ring and slunk beneath the ropes. When he straightened, he bounced in the middle, warming up his muscles. "Because I think you have what it takes to be a great alpha. You have the determination and desire to protect."

My eyes widened. "I don't want to protect anyone."

"You want to protect *everyone*," Cole corrected. "Tell me something. Why do you want to learn to fight?"

"So I don't die, so—"

"No, don't give me that crap. Be honest, even if it's only with yourself. Why are you really here?"

My mouth twisted, and I gnawed at my inner lip. He wanted the truth? Fine. "Because I want to kill Corbin."

"And why do you want to kill Corbin?"

Rage heated the back of my neck. "Because he's dangerous. Because he wants to hurt people. He *did* hurt people. People I care about." My mind flashed to Sam's face when he'd first laid eyes on his brutalized sister. Corbin had taken great pleasure in hurting her. For that alone, I wanted his head.

Cole nodded. "Don't forget, he hurt *you* too. But this is what I'm talking about. You don't care that he hurt you. You care that he hurt others. You have this desire to protect—I saw it in you the day we came to New Orleans. You didn't want to leave, but you did. Because you feel responsible for Corbin. You have the heart of an alpha. You may not be physically strong enough yet, but I can help with that. We can change that."

I pressed a hand to my chest. I'd never heard someone speak of me like that.

"Let me guess, you've always cared about people. Always gone out of your way to protect them."

My mind leapt to all the times Anna had called me a mother hen and told me to stop fretting so much, to stop trying to control everyone and let them have fun. When she'd been turned into a vampire, I'd wanted to find and kill Petrik myself, so long as it meant protecting her from further harm. When Corbin went after the New Orleans human-borns, I'd gone against my own alpha's wishes and refused to come home, so I could help protect them.

"You have what it takes," Cole said. "There are some alphas who are physically strong, but lack that empathy and compassion. That can't be taught. But I can make you strong. I can teach you how to fight and defend."

"You want me to stay?" I asked, my voice barely more than a whisper. "Remain the alpha?"

"I think you'd make one hell of a leader," Cole said. "And I'll do whatever I can to make you see that. Our pack needs someone strong who cares about their people. Reginald was strong, but he was neglectful, which I don't need to tell you."

"And you don't think you'd make a good alpha?" I asked.

Cole shrugged. "I wouldn't turn the position down if you decided to offer it to me. But I don't think I'm the best person in this room for the job."

It felt as though my entire world had flipped on its side. I'd never considered that I might actually make a good alpha. I'd only cared about going home and being with Sam and Anna. Cole was right, though. These people needed a strong alpha. And if I really wanted to choose the best person, then I couldn't take myself out of the running. I needed to consider everyone. That didn't mean I wanted the job. Heck, I didn't know what I wanted.

"Let's get this party started," Cole said. "Since we have a limited amount of time, we shouldn't waste any of it chatting."

No, he was right. We shouldn't. For this, every second counted.

I slipped beneath the ropes and faced Cole. Then I lifted my arms and readied myself. Come h-e-double-hockey-sticks or high water, I *would* learn to fight. Because even if I didn't remain alpha, I still had a duty to all the human-borns. To protect them from Corbin. And so help me, I'd put that murdering wankhammer down before I let him hurt anyone else.

FOUR

Every inch of me hurt.

I took stock of my condition, pain erupting everywhere I touched. I knew even without looking in a mirror that my bruises had bruises. Cole had thoroughly whooped me, to the point where I couldn't find a single place that didn't ache. He hadn't done any lasting damage, thank goodness. But my split lip and tender nose told me I'd taken a few hits that I should have tried a little harder to dodge. He hadn't been kidding when he'd said I needed to learn to fight. Anna's training had done nothing to protect me.

I limped to Cole's nearby kitchen table and slumped into one of the chairs. Then I leaned my head back against the wall and released a long, slow breath. One that set my ribs on fire. Not broken, but certainly injured. I'd never known a body could hurt like this. I mean, I'd obviously sustained injuries before, but this went above and beyond that. Even my scalp ached.

"You okay?" Cole asked, his voice growing closer.

I waved a weakly dismissive hand and closed my eyes. "Oh, sure. Right as rain. Give me two minutes, and I'll be fit as a fiddle again."

His chuckle made me smile. If I could joke about it, I was fine, right?

I definitely needed another bath tonight. One loaded with Epsom salts and bubbles and maybe a quart of lidocaine. Anything to dull this endless throbbing. Wine would help with that. I hoped. Our metabolisms burned through alcohol super quick, but maybe if I just didn't stop drinking... maybe a buzz would soothe my abused muscles.

"You did really well," he said reassuringly. "Better than I expected. Your vampire friend did a good job teaching you the basics. It's just a matter of implementing them in true fights now."

I slitted an eye and glared at him. That was exactly what Cole and I had just done, and I was paying the price for it. My gaze flicked to the clock above his stove, which revealed that it was early in the afternoon. We'd spent hours—*hours*—in his boxing room of doom. No wonder I hurt.

"Meet me here every morning for the next week, and I think you'll stand a chance."

Gentle laughter shook my shoulders, which immediately protested their dislike of the movement. "That seems..." Unbelievable? Unrealistic? Impossible?

"I didn't say you'd win," he said, also laughing. "Just that you'd stand a chance. And I truly believe that. You have great instincts. You just need to trust yourself more. I'm hoping I can help you with that."

I closed that one eye and resumed resting, all the while measuring Cole's words and wondering something. "What will the pack think if they learn you're helping me?"

"Who cares?"

"Aren't you worried they'll hold it again you? Or call you a traitor or something?"

I caught the sound of a chair scraping against the floor, and I pried open my eyes to find Cole sitting across from me, his elbows balanced on the table. "The pack doesn't get to dictate my life choices. And if they have a problem with me helping you, that says more about them than me. However, since I'm second in command, there's really nothing they can do about it. Except challenge me, and believe me, no one is willing to do that."

"Ah. So your ego is bigger than your muscles," I mused.

Cole barked out a rough laugh. "Hardly. Just stating a fact. Listen, the only reason Bryn and Marcus want to challenge you is because they don't know you. You spent a year here, but you barely interacted with any of us. You kept your distance, which we understood, since you were grieving your human life. But then you up and left us. Abandoned us for New Orleans. And when Reginald died, we had to drag you back. Everyone knows you don't want to be here. And that creates this hole in the pack. One that any dominant wolf will crave to fill by ousting you. Right now, you don't fit. They see you as *other*. And until that glitch is repaired, they'll keep challenging you."

I didn't speak.

"If you spent some time with them," Cole hedged, "showed them that you want to be here, that you're the right person for the job, I think they'd come to like you."

"I'm their alpha, not their friend," I said. Even I knew an alpha couldn't be friends with their subordinates. Especially in a wolf pack.

"They don't need another friend. But they do need to respect you. And right now, they don't. You need to put a stop to these challenges before Marcus or Bryn can formally issue them. Because once they do, there's no rescinding them."

"And if I don't want to be the alpha?"

Cole sighed and leaned back in his chair, disappointment crossing his face. "If you refuse, then you know what you have to do."

"Name a successor," I said.

"Name a successor," he repeated, his fingers gently drumming against the table. "Either way, I'm going to teach you how to fight. Whether or not you remain the alpha, you need to be as physically prepared as possible if you're going after Corbin. That mutt needs to be put down ASAP, so I'll do whatever it takes to help you with that."

Corbin's name unleashed a fury within me that beat back the pain. For a moment, I felt as though I could go another round in Cole's torture ring.

"Have you heard anything yet?" I demanded. "Any whisper of his location? Or what he might be up to?"

Cole shook his head. "We have quite a few people looking for him. But he hasn't resurfaced since killing Reginald. We haven't been able to track any new credit cards or find any new leads. I don't know what he's doing, and that worries me more."

I nodded. The not knowing drove me insane. After Corbin killed Reggie, he'd just up and vanished. Part of me hoped that Reggie had done enough damage to Corbin that he'd slunk off somewhere and died. But life wasn't that kind. No, he was alive, and out there somewhere, biding his time. I just wish I knew what for.

"It's been almost two months," I said, sighing.

"I know. But let's use this time to our advantage. We'll get you into fighting shape, take care of our pack squabbles, then handle Corbin."

I didn't much like that sequence of events. In my mind, Corbin was the bigger risk. Yes, I had two pending death matches. But Corbin affected everyone. Not just me. My preference was to first take out Corbin, then deal with pack politics.

Either way, next time I faced off against Corbin, he would be the one left bleeding at the end. Not me.

Pressing my palms against my trembling thighs, I pushed to my feet and started to slowly limp toward Cole's door. Oh yeah, my muscles were definitely crying out in pain. "Thanks again, Cole." I paused and cocked my head. "It feels weird to thank you for kicking my butt."

His deep laughter echoed through the hallway. "We heal fast. You'll feel better in the morning."

"Only for you to lay another ass-whooping on me."

"Tomorrow, you'll block my attacks better." He clapped a hand on my shoulder and my knees nearly buckled.

"No touchy," I mumbled. "Not until I'm healed."

"Go home and fry yourself up a couple steaks. Protein helps us heal faster. Then soak in a tub or something. Tomorrow, your bruises will be much improved."

"Just to start fresh again," I said, groaning.

"Suck it up, alpha," Cole teased. "See you tomorrow?"

I nodded. As much as my body ached, I needed this training, and I refused to wuss out. The stronger I got, the more I could help. I wouldn't need to rely on someone else to protect me anymore. I hated thinking that I was a weakness, and the thought of Sam dying to protect me set off my inner wolf. He was a strong and powerful heir. It only seemed fair that I mold myself into something similar.

A thought came to mind. Fighting wasn't the

only thing I needed to practice. Over the past seven weeks, I'd been remiss about shifting. First, it'd been so I could heal. But afterward, I just hadn't found the urge to shift. With Sam traveling back and forth to New Orleans, I'd had no one to shift with, nor the desire to do it alone. But it was another weakness of mine. One I needed to correct. Tonight, then. And I'd take Anna and Vlad with me to watch my back.

"About the pack," I said, pausing at the door. "I want to arrange a gathering."

Cole's brows shot upward. "You do?"

"You were right. I don't know them, and they don't know me. They saw me at Reggie's funeral, but after that, I've been AWOL."

He gave a slow nod.

"So, let's call a pack meeting, but make it fun. Music, snacks, the works. Is there someone I can appoint to arrange all this? I assume as the alpha, I can't do it."

Cole's mouth tugged upward. "Yeah, you definitely need to delegate. Darla's our pack's party planner. She arranges all our gatherings whenever we have one. She knows everyone's likes and dislikes, and she has access to the funds. I can reach out to her." He pulled up his phone and started typing out a message. "Is there a specific location where you'd like to hold the event?"

"Reggie's house—er, my place. In five nights."

"Five?" Cole's head snapped up, and he shot me a startled look. "That's the night before the full moon."

I nodded. "I know. I want to hold the event before the meeting, before Bryn and Marcus can formally challenge me. I want the gathering to be lighthearted, so we can all get to know one another."

A knowing light entered Cole's eyes. "And so you can have a chance to hopefully persuade them not to challenge you."

"That, too," I said, winking. "Don't let it be said that I'm not a thinker."

Approval smoothed Cole's expression. He finished typing out his message to Darla, then pushed open the front door for me. "Alright. All done. I'll let you know what she says when she responds."

"Thanks."

Just as I was about to leave, Cole placed a hand on my arm, staying me. I glanced back with a raised brow, my gaze quickly dropping to his hand.

"If I could make a suggestion?"

"Sure?" I replied.

"I know Sam is your mate..."

My brows slammed into a frown at the sound of Sam's name. Somehow, I suspected I wasn't going to like this suggestion, and my battered muscles tensed in anticipation.

"Don't bring him to the gathering," Cole finally said.

"Excuse me?" My wolf reared her head, anger lifting her hackles. Neither of us liked the thought of leaving Sam out of anything.

"Just hear me out," Cole said, clearly sensing my rising anger. "Sam isn't one of us. We need to get to know *you*. *Our* alpha. Not your mate. He doesn't even belong to our pack. He's an outsider. Bringing him isn't going to help your cause."

I bared my teeth. "And what cause might that be?"

"Swaying opinions in your favor."

"I don't care what other people think. He's my mate."

Cole sighed. "I know. And I also know how protective mates can be with each other. I'm not trying to upset you or your wolf. I just want you to see reason here. If you want to stop Bryn and Marcus from challenging you, we need to feel like you're one of us. And right now, you don't. Bringing your mate, another outsider, only widens that gap. We need to bridge it."

"He's my mate," I growled, my wolf growing agitated. "If you think for one moment that I would leave him—"

"I never said leave him," Cole replied, raising his hands defensively. "I'm just suggesting you don't bring him to the gathering, that's all. Our pack knows you have a mate, and that he's from the New Orleans Pack. We know the two of you are bonded. We would never ask someone to leave their mate, but we can ask you to give us time to adjust to everything without you forcing him on us."

My mouth twisted, and it took every ounce of restraint I possessed not to bare my teeth at him. Neither myself nor my wolf appreciated this suggestion of his. "I'll think about it."

Cole's shoulders relaxed. "That's all I can ask. I'm just trying to help."

I knew that. And his suggestion wasn't... *terrible*. Even though I desperately hated it. Either way, my wolf needed to calm the eff-train down before I did something stupid.

"Anyway, think on it, and I'll see you tomorrow," Cole said.

I stormed out of his house, still fuming. The

logical, human-brained Lucy might have recognized the logic in his suggestion. But rational Lucy had left the building, leaving behind a possessive, territorial alpha werewolf who greatly disliked being told what to do.

Shaking my head, I limped to my car and flopped into my seat, all the while focusing on my breathing and calming my nerves. I couldn't let my wolf take control like that. I needed to keep a clear head at all times, but she made it difficult, especially when Sam was involved.

CHAPTER
FIVE

AFTER A WELL-DESERVED NAP AND A LONG SOAK
in a blistering hot bath, I stood in the kitchen and
stared at my phone. Thanks to my notifications being
on silent, I'd missed a call and several texts from
Sam. In the last message, he mentioned he'd be out
for a pack run this afternoon, so he might not be near
his phone, but he'd try to catch me tonight.

Cursing under my breath, I dialed his number,
and listened as it rang and rang and rang some more.
When his voicemail picked up, disappointment
crushed my chest. I hated this. Hated that we never
seemed to be able to connect. In the past five weeks,
we'd spent a total of a week together at most. While
he'd intended to stay with me when we'd first arrived
in Mississippi, it hadn't been long before Adrien had

summoned him home. His pack needed their heir—
and I completely understood. His pack was family,
and I would never make him choose. I loved him far
too much for that. We'd make it work, I had no
doubt. But in the meantime, I just... *missed* him.
Deeply. Keenly. I ached for him. Being parted from
your mate was a fate worse than death.

"Calling Sam?" a voice rose behind me.

I glanced at the time, then smiled. Half past four.
Anna was awake.

I turned and found her standing in the small
hallway that connected to the kitchen. She couldn't
come any closer, thanks to the massive bay windows.
At first, I'd intended to buy some blackout curtains,
but Anna had asked me not to. Being that she was a
vampire, she was allergic to sunlight. In a deathly,
cooked to a crisp, sort of way. That didn't stop her
from insisting the house remain bright and cherry,
though.

Anna skidded to a stop and gasped, her fingers
touching her lips. "What happened?"

Oh right, my face. I'd stared at my reflection for
quite some time in the bathroom, touching all the
puffy, bruised bits. I looked like I'd gone toe-to-toe
with an MMA fighter.

When I stepped into the hallway and out of

direct sunlight, Anna rushed toward me with her vamp quickness. Her hands gently cupped my cheeks, and she turned my head side to side, appraising the myriad of bruises. My skin was a rainbow of maroons, purples, and reds. Bruising had set in beneath one of my eyes, and my split lip had swelled to the size of a small grape. And that was just my face. The rest of me held a litany of injuries, from bruised ribs to darkened fingerprints marring my sides.

"I'm fine, I promise. Just leftovers from Cole's training."

Anna whistled between her teeth. "Holy shit, girl."

"It looks worse than it feels," I assured her.

"Well, it looks awful."

"Then maybe it feels exactly like it looks," I said, grinning. My lip protested, but ah well.

"Werewolves are brutal," she mused.

Now there was an assessment I could agree with. Perhaps Cole could have gone a little easier on me, but I almost appreciated that he hadn't. Marcus and Bryn certainly wouldn't pull their punches. I needed to prepare. And if that meant beating me black and blue, so be it.

"Does Sam know about this?" Anna asked.

I shook my head. "We haven't been able to connect with each other today or yesterday. And honestly, with how protective Sam has become, I'm afraid this would set him off."

"You're keeping this a secret from him?"

"Not a secret. I just don't plan on bringing it up."

Anna's mouth pursed. "I don't know, Lucy. I don't think that's such a great idea. Sam isn't going to be happy if he sees you like this."

"I know. But I have a lot to focus on right now, and Sam's reaction won't help at all. Besides, he's with his family right now. With luck, next time we see each other, I'll be all healed."

"Does he even know about the challenges yet?"

Shame heated my cheeks. "No. I didn't think that was a good conversation to have over text."

"Lucy, oh my god!" Anna shouted. "You can't keep stuff like this from him. Vlad would kill me if I pulled this sort of shit."

I winced. I knew that—I *did*. I just... dreaded that conversation. And having it in person really did seem best. "Don't worry," I told her. "I have everything under control."

"No, you don't."

"Well, I can pretend. And don't worry,

werewolves heal quickly. So I won't look this way for too long."

"How quickly?"

"Cole assures me I should be looking like my fine self again in a few days," I said. I didn't bother mentioning that tomorrow's training session would only compound on today's damage. "I just need to get better at blocking and dodging."

"I'd say," she muttered. "I don't like this. Have you looked at yourself in the mirror?"

"Of course."

She sighed, then reached for the small shelf we kept stocked with bottled blood. Upon Anna's arrival, I'd contacted one of the new local businesses that guaranteed delivery of fresh blood. I didn't know all the details—something about reagents and chemicals to keep it fresh for an extended amount of time. Anna hadn't choked and died yet, so clearly the business knew what they were doing. I did need to make a mental note to call and order more, though, now that Vlad was here.

Grabbing a bottle, she cracked the lid and took a small sip, still appraising me. "I don't want to be here when Sam finds out. My god, he's going to lose his mind."

Anticipation frayed my nerves. "Really, Anna.

I'm fine." Then, deciding to change the topic, I winked and said, "Not as fine as you, though, I'd wager. Had a good night last night, did'ya?"

Anna's eyes widened. She tucked her hair behind her ears and shrugged. "Same as any other night."

"Oh, really?" I approached her, imitating her voice. "*Oh, Vlad. Right there. Don't stop. Yes—*"

"Lucy!" she shouted. If she'd been human, blood would have rushed to her cheeks. As it was, her mouth gaped open, her fangs flashing at me. "You *listened?*"

Laughter erupted from my mouth. "Sweetie, I'm pretty sure the whole neighborhood heard you."

Mortification twisted her expression, and she lifted a hand to her brow. Slowly, she shook her head, then stepped back into the hallway.

"Oh, come on, it's not a big deal," I told her. "You guys haven't seen each other in nearly two months. I expected an... enthusiastic reunion."

"Oh god," she moaned. Then she spun around and pinned me with a severe glare. "Do *not* mention this to Vlad. Promise me."

I chuckled. "Why not? I could critique his performance. Give him some tips. Think it might help?"

"Help?" Anna shrieked. "We don't need *help*, thank you very much!"

No, they certainly didn't. But it was fun to see that look in her eyes—the one that said she would have murdered me if I weren't her best friend.

"Oh, I don't know. I think he could have got you screaming a little sooner."

"Lucy!" she shouted.

"See? It only took me a few seconds."

Anna's mouth snapped shut as she glared daggers at me. After a few seconds, her mouth curled into a grin. "You're a wretch, you know that? Don't think I haven't heard you and Sam going at it."

I shrugged. "I already suspected that, considering we all sleep in the same house."

She shook her head. "You're terrible."

Together, we headed into the living room and took a seat. I'd insisted on blackout curtains for this room. She needed somewhere to sit during the day, somewhere safe from the sun. And I didn't want her confined to her bedroom all day. With the kitchen nearby, the living room possessed enough ambient light to appease her. It always cracked me up how much sunlight she required.

Done teasing, I decided to approach a more

sensitive topic. "There is something I could use your help with, though."

She took another sip of blood, her eyes locked on mine.

"I need to practice shifting. Cole told me that the challenger gets to choose which form we fight in. And apparently, the entire pack knows shifting is one of my weaknesses."

Anna froze, the bottle hovering at her lips. "They're really out to kill you, aren't they?"

Well, I mean, yes? That was the point of these challenges. But I didn't answer her question. Instead, I continued my explanation. "If it's okay with you and Vlad, I'd like you two to come with me tonight. You don't need to do anything other than watch my back. Make sure nothing surprising happens while I practice shifting."

"Nothing surprising like..."

"Mainly Corbin. We still don't know where he is or what he's up to, so I don't want to be caught unaware. I'm trying to be smart about this."

Anna nodded. "Of course we'll help you. Vlad adores you. He'd likely insist anyway if you'd told him what you were doing."

"Thanks." Relief loosened my muscles and a faint smile crossed my face. "You're the best. I know it's against the law for any werewolf to challenge me until the next full moon, but I just want to be prepared in case someone does something reckless."

"Like arrange your death beforehand."

I nodded. I didn't relish the thought of anyone in my pack behaving so abhorrently, but after everything I'd been through in the past year, I refused to take any chances, needed to think it all through beforehand.

Draining her bottle, Anna placed it on the table, then gestured toward me. "Okay, so what can we do about... *this*?"

"About what?"

"Those bruises. Babe, you look just terrible. Will makeup help?"

I waved off her concerns. "There's no one here for me to impress with my looks."

She touched a hand to her unbeating heart and scoffed. "What about me?"

"Pfft, you've seen me far worse than this."

Chuckling, she leaned forward and scooped up the television remote. She turned on the TV, then sat back and navigated us to the movie section. "Alright. Well, if you refuse to make yourself look pretty, then let's watch something. I'm tired of looking at your grotesque face."

I choked out a laugh.

"Now, which movie are we on?"

"Number three," I told her. *Bridget Jones's Baby.*"

"Right. Baby time it is." Anna clicked the remote, then tossed it next to her on the couch and settled in.

I did the same, tucking my legs up under my rear, then covering myself with a blanket. Nothing like a little romance and comedy to lighten the mood.

WE STOOD AT THE EDGE OF A NEARBY FOREST, the soft caress of moonlight illuminating the lush grass. This late at night, I didn't expect any visitors, but we still had to be careful. Humans didn't know about werewolves. Thankfully, I'd brought along two vampires, with ears like bats, to tell me if anyone was nearby. My hearing was just as sensitive, but I'd be too distracted with shifting to pay attention.

A warm breeze drifted by, carrying the scent of nearby swamp water to my nose. My wolf pawed at the edge of my consciousness, eager to tear free of my skin and *run*. It'd been weeks since she'd last been let out to play, and her excitement was contagious. I smiled as I stared into the trees.

"What?" Anna asked, catching my grin.

I shrugged. She wouldn't understand. It was a wolf thing.

"Um." I turned and faced Vlad. "Sorry, but I gotta... kinda..."

"Ah." Ever the gentleman, Vlad turned and gave me his back. "Feel free to disrobe. I won't look."

"Better not," Anna growled possessively.

Vlad chuckled and reached for Anna's face, stroking her cheek lovingly. My heart fractured at the sight. I missed Sam. I'd tried to call him once more before heading out with the vamps, but the call had once again gone to voicemail.

I stole another quick glance around the wooded area, then quickly shucked my clothes. I fought the urge to cover my breasts and instead, crouched low to the ground. My body knew what to do. I merely had to get out of the way.

Anna, who had never seen me shift before, watched with an inquisitive expression. I forced myself to ignore her and instead focus on my body. I drew in a deep breath, then lowered the shield in my mind, allowing my wolf to surge forward. She pranced toward me, her tongue lolling happily out of her mouth. I reached into my mind's eye and offered a hand, stroking her smooth, supple fur. A silent apology for keeping her locked up for so long.

Her hot tongue lashed my hand, then she lunged forward, our bodies merging.

My legs snapped first, and I bit back a pained cry. The less often a werewolf shifted, the more painful the experience. I knew that, and yet I'd still refrained from changing.

Next went my arms, the elbows jutting backward with deafening cracks.

"Jesus," Anna whispered. "You okay, Luce?"

I merely grunted and kept my head down, a curtain of hair covering my face. I couldn't speak right now, even if I wanted to.

Closing my eyes, I succumbed to the change, giving myself over to my wolf. She knew what to do, and she would take care of me if I allowed her to. When I stopped resisting, the shift became fluid. My bones broke and reshaped themselves until finally, I stood on all fours, my claws curling into the earth.

I drew in a deep breath, raised my furred head...

And sneezed.

Gah! I'd purposely taken allergy pills before heading out tonight, but either I hadn't waited long enough, or the damn things were ineffective.

Considering our metabolisms, I supposed it was possible, though horribly annoying.

Another sneeze ravaged me. Then another. But it was the sound of Anna's gleeful laughter that had me swinging my head her way with bared teeth.

At the sight of her phone out and recording, I snapped at her.

"Oh, calm down. It's just for me," she said, laughing. "I won't out you to my followers."

She'd better not. The woman was a damn social influencer with nearly ten million followers. If she showed this video to anyone, our secret wouldn't be a secret anymore.

I gave another sneeze, then shook out my fur. Damn allergies. How the hell was I supposed to fight other werewolves when I suffered from sneezing and watery eyes in wolf form? I suppose I could double the dose to compensate for my metabolism.

"Okay, so now what?" Anna asked.

With a shuddering breath, I sparked the shift once more, forcing myself back into human form. This was what I needed to practice. I needed to perfect the art, to quicken the process. I needed to be able to practically melt from one form into another.

Once I stood on two legs again, I breathed a sigh of relief and rolled out my shoulders. Every inch of me burned and ached, compliments of the shift and Cole's training. But I couldn't allow a little discomfort to stop me.

"You okay?" Anna asked.

Vlad remained stock still, his gaze trained on the field behind us.

"Yeah," I wheezed. "It's just a tiring process."

"I bet."

"There's no one around," Vlad told us. "Feel free to keep going."

"Keep going?" Anna shot me a startled glance. "You're going to shift again?"

"And again and again, until it no longer hurts."

Her eyes widened, the moonlight catching her blue eyes. "Is that possible?"

"I have no idea," I mumbled. "But the more I shift, the better at it I'll become."

I crouched on all fours again and allowed my wolf to roam freely. She came happily, eagerly, and the shift swept over me. This time, I didn't flinch at the sound of my breaking bones. Maybe one day it would become second nature. That day wasn't today though.

Now returned to wolf form, I plopped my butt down in the grass and panted for breath. Holy crap on a cracker, I was exhausted. My poor legs trembled just from the effort of holding myself up.

"That was quicker, I think," Anna said. "Maybe by a few seconds?"

My furred head dipped. At least this time I wasn't sneezing. Not yet anyway.

Heaving another breath, I pushed back up onto all fours and changed back to human form.

Again and again, I shifted. Each time, I nearly collapsed with exhaustion, but with gritted teeth, I forced myself to keep going. My life depended on it. I couldn't give up now.

But when I shifted into wolf form for the fifth time, my legs gave out and I toppled over with the weakest sneeze.

"Luce," Anna murmured. She dropped to her knees beside me and ran her fingers through my damp fur. "Let's call it a night. You've done enough."

"Anna," Vlad snapped. "Lucy."

For a moment, I thought he was admonishing us. But then I heard it. A twig snapping in the distance and the sound of footsteps. With a low, threatening growl, I struggled to my feet and drew in a deep breath. But only the scent of forest tickled my nose. Downwind, then.

Footsteps approached. Heading right in our direction.

I limped in front of Vlad and Anna, my head coming up to their waists.

"Who is it?" Anna whispered.

"I can't catch their scent," Vlad replied. "It's nearly impossible when surrounded by all this." He gestured to the marshlands.

Their bodies tensed as one, and together, we presented a united force. Whoever was approaching would have to face the three of us together. The feel of them at my back bolstered my confidence. I wasn't alone. I wasn't weak.

A shadow moved in the distance as it slunk ever so carefully through the trees. But I couldn't make out anything beyond the sound of four feet padding through the underbrush. A werewolf, then. It had to be. The steps were too slow and loud for a wild animal.

My lips curled up over my fangs and I crouched low, my aching muscles bunched in preparation. The instant the wolf showed its face, I'd tear it off.

Finally, the wolf stepped out of the trees, and I lunged.

CHAPTER
SIX

THE TWO OF US COLLIDED IN A TANGLE OF LIMBS and fur. I hadn't given this any thought other than *attack*. But when I slammed into the massive wolf and rode him down to the earth, my senses finally snapped into place. A familiar scent—as familiar as my own—rose to my nose. One that called to me and made me yearn. One I had desperately missed over the past week.

With an amused huff, I rose from the enormous white wolf, my mouth opened in a wolfy grin.

Sam.

My Sam.

Laughter shone in his amber eyes as he picked himself up and shook out his fur. The two of us were like mirror images of one another—me with my black fur flecked with white, and him with his white fur stained with black. A perfect complement to each other.

Sam rose to his full height, his head towering over me. I stretched my neck and butted my head under his jaw, snuggling close to his throat. I couldn't believe he was here! I hadn't even known to expect him. But, oh. My heart pounded with excitement, and my pulse raced. His scent encircled me, seeping into my bones, reminding me of what we meant to one another.

He leaned his head down and lashed his hot tongue across my cheek. I barked out a laugh, then stepped back, drinking in the sight of him. He lifted a furry brow and cocked his head toward Anna and Vlad.

When I turned, I found her smiling, her hand clasped within Vlad's.

"*Did you know he was coming?*" I asked her.

One of Anna's vampiric powers was the ability to speak to animals. Apparently, that power extended to werewolves as well. It was a handy little talent, especially for moments like these.

"*No. I had no idea.*" She released Vlad's hand, then strode forward and placed a hand on Sam's back, before saying aloud. "It's good to see you, Sam."

He butted her hand and offered his own wolfish grin.

Vlad, however, hung back. He and Sam didn't get along on the best of days. Too much history between them. History that, to this day, still made me snicker. Ever the vampire and the werewolf, the two were practically frenemies. They worked well together when the situation called for it, but beyond that, they preferred to maintain a distance.

Anna faced me, still grinning as she said aloud, "We'll leave you two to catch up then, okay? See you back at home."

I nodded, then touched my nose to her wrist, silently thanking her. She and Vlad took each other's hands once more before vanishing in the night.

Once alone, I turned back to Sam, and, with an elated grin, leapt onto his back. I opened my mouth and pressed my teeth to his neck but didn't bite. More of a playful nudge than anything.

Sam let loose a nonthreatening growl before shaking me off. I tumbled to the ground, still chuckling, then clambered to my feet and took off into the woods. Now that he was here, I didn't care about shifting back into human form. Not yet anyway. I wanted to run and play and enjoy his presence. Hopefully he could stay longer than the night. But just in case, I needed to make every moment count.

The instant I hit the tree line, I felt Sam's looming presence behind me. He was faster and stronger than me, thanks to years of practice, but that didn't mean I couldn't give him a run for his money. I wove through the trees, ducking beneath low branches and hopping over felled logs.

A sense of serenity filled me, now that my mate and I had been reunited. It was unlike anything I'd ever experienced before. This feeling of contentedness and fulfillment. As though half of my being had been missing and was now returned. Happiness ran rampant within me, to the point where I wondered if my heart would burst.

Sam's footsteps thundered behind me. Always close, but not overtaking me. Clearly, he enjoyed the chase as much I did.

I raced through the next copse of trees, then pivoted on my paws and circled around a thick trunk. I caught wind of Sam's grunt, but before he could follow me around the bend, I came up behind him and leapt, my paws slamming into his side. We toppled to the ground in a jumble of limbs.

Sam lifted his head, his amber eyes aglow with humor. After a few playful nips, we rose to our feet and returned to the clearing. I wasn't where Sam had left his clothes, but mine lay scattered across the grass, exactly where I'd left them.

Sam trotted off, then returned a few moments later with his clothing in his mouth. He must have shifted once he'd spotted us through the trees. Dropping them to the ground, he started to shift. Human time, then. I immediately did the same. My change, while still slower than his, was faster than before. Good. It was working. If I spent the next few nights shifting back and forth, I'd hopefully become as quick as everyone else. One weakness tackled.

Wholly human and now standing on two feet, I turned toward Sam, all while idly running my hands through my hair. But the sight of him staring at me, eyes wide in horror, reminded me that I wasn't a pretty sight to see at the moment.

My hands froze, and I quickly glanced down, taking note of the colorful bruises marking my body.

"Ah, shit," I whispered. In all the excitement, I'd forgotten.

And Sam... looked murderous. Jaw tight, nostrils flared, eyes burning brighter than any moon I'd ever seen. He stalked toward me, half-clothed, and gently lifted my arm.

"Who. Did. This?" he snarled, his voice deadlier than I'd ever heard.

I didn't immediately answer, not really sure what to say.

"Who did this to you, Lucy?" Sam demanded.

I pulled my arm free from his grasp. He didn't grab me again, but his gaze still burned into mine.

"Sam, it's okay—"

"Like hell it's okay!" he rasped, his wolf rumbling deep in his throat. "Who hurt you? Why didn't you tell me? What the *fuck* is going on?"

I backed up a step. I knew Sam would never hurt me, but I needed a bit of space. The intensity in his eyes, the snarl on his lips, it was too much.

"Cole—"

With a savage snarl, Sam turned and stalked through the clearing, moving with a liquid quickness. He wrenched his shirt on as he moved, his steps purposeful. It took me a moment to process everything. He hadn't even let me explain.

Shaking my head, I took off after him. "Sam!"

He ignored me, completely lost to his rage. I could scent it on the air, its bitter perfume assaulting my nose.

"Sam, stop!" I shouted.

He didn't.

Damn it. I knew mated werewolves were territorial and dangerous, but he hadn't even allowed me to explain. I bolted into a run. My muscles protested, especially considering all that shifting, but I couldn't let that slow me down. Sam looked positively lethal right now, and with every fiber of my being, I knew he was heading for Cole's place right now.

"Sam," I panted, still chasing after him. "Damn it, Sam! Wait!"

We neared my car, parked on a dirt path. Sam reached it first, and when he ripped open the driver's side door, I thought for sure he'd torn it off the hinges.

With a soft curse, I dove under his arm and placed myself between him and the car.

Light burned within his eyes, his jaw so tight, I thought it might shatter. "Move."

A shiver screamed down my spine. I'd never seen him like this before—this feral. "No. Not until you listen to me."

His nostrils flared. "Move. Lucy."

Okay. He was in a mood. A dangerous mood. I

needed to navigate this carefully. And fast. Before this got out of hand.

I cupped his stubbled face and forced him to look at me. "Listen to me." My words dripped with every bit of authority I could muster. "No one hurt me."

Sam growled, and the sound lifted the hairs on my arms.

"No one *hurt* me, Sam!" I repeated. "I agreed to this. Cole asked if he could teach me to fight so I could learn to protect myself! That's all this is! Yes, I'm bruised. Yes, I'm sore. But we *agreed* on this. He's teaching me how to be an alpha."

The blinding light in Sam's eyes flickered briefly. "He hit you."

We were definitely in full werewolf mode here. For a moment, I wondered if Sam was even home right now, or if his wolf had taken full control without shifting.

"Yes, and I hit him back," I said, my tone softening. "Cole didn't attack me. Do you hear me?"

Not even a twinkle of recognition.

"Sam..." I stretched up onto my tiptoes and pressed my mouth against his, ignoring the lick of pain in my split lip. His emotions were spinning wildly out of control. I needed to break past his wolf and make him see reason. I inched back from the kiss. "I promise you, no one hurt me. Cole was just teaching me how to fight."

"Why?" he demanded, his voice still rough.

Sighing, I ran my fingers through his silken hair, smoothing it back from his face. A gentle smile curved my lips. "Because I'm an alpha who doesn't know the first thing about fighting."

"Anna—"

"Taught me everything she knows. But it isn't enough," I said. "And in one week, I'm going to be challenged. I need to know how to fight."

He jerked at the word challenged, his eyes slitting. "I would have helped."

"We tried that, remember?" I met his gaze and offered another smile. His eyes dimmed, the power of his wolf ebbing. Good. I was getting through to him. "You were afraid to hurt me. And you've been back and forth to New Orleans a lot. I need someone who can teach me to fight without pulling their punches. Because anyone who challenges me isn't going to pull theirs."

Anguish rippled across Sam's face. I framed his face with my hands and brought him down for another kiss. This time, I parted my lips. Sam instantly responded, his hands gripping my hips tightly as his tongue swept into my mouth. I sucked in a sharp breath, startled by his almost violent reaction. But instead of fighting it, I gave in. I let him push me back against the car as he deepened the kiss.

His touch softened then, as though remembering my bruises. His fingers ghosted up my side, lingered on my arms, before finally combing through my hair.

"Lucy..." he whispered against my mouth. His forehead rested against mine, and his eyes fluttered closed, effectively smothering the light. "I'm sorry. I shouldn't have... seeing you like that... you're so..."

I chuckled and brushed another kiss across his lips. "Is this your way of telling me I'm gorgeous?"

A devastating growl ripped free of his throat. "Don't make jokes. Not now."

Okay. I could do that. If he didn't want humor, I'd give him something else to focus on.

My mouth returned to his just as my hands slid beneath his shirt. Sam's breath quickened when I ran them along the edge of his jeans until they came together at the fly. I popped open the button and slowly unzipped them.

"Luce..." he rasped. "What—"

"You said no jokes." I pried open his pants, then slid them down his legs.

He hesitated for the briefest moment, as though debating his options. Whatever thoughts ran through his head, he came to a quick conclusion, one that had him stepping out of his jeans. His shirt went next, tossed onto the roof of the car. Just like that, he stood naked in the clearing. Thankfully, I couldn't hear anyone for miles, so I knew we were safe. Voyeurism wasn't usually my thing, but I needed to be with Sam right now, and I had a feeling his wolf needed the same. And home meant Anna and Vlad. After their reunion last night, I didn't exactly relish the thought of them overhearing us tonight.

He dipped his head then, his dark hair falling in front of his eyes. "Here? Now?"

"Here. Now. Everywhere. Always," I whispered.

Grasping his hand, I drew him down to the ground. For a moment, I'd considered ducking into the car, but my little beater barely fit Sam at the best of moments. The man was a beast, after all, standing somewhere around six-foot-five. I couldn't expect him to be able to perform well in such tight confines. Nor was I in the mood to knock my head off the roof. So, out here it was. Beneath the moonlight. With nothing but the cool night air kissing our skin.

Poised above me, Sam lowered his head and kissed every single mark on my face. His lips feathered the skin beneath my eye, my puffy cheek, my swollen lip. His hands swept down my body, reveling in every curve, his fingertips brushing my bruised ribs and thighs. I must have looked quite the sight right now, but I chose not to let that bother me.

Sam's fingers swept up my thighs and settled between my legs, his touch soft and gentle. This felt different than the other times we'd had sex. Those had been hurried and passionate. Sam seemed determined to go slow tonight, though. Perhaps he was afraid of hurting me. I didn't mind.

His thumb brushed against my core, and I shuddered, my back arching off the soft grass. It'd been for too long since we'd been together, thanks to Sam's travels. And I almost came apart the second he touched me.

With a possessive smile, Sam slipped a finger inside me, exploring and teasing. I moaned and gripped his back when he inserted a second finger. The feel of him inside me, caressing my inner walls, made me tremble.

"Lucy," he whispered again, his head lowering to mine. The tips of his hair brushed my cheek as his mouth found my neck, nibbling and biting. "God, I missed you."

And I missed him. So much.

His fingers quickened, and he added his thumb

into the mix, gently circling my clit. I gasped, my hips bucking up from the ground.

"Sam," I murmured.

"Mm?" He lifted his head and gazed down at me, his wolf completely gone from his eyes. Just the two of us now—exactly as I preferred it.

"I don't want to play," I told him. I meant it too. I wanted him. We could play later, after satiating ourselves.

He claimed my mouth in a long, possessive kiss, then settled between my legs, clearly content to give in to my demands. He reached between us and gripped his length, guiding himself toward me. He didn't slide within, though. Not yet. He teased my entrance with his length, exciting me to the point where I nearly begged him to take me right now. On and on he teased. Just barely stroking me, working me into a frenzy. I wanted him inside me, wanted him to fill that yearning emptiness. Wanted him to fuck me.

With an animalistic growl, I took matters into my own hands and lifted my hips, grinning triumphantly when he slid inside. Sam's breath caught and amusement twinkled in his eyes, both a result of my brazenness. I was starting to learn, though, how to get what I wanted. Before being turned into a werewolf, I'd been content with my life. But now, I possessed the courage to go after what I desired. And right now, I desired Sam.

"Move," I ordered him.

Sam gave another wicked grin, then dropped his head closer to mine, his lips pressed against the shell of my ear. "As you wish, my alpha."

Oh. My. God. That nearly undid me right there. I slammed our mouths together just as he obliged my last command and started moving. Our breaths joined, our heartbeats pumping as one. The feel of his length gliding into me sent my back bowing off the ground.

Sam quickened his pace, settling into a fast rhythm that forced the air out of my lungs. I lay beneath him, clinging to his arms, his sides, wrapping my legs around his hips. I couldn't get close enough, couldn't find that perfect position. Until his hand found its way between our bodies, his thumb landing on that one special spot.

I purred beneath him, more kitten than werewolf, and let the sensations sweep me away. My body gave little warning before pleasure surged through me, flooding every inch of me with delirious ecstasy.

Sam's mouth found mine the instant I cried out

my release, muffling the sound. I didn't want to be quieted, though. Didn't want to be stifled.

I unwrapped my legs from his hips and, using a move Cole had taught me earlier this morning, flipped us over. With Sam now on his back, I started riding him, rocking my hips. He cupped my breasts, but I took hold of his wrists and pinned them to the soft earth, my breasts now displayed before his mouth like hanging fruit.

Sam's mouth found my nipple, his tongue swirling across the peaked flesh. I moaned, allowing myself to enjoy his attentions a moment longer before seating myself upright.

I gave Sam a mischievous grin, then flattened my hands against his chest and quickened my pace. Every downward thrust had his breaths growing ragged. His eyes rolled backward, and he clenched his jaw, likely trying to stave off his climax.

I didn't want that though.

I craved his release. There was a special power that came with making someone orgasm. Knowing you were the one to throw them over that cliff. To make their hands clench and toes curl.

I wanted him to succumb. Wanted to feel him swell and spill inside me. Wanted to ride his pleasure and take my own.

So I didn't relent.

Sam's hands shot to my waist, attempting to slow me. But I refused. Instead, I brought his hand to the apex of my thighs and increased my pace. His thumb circling my clit as I rode him brought me to the heights of ecstasy.

And just as colorful lights burst behind my eyes, Sam stiffened beneath me, his fingers reflexively gripping my hips as he groaned. I moved at a slower pace, drawing out his orgasm. Only when we were spent did I slowly climb off and curl up next to him, our chests both heaving.

Sam turned his head, the grass ruffling his hair, and stared at me, a look of incredulous wonder widening his eyes. "That was…"

I gave a weak laugh and cuddled into his chest, drawing idle images on his flesh. He didn't bother finishing his sentence, and he didn't need to. I could practically taste the contentment pouring off him. Instead, I tucked myself closer and reveled in the blissful aftermath.

CHAPTER
SEVEN

AFTER STROKING MY HAIR FOR A FEW MOMENTS, Sam leaned over and placed a light kiss on my forehead. "We should get dressed before someone spots us and calls the cops."

Unfortunately, he was right. I sighed, then tilted my head to meet his gaze. I didn't want to leave. It was peaceful here, beneath the faint moonlight. But I understood his concern. A public indecency ticket didn't sound all that appealing. Thankfully, the late hour protected us from prying eyes, but it only took that one person to spot us stretched out naked next to my car to ruin the night.

I leaned in for another kiss, then climbed to my feet, my body deliciously achy. It didn't take long for me to locate all my clothing and dress. When I finally turned, I found Sam fully clothed, much to my dismay. With a body like his, he needed to be naked twenty-four-seven.

He approached me slowly, his steps light. His gaze raked over my face, concern lining his eyes as he catalogued every mark.

I stretched onto my tiptoes and brushed a third kiss across his cheek. "It looks worse than it is. I promise."

Disbelief darkened his expression. "Maybe you should tell me the whole story now."

Yeah, probably a good idea. I had no desire to see Sam slip into territorial werewolf mode again. I preferred my mate calm and happy. So with his hand tucked into mine, I led him back to the car, and as we walked, I filled him in on everything. His shoulders tightened when I reached the part about the upcoming challenges. They didn't loosen until I explained how I planned to persuade Bryn and Marcus to back down before they issued their irrevocable challenges. I even told him about Cole's and my conversation, and how he believed I would make a wonderful alpha. Sam's body tensed once more when I mentioned Cole's request to mold me into a fighter.

I knew from the emotions scouring his face that

Sam didn't like any of this. Not that I blamed him. Were our roles reversed, I'd probably hate it too. It couldn't be easy listening to me casually discuss all the people who wanted to kill me. I assured him I needed to train no matter what, because even if I did manage to convince Bryn and Marcus to back down, that still left Corbin to deal with. And I refused to face him unprepared again. There would be no more stabbings, thank you very much.

"I'm sorry," Sam murmured, breaking his silence. "I'm sorry I didn't better prepare you for any of this. I'm sorry I can't fight on your behalf. And I'm sorry I failed to kill Corbin."

"Hey." I stopped him with a gentle squeeze of his hand. "You didn't *fail* at anything. And you have absolutely nothing to apologize for. None of this is your fault."

My words went in one ear and out the other—I could tell from the twisting of his lips. Then he shot me a scowl. "You should have told me about all this."

Guilt speared my heart. "I'd planned to, I swear. We just kept missing each other's calls. I definitely wasn't going to text you about all this. Can't imagine *that* would have gone well."

A deep chuckle rose in the night air, relaxing my shoulders. "No, I suppose not."

"I hate being apart from you," I admitted. "But I understand. Your pack and family need you."

"That's actually why I'm here," Sam said. "I couldn't stand being away from you anymore. So tonight, I told my father I was leaving, and I wasn't coming back, not without you."

My head snapped up and I stared at him, studying the silver moonlight tracing his face. "What?"

"Daniel and Brenda are progressing well," he said, shrugging. "And while my family is still hurting, they're also starting to heal from Izzy's death. It's time for me to be where I'm most needed, and that's here. With you."

I blinked, convinced I'd misheard him. "You mean that? You're staying? For good?"

"I'm not leaving your side again," Sam vowed, his voice deep and deathly. "I'll be there for the fights, and intend to help you track down Corbin too."

Help you. Not protect you. I grinned, grateful my mate understood that this was something I needed to do. But I didn't need to do it alone. Those were two very different things, and I wasn't stupid enough to go after Corbin without backup. We would do this. Together. As we would do all things.

"I love you." A peaceful smile flirted with my lips, and I leaned in and kissed him.

Sam's face softened, his mouth warm against mine. "And I love you."

I stroked his cheek before stepping back and reaching for the driver's side door. "How did Adrien take the news that you weren't planning on coming back anytime soon?"

"Oh, he understands," Sam said, striding toward the passenger side. "He knows I'm not needed as much anymore. He also asked me to reassure you that there will always be a place for you in our pack, no matter how long it takes us to sort out this mess. Once it is, though, we can go home."

Home. Yeah, I loved the sound of that.

Now I just needed to make it happen.

THE MOST IMPORTANT POST-SEX RITUAL, FOR ME, was sleep. Or maybe delicious food. Or both? Both. Definitely both. Especially at the same time. Cookies in bed. Oh, yes. The thought of cookies made my mouth water. And I suddenly pictured the bag of cinnamon roll cookies—sans chocolate, of course— sitting on the top shelf of the kitchen pantry. High enough to keep them out of easy reach of my grabby little hands. Self-control and all that nonsense. I might be a werewolf whose metabolism ran three times hotter than the average human's, but I still needed to watch the sugar intake.

"Let me guess. You're thinking of something sweet. I'm guessing either cookies or cupcakes."

I jerked at the sound of Sam's voice, then shot him a startled glance. "What makes you think that?"

"You get this look"—he gestured toward my face—"that's almost serene." He laughed while pushing the hair back from his face. "And you always snack after we have sex. Which leads me to believe you're thinking about cookies or cupcakes."

Heat blasted my cheeks. The man knew me well. "Cookies."

But my daydream vanished from my mind when we pulled up in front of the house to find Cole sitting on the front porch steps. The instant Sam spotted him, a low growl trickled out of his lips. Oh no. Oh no, no, no.

"Sam." I parked the car, then turned in my seat and grasped his hands. "Do *not* start anything. Please? I need Cole on my side. I can't afford to ostracize him."

Sam's jaw clenched and that otherworldly light

flared in his eyes, but after a brief pause, he nodded. I didn't take much stock in that nod. Especially considering my mate looked downright murderous. But even though his werewolf instincts were running the show right now, I had to trust him, had to trust he would hold to his word.

"You got this?" I asked.

Another clipped nod.

That was as good as I was going to get. So, with a deep breath, I popped open my door and slipped out of the car. The cool night air greeted me, chilling my flushed skin. Cole sat beneath the porch light, his eyes grim and expression bleak.

Something bad had happened.

I could read it on his face.

His narrowed gaze shot to Sam, then back to me, as though trying to silently communicate something. I didn't need to be a mind reader to understand, considering our conversation this afternoon.

Sighing, I glanced back at Sam. "Would you mind giving us a few moments?"

Sam balked at the question, as though shocked I'd even consider requesting such a thing.

"Please," I implored.

Mouth twisted, Sam sighed, then stormed toward the street. I watched him for a moment, noting how he raked a frustrated hand through his hair and cursed under his breath. I hated that I might be alienating Sam. Not when he and his pack had done everything for me. I'd make it up to him. And then I'd make sure my pack offered Sam the same courtesy. I refused to choose between the two.

Shaking my head, I turned back to Cole, my voice coming out a bit harsher than I'd intended. "What do you want?"

"Huh, one would think you'd be in a more pleasant mood. You know, considering..." He gestured to Sam and shot me a knowing glance.

"Gross," I said. It shouldn't have surprised me, though, considering werewolves had such a heightened sense of smell. But I really didn't need Cole pointing out that he knew Sam and I had slept together. That had to be bad manners or something.

He shrugged and stood. "I didn't mean to start anything. I just came to tell you..." He drew a deep breath, then shook his head, his shoulders rounding. "One of our pack members is missing."

I instantly went on high alert. I closed the distance between us in three quick steps, my heart racing in my chest. "What? Who? When? Why wasn't I immediately called?"

Cole shot a glance over my shoulder, likely

gauging the distance between us and Sam, as though he wanted to keep this conversation private. Sam would have to give us a hell of a lot more space to accomplish that.

I growled an impatient warning. "Cole."

His gaze snapped back to mine. "It happened around eight p.m."

I flicked a glance at my phone and snarled at the lack of missed calls. "Which has me asking, *again*, why wasn't I called?"

Cole shot me a look, one that I interpreted as *you know why*. Right. Because the pack didn't trust me. But that didn't explain why *Cole* hadn't called me. It was half past eleven, for crying out loud. Three and a half hours had passed before anyone had deigned to inform me of this. I should have been the first person they contacted.

I growled my annoyance. "Tell me exactly what happened."

Cole plopped back down onto the porch steps, his hands dangling between his thighs. "The third Tuesday of every month, our outer pack members get together. If you remember, our outer pack members are the—"

"Human-born. Yes, I know, Cole. I spent a year here, remember?"

The Mississippi Pack operated differently from the New Orleans one. While Adrien maintained a tight familial bond among all pack members, the Mississippi Pack had two "circles"—an inner and an outer. The inner circle consisted of all the wolf-born members who wished to be involved in everything. They attended every pack meeting and were closest to the alpha. The outer circle consisted of the human-born members and any wolf-born who didn't necessarily wish to actively partake in the pack but still wanted to be a member. They gathered once per month, where they received detailed updates regarding the pack's dealings. Wolf-born members could pass between circles as they desired, but the human-born belonged only to the outer. They weren't allowed to join the inner workings, since they weren't technically werewolves. It was all very political, and I hated it.

"Well, tonight's the third Tuesday," Cole continued. "The outer circle had arranged to meet for a night of bowling. But first, they gathered at Patricia's house for the meeting. Afterward, on their way to bowling, a human-born named Laini vanished."

"Vanished? How do you know she didn't just decide not to go bowling?"

Cole nodded, as though he'd wondered this question himself. "Apparently, Laini told everyone she'd meet them at the bowling alley. Some people carpool to these events, but she often drove herself so she could leave whenever she wanted."

I tapped my foot, anxiously awaiting any relevant information that proved she hadn't simply changed her mind at the last second.

"When she didn't arrive at the bowling alley, a few of her friends tried to call her. She didn't answer, so they backtracked to look for her. They were worried her car had broken down or her phone had died or something—"

"Get. To the. Point," I bit out.

Cole shot me a glare, but thankfully, moved on. "They found her car abandoned on a dark road a few blocks from her house. The driver's side door had been almost torn off the vehicle, and there were claw marks on the seat and steering wheel."

A weight crashed down on my shoulders. "Taken by a werewolf, then."

Cole sucked in a deep breath, then rubbed his brow and sighed. "Not just any werewolf. Corbin."

I jerked at that dickladle's name. "You sure it was him?"

"Yeah. When we found Reginald's body, we had

most of our pack memorize Corbin's scent. That same scent was in Laini's car."

I frowned. "Human-borns don't have strong enough senses of smell to know it was him."

"They don't. But once they saw the state of Laini's car, one of the human-borns phoned her brother, Lee. He's—"

"Fifth in the pack and werewolf-born, yes I know," I growled.

Cole nodded. "He picked up Corbin's scent and phoned me."

"And you're sure Corbin took her?" That went against his typical modus operandi. In the past, whoever he'd attacked had been left at the scene.

"We don't know anything for sure right now. But we didn't find any blood in the car. Nor did we find a body anywhere nearby."

I pressed a hand to my brow and cursed more than once. So, Corbin had finally made his move. And he'd taken one of my pack members. While Corbin had committed some heinous acts in New Orleans, he'd never abducted anyone. Why start now? Was this to get back at me? To show me I had no control over my pack? That I wasn't strong enough to face him? If so, he was in for a whole world of hurt. I would rip him to shreds myself.

"Sam?" I called out.

Cole immediately shot to his feet.

I jabbed a finger in his direction and curled a lip, anger simmering in my voice. "Do *not* question me on this. Sam has been involved with this since day one. He knows what's at stake better than anyone else."

Sam approached, his brows furrowed as he took in our expressions.

Cole didn't back down, but he didn't argue either.

"Corbin," I growled. "He took someone."

Sam nodded, his hand brushing the small of my back. "I heard."

I squeezed my eyes closed and took a few slow breaths. But rage churned in my veins. I'd known Corbin wouldn't stop, known this matter wasn't over. I hated that bastard with every fiber of my being. I wanted him dead. And that craving made my fingers burn, as though they might split and grow claws right this second.

I whirled back toward Cole. "Next time, I'm the *first* person contacted," I snarled. "I don't care if the pack has a problem with me. I'm their *alpha*."

Cole nodded, wisely keeping his mouth shut.

I blew out a breath and turned to face Sam,

searching his face for answers. Not that I found any. If this had been happening to Adrien, the first thing he'd do was call a pack meeting. But it was almost midnight. Too late to drag everyone out of their beds and insist we meet—especially when we had no information to pass on. At the very least, I needed a game plan before I spoke to the pack.

Steeling my nerves, I turned back to Cole. "Remember that pack meeting I had you ask Darla to arrange?"

He gave another nod.

"Change of plans. Call everyone and move the meeting to tomorrow morning at eight a.m. Hopefully we'll have found something by then."

"Many of our pack members work day jobs," Cole said. "And they can't just skip work."

I considered his comment. "Understandable."

"Do you have a pack forum?" Sam asked. "We keep one active for those in such situations."

Cole's jaw tightened, but thankfully he answered. "We do."

"Good," I said. "Put someone in charge of updating the forum after the meeting."

Cole opened his mouth. I wasn't sure if he intended to argue or agree, but I wasn't in the mood to listen. Instead, I jabbed a finger in his direction and said, "Call the meeting, Cole. Now." Then I stalked into the house.

Anger burned within me, and I needed somewhere to unleash it. A focal point. I stormed upstairs, into the small gym Anna had set up for me weeks ago. I needed to cool off, needed to handle the raging inferno blazing inside me. And the only place I could think of was the punching bag. Cracking my knuckles, I readied myself.

Then I faced the bag, and unleashed the beast.

CHAPTER
EIGHT

"Well, now. Aren't you in a rotten mood?" a far-too-cheery voice rose behind me.

I snarled, but kept my eyes forward and body primed, ignoring Anna. I lashed out hard, connecting with my top two knuckles, exactly as she'd taught me. One, two. One, two. One, two. Right in Corbin's hideous little face—or so I imagined. With each strike, the bag shuddered under my assault.

"One would think a little sex would mellow you out," Anna continued, clearly oblivious to the line she walked.

"Always knew you were a perv," I ground out. "Did you stay and watch or something?"

Her laughter rang in my ears, but rather than

calm me, it increased my blood pressure. I wasn't in the mood to laugh or joke around.

"Please. I have better things to do than stand around and watch my friend get laid."

I ignored her jibe and continued assaulting the bag. Clearly, she didn't know about the recent events. So, I told her about Laini in between strikes.

"Oh," she said, her voice softening. "I'm sorry to hear that. But everything will be okay."

Her words were like tossing gasoline on a fire. I whirled around, heat blazing through my cheeks. "Everything will be okay? Are you fucking kidding me right now?"

Her eyes widened the instant the curse slipped past my lips. I didn't swear much. Only in dire circumstances—like right now.

"A member of my pack is *missing*," I hissed. "Taken by Corbin. And you're telling me it'll be okay? Need I remind you what that prick did in New Orleans? The people he hurt? Sam's little sister is *dead* because of this asshole. It wasn't an easy death, either. He savaged Daniel and Brenda. Laini is someone's sister too. Mother. Daughter. Friend. So don't stand there and tell me this isn't bad. For her, it's catastrophic. Traumatizing. Who the hell knows what Corbin's doing to her right this second?"

"I'm sorry," Anna murmured, her hands lifted in placation. "I didn't mean to make light of the situation. I just meant, she's not dead. So we have time to find her. To help her."

I flashed my teeth, then returned to the punching bag and continued unleashing the rage within. With every hit, thoughts crept into my mind. That I wouldn't find Laini in time. That I'd never be able to take out Corbin. That I wasn't fit to be an alpha, regardless of what Cole thought. That I would fail miserably and let everyone down. On and on the thoughts festered, like poisonous roots burrowing deep into my consciousness. They dug deep and needled me until my fists became a flurry of movement. Hit after hit. Punch after punch. Grunt after grunt. It wasn't until the punching bag suddenly exploded in a sandstorm that I stopped.

I gasped and stumbled backward, waving my hand in the air.

"Whoa," Anna murmured. "I've never seen someone break one of those before. Except in the movies."

I stared at the mess on the floor, panting for breath. Now that I was a werewolf, I sometimes underestimated my strength. My arms burned and my muscles ached, but it'd felt so good to unleash myself like that, to direct all my anger and fear and frustration at something inanimate.

Before all this, violence had never been my go-to when angry. In fact, people had often said I was a pacifist, always searching for peaceful resolutions when people argued. I was the calm and rational one, the one to think things through before responding. As a child, Anna's mother had always told her to "think before speaking." I'd never received that admonition.

Sadly, I didn't feel like that person anymore. Now, the anger always seemed to ride close to the surface, almost as though it'd become my default response, and I wasn't sure how I felt about it. Or if I even liked this new me.

I stared at my hands and contemplated that last thought.

I *did* know how I felt about it. This new me felt strong, capable, and people depended on me. Those were things I hadn't felt before, and I *liked* it. I liked being a leader and protecting people. Maybe Cole was right, and I did have potential to be a good alpha after all.

"Feel better?" Anna asked.

"A bit," I admitted. The anger still sang in my

blood, but I could think clearly now. "I'll feel a lot better when we find Laini and Corbin is dead."

"I bet. If you're ready, how about we head downstairs then and discuss our options? Before your two werewolves rip each other to shreds."

Ah, crap. I'd left Sam and Cole alone together. Probably not a wise idea, considering everything that was going on. I only hoped Sam was able to control himself. Better than me, anyway. Someone had to be the sensible one in the relationship, and right now, that didn't describe me.

"Were they fighting?"

"No, not fighting." A faint smile twitched on Anna's lips. "More like, standing very still and glaring daggers at each other. I honestly don't think either of them blinked the whole time I watched them. I *did* suggest they eye-hump each other elsewhere, but neither seem inclined to take my suggestion."

I couldn't help but laugh. And once I did, my body released the remaining tension.

"There we go," Anna said. "You just needed to pummel the shit out of a punching bag."

Shrugging, I flexed my fingers, stretching them in and out. My knuckles ached, but otherwise seemed perfectly fine.

"Where's Vlad?" I asked.

"He's downstairs, monitoring the situation, and keeping your naughty boys in check."

"Only one of them is mine," I reminded her.

"Technically, they're both yours. One's just yours in a far more intimate capacity." Anna's brows shot upward, and she stared at me. "I hope?"

I snorted. "Oh, Jesus, Anna."

"Just checking! You never know. A girl's preference can change, and I must say, they're both quite the beautiful specimens. If you wanted—"

I wasn't remotely surprised when *three* growls rose to my ears. I pressed a hand to my mouth and laughed. All three males had overheard the comment, and none had been pleased with her assessment.

"Come on," I said, chuckling. "Let's get down there before *you* cause a fight."

She winked, then ducked her head close to mine and whispered, "Just think. A hunky man sandwich," before dashing up the stairs.

TENSION RANG IN THE AIR AS ANNA AND I entered the living room. Vlad leaned against the farthest wall, amusement carving a rare smile into his face. Sam and Cole stood practically nose to nose, glowering at each other. The sight of Cole holding his own against my beast of a mate almost made me laugh. It wasn't often I witnessed someone stand up to Sam, but Cole seemed determined, even though he had to practically strain on his tiptoes to hold eye contact.

"Okay, enough," I said, choking back a laugh.

Neither budged an inch.

Shaking my head, I strode between them, then place a hand on each of their chests and *pushed*. Even though I'd just demolished a punching bag, my strength still surprised me, especially when both men staggered backward.

"Go to your corners," I muttered.

The hostility in the room dipped a few levels as the two retreated to opposite sides of the room. I released a long breath, then glanced at the grandfather clock the instant it chimed. One o'clock in the morning. No wonder I was exhausted. Especially after all the shifting I'd done earlier this evening. Unfortunately, we still had a long way to go before we could call it a night. And I had absolutely no idea where to even begin. I wasn't a detective— nor did I play one on TV—so I'd never dealt with a missing person before.

Raking a hand down my face, I faced Cole. "Did you call the meeting?"

Guilt flashed in his eyes, and he shot Sam an accusatory glance. "I haven't had a chance yet."

I bristled with annoyance. I'd given him a command, and he hadn't followed through. Unacceptable. The pack needed to follow my instructions without delay or question. Instead, he'd allowed himself to get caught up in a silent pissing contest.

"What's Laini's family doing right now?" I asked.

"I told them to go home and wait for word from you."

I nodded. If it were me, and my daughter or sister was missing, I wouldn't be able to sleep. I'd be wearing a track in my floor, demanding answers. And I would bet any amount of money that Laini's family was currently doing the same.

Even though Laini had been born human, we still couldn't call the police. We couldn't risk exposing ourselves to the authorities. Which meant rescuing her was up to us.

I heaved a sigh, then lumbered over to the couch and took a seat.

"Do you have a plan?" Cole asked.

I really, *really* didn't. But I couldn't let that stop

me. Hopefully I'd figure this all out as we went. "I want you to do as I asked earlier and call that meeting. Inform those who can't come that the forum will be updated immediately afterward. I want both the inner and outer circles present, as many as can come."

Cole nodded. "Where would you like to hold it?"

"Here," I said. Thankfully, Reggie had bought land along with the house. Three acres gave us enough space to hold pack meetings without neighbors peeping in on us.

Cole immediately started typing into his phone.

Now, all that remained was actually *finding* answers. And truthfully, I had no clue where to even begin. If TV shows were to be trusted, then we needed to start at the scene of the crime.

"You said Lee was the one who picked up Corbin's scent. Did he track it?" The problem with scents was that they faded quickly, especially when outdoors.

"He tried but didn't get very far. Laini and Corbin's scent disappeared ten feet away. We suspect Corbin loaded her into a different vehicle and drove off."

Cole had mentioned earlier how they'd found her abandoned car on a dark road. Telling me we likely wouldn't find any witnesses. Corbin would have orchestrated that. Our first dead end.

"What about security cameras?" I asked. "Highway cameras? Satellite images? Anything that might have caught this on camera?"

"Maybe. I already have our tech guy on it. Unfortunately, there aren't many cameras in the area. And the road isn't a busy one, which is likely why Laini had taken it, to avoid traffic. I mentioned satellite imagery, but it isn't like he has an all-access pass to those."

Understandable.

"So, why Laini?" Sam asked. "Why target her?"

I watched as he crossed the room and took the seat next to me, his thigh brushing against mine. As though sensing I needed comfort, he clasped my hand tightly.

"Maybe she was the simplest target," I replied. "The others had grouped together in a carpool, but she'd gone off alone."

"Which suggests he's watching the pack," Vlad offered.

Oh, I didn't like that. For nearly two months, we'd been searching for this bastard and hadn't once laid eyes on him. But the thought of *him* watching *us...* My wolf unleashed an unsettling growl in my head, one I wholeheartedly agreed with.

"It wouldn't have been too difficult to take her, either," Vlad continued. "Human-borns are no stronger than humans themselves. She would have been easy prey. Especially on a dark road with no witnesses."

I nodded, ignoring that I used to be a human, and that his assessment would have once included me. Instead, I focused on our path moving forward. Back in New Orleans, Adrien had made the decision to pair his pack members off. The strategy hadn't been foolproof, considering his daughter and her protector had died, but it still felt better than doing nothing.

"Cole, do we have a pack roster?"

"Of course," he said.

"Perfect. Let's get a copy of it and have someone go through the list and pair as many people up as they can. One human-born to one wolf-born."

Cole's expression showed a momentary flash of surprise before he nodded and reached for his phone yet again. "Dominic can handle that."

I nodded. I knew that name. He was the pack's third in command.

"If we have any human-borns left over without a wolf counterpart, let me know."

"We shouldn't," Cole said. "At last count, we had more wolves than humans in the pack. We could even do two wolf-borns to one human-born for some."

Good. That made things simpler.

Next on my list... "Who's the techie guy? The one you mentioned earlier?"

"Jorge," Cole said.

"When he's done looking into the satellite imagery, see if he can track down Corbin's name on any real estate. Maybe he's using a place he owns."

"He'd be stupid to use his own property," Sam commented.

I nodded. "Agreed. But it's worth a shot." We couldn't track Laini and Corbin by scent, so we needed to be smarter about it. "Sam, can you contact your father to get everything they drudged up on Corbin? His past, any run ins with the law, et cetera." Know thy enemy, and all that.

"Of course," Sam said.

"Anything else?" Cole asked, hardly batting an eye at the list of assignments I was leaving him.

At the moment, I couldn't think of anything else.

Not until we first gathered the basics. "We'll meet with the pack in the morning, where we can impart upon them how important it is that they remain together. We can also take that opportunity to ask if anyone has anything to add to the investigation. If anyone's heard or seen anything. Could be someone saw something but is too afraid to speak up. Or saw something that they didn't know was relevant at the time."

"Agreed," Cole said.

"Keep me apprised of everything," I said. "The instant Jorge knows anything, bring that information to me."

Cole nodded.

"In the meantime, everyone try to get some sleep," I said, rising to my feet with Sam's hand still clasped in mine. "The next few days are going to be intense. We'll need as much rest as possible."

Cole left without a lengthy goodbye, leaving me with Sam, Anna, and Vlad.

I caught their expressions and grimaced. "I have no idea what I'm doing."

Sam's hand found the small of my back. "None of us do. My father didn't know what to do either. You're trying, and that's all that matters. You can do this, Luce."

His comforting words sent a rush of warmth through me. "Thanks, Sam."

"If you're finished with us, I could use a drink," Vlad said.

Anna nodded, clearly feeling a little peckish herself. "There isn't any blood left from tonight's delivery."

"Right." I still needed to call and change that order. "Sam's here, so why don't you two go out to get some. I'm sure you wouldn't mind a little fresh air."

"Thanks, Luce." Anna swept in for a gentle hug, then she and Vlad disappeared.

I stared up at Sam and forced a small smile. Only a few hours ago, I'd been so happy to see him. I still was, but that happiness was tainted now. After two months, I'd taken the peace and quiet for granted. And now we were right back at the beginning, trying to find Corbin so I could plunge a silver knife into his heart.

"Come on," Sam said. He lifted our joined hands to his chest, then led me through the house. "Let's get some sleep. Lord knows we'll need it."

CHAPTER
NINE

WHY IS IT EVERY TIME SOMEONE *NEEDS* TO SLEEP, they can't?

I tossed and turned on my bed, sighing every single time I failed to get comfortable. At this rate, I couldn't believe I hadn't woken Sam. He laid sprawled next to me, snoring softly under his breath, and completely oblivious to my restlessness. For a month and a half, I'd slept comfortably on this mattress, but tonight, I felt like the girl in *Princess and the Pea*. Every time I found a somewhat decent position, something dug into my back. Or my body started to ache. Or the covers grew too warm. Or the fan whirled too loud.

I flopped on my side and stared at Sam. *Glared* more like. Typical man. We hadn't been in bed for five seconds before his breathing deepened and his muscles started twitching. Not me, though.

A part of me wanted to thwack Sam in the head with my pillow. *Oops, sorry, did I wake you? Well, now that you're up...* Maybe if we did the *diddly do*, I'd be able to sleep after. Sam had this marvelous way of wearing me out. Then again, never-ending orgasms did that. Made me pleasantly sleepy and oh, so happy. Less anxiety, more ecstasy. Hmm, I needed to put that on a shirt.

Grumbling under my breath, I rolled onto my back and stared at the stucco ceiling. Ugh, I didn't have time for this. I had things to do, people to find, and a turd-nugget named Corbin to thoroughly kill. On my to-do list, sleeping ranked fairly low.

The sound of a soft, girlish giggle coming from the living room made me groan and flip onto my stomach. If Anna and Vlad had returned home, it had to be near sunrise, and that angered me all the more. Had I truly spent the entire night rolling around, begging myself to fall asleep?

I fumbled for my phone on a nearby nightstand, but was dismayed to find it dead. Apparently, I'd forgotten to plug it in. I lifted my head from the pillow and scowled at the nearby clock. Lucifer's sweaty balls, it was after five in the morning. Ugh.

Maybe I could convince Vlad to knock me out. At least then, I'd finally get some rest.

Footsteps shuffled through the hallway, and I uttered a small groan. I couldn't handle it if Anna and Vlad chose to play *hide the wiener* again tonight. And if they did, I fully intended to lace their undergarments in garlic. I absolutely refused to listen to them get freaky again. Once was enough, thank you very much.

"Did you hear that?" Anna's whispered voice rose outside my door.

Vlad shifted his weight but didn't speak.

"I think Lucy's awake," Anna continued.

Relief lifted my agitated mood. At least there wouldn't be any hanky panky if Anna knew I was awake.

Sighing, I climbed out from under the covers, threw on the closest clothes I could find, then strode to the door. My fingers touched the doorknob, and I glanced back at Sam. He lay, undisturbed, snoozing away to his heart's content. I kinda hated him a little bit. Except, not really. I could never hate him.

With one last glance, I slipped out of the room.

"Luce, what're you doing up?" Anna whispered.

"Couldn't sleep," I grumbled, stumbling blearily toward them. "My brain won't shut up."

She gave a sympathetic nod. "Do you want me to make you something to eat? Or get you something to drink?"

I winced at the thought of Anna making me food. Since becoming a vampire, she'd lost all ability to cook. Flavors seemed foreign to her now that she couldn't taste things.

"Thanks, but no," I said.

"You sure?"

With a forced smile, I nodded. The thought of eating turned my stomach. I couldn't get Laini out of my head. We'd never met—I'd never met *any* of the human-borns—but that didn't matter. As the alpha, whether interim or not, she was my responsibility. How could I eat or sleep knowing one of my pack members was missing? God only knew what Corbin was doing to her, and it was driving me crazy.

"I think I'll go for a walk," I said. "Get some air and hopefully clear my head."

Concern flashed across Anna's face. "I'll go with you."

Vlad laid a hand on Anna's arm, drawing her attention. "The sun's about to rise, my love."

"Shit." Anna turned back to me. "What about Sam?"

"He's sleeping and I don't want to wake him.

One of us needs to be rested today. Don't worry, I'll be fine. I won't go far." I skirted around the two and reached for my sneakers. Hopefully the fresh air actually helped. I needed to sleep, but I couldn't lay in bed anymore.

I slipped on my shoes and gave the laces a quick yank before waving at Anna and Vlad, then dashed out the door. Cold rain immediately splashed my face, and I glared up at the dawning sky. Normally I didn't mind a little rain, but I wasn't in the mood for it this morning.

I ducked back inside to grab a rain jacket, then returned outside, my steps quickly carrying me down the sidewalk. I knew a few paths and trails to take, thanks to the year I'd spent here, so I let my memory carry me toward LeFleur's Bluff Park. The scent of swamp and cypress trees made me feel a little nostalgic for New Orleans.

The fresh air only seemed to reinvigorate my brain, which raced with all the thoughts. What the hell was I doing here? Did I honestly think I could help Laini? Or stop Corbin? Or be an alpha? Every single doubt I'd ever suffered came spewing out the dark recesses of my mind again. I was just me—Lucy. A girl who'd been barely more than Anna's shadow her entire life. Even in school, people had only known me through her. They knew her as the outgoing extrovert, and me as the complete opposite. The antisocial introvert. It wasn't that I disliked people, but rather that Anna shone when in the spotlight. She always had. I'd never begrudged her for it though. That was our relationship. Two extremes. And I'd never had a problem with it.

I shook my head and banished those thoughts. I couldn't let the negativity suck me down into the muck. I had to believe in myself. But how could I do that when no one had ever believed in me?

No. That wasn't true at all.

Sam, Anna, Vlad, and Cole all believed in me.

Now, *I* had to believe in me.

I kept repeating those words over and over under my breath, forging it into my new mantra. It didn't matter if the rest of the pack didn't believe in me. I had to believe in myself. No one could do that for me. If I wanted to be an alpha, then I had to take those steps. I had to make myself *into* an alpha.

I could do that. I just needed to break everything down into baby steps. If I made myself a plan and stuck to it, I could accomplish anything. I just... didn't know where to start. Cole had already begun teaching me how to fight. One lesson wasn't enough, of course, but it'd given me a new appreciation for a werewolf's abilities. Next came understanding the politics and rules. Adrien had given me a decent foundation, and Sam would help. I wasn't alone. That was all that mattered.

A sense of calm washed over me as I laid all this out in my head. Almost as though my inner wolf approved of these thoughts. Knowing the two of us were in understanding gave me another sense of peace. I'd spent a year fighting with what I believed was the monster in my head—restraining it, controlling it, hating it. Appreciating it unlocked a new feeling within me, a sense of power I hadn't possessed before.

And I liked it.

"You know, it really isn't safe for a little girl to be walking through these woods alone."

I went rigid at the sound of that horribly familiar voice. My head snapped up and my eyes narrowed on the thatch of trees ahead of me. So lost to my thoughts, I hadn't sensed Corbin's approach. Or the two lackies behind him. How on earth had they found me here? Had they followed me from the house?

I immediately reached for my phone, then grimaced. The damn thing was still sitting on my nightstand, battery completely dead. I was so used to always carrying it on me that I hadn't realized I'd left without it. Great. Just freaking great.

A low, threatening growl rumbled up my throat and my hands fisted as the three Musketeers fanned out around me. Cole had shown me a few things about defending myself, but not against multiple opponents. Heck, I was still learning how to fend off one.

"My, my, what big teeth you have," Corbin taunted.

I rolled my eyes. He could quote *Little Red Riding Hood* all he wanted. I refused to play this game of his. Instead, I analyzed the situation. Three against one, and me without any way to call for help. The odds certainly weren't in my favor. But I didn't necessarily need to take out all three. Just one. Enough to break free and retreat—a lesson Cole had taught me. Being an alpha meant being smart enough to know when to retreat. And right now, I knew I couldn't handle all three of them. Not alone. Not yet.

My wolf pawed at the edge of my mind, demanding I release her. I couldn't, though. Not yet. Shifting would cost me precious time. Time Corbin could take advantage of.

I curled a lip and glared at the asshat. "Where's Laini?"

A vicious grin claimed his lips. But rather than answer, he stalked closer, his narrowed gaze tracking my every move.

I stepped back, only to bump into one of Corbin's men, who'd circled behind me. Long fingers curled around my forearms, locking me in place. My instincts instantly kicked in, and with one sharp jerk, I snapped my head back, smashing the back of my skull into his nose.

A sharp cry rose behind me, and the hands vanished from my arms. I didn't need to glance back to know my attacker had stumbled backwards. His blood perfumed the air and his wheezing breaths filled the silence.

Pleased with myself, I rolled out my shoulders, then inched away from the other two. I'd given myself an opening. But I couldn't leave yet, not without finding out where Laini was.

Corbin's gaze leapt between me and his injured lackey, his eyes widening in delighted surprise. "I must say, I didn't expect that."

"I've learned a few tricks," I snarled.

Amusement brought a grin to his lips. "So I see."

"Where's Laini?" I demanded again.

He waved a dismissive hand. "She's around."

When he didn't elaborate, I released another growl. I was going to enjoy tearing him to pieces. Even if I failed to take out all three, I'd die happily if I dragged Corbin to hell with me.

"Temper, temper," he taunted. "I thought you'd be happy. One less human-born to worry yourself over."

Ice crackled in my veins. What did that mean? Had he killed Laini?

"You don't know the first thing about me." I lifted my fisted hands in front me and eyed Corbin and his backup. It hadn't taken long for the third to recuperate. Werewolves healed fast, and a broken nose was a minor nuisance.

"Indeed." Corbin asked, his inquisitive stare roving over the woods. "I'm surprised lover boy let you out of his sight. Last time we all met, it hadn't ended well for you."

Anger melted the lingering chill in my blood, and I lifted my chin a notch. "Sorry, but it's just me here. Guess I'll have to do."

Corbin winked. "Guess so. That's okay. I have a feeling once I'm done with you, lover boy will find me."

A murderous rage swept through me. He could

threaten me all he wanted, but if he so much as laid a finger on Sam, I'd rip it off and stuff it down his throat.

In any other situation, my reaction to Corbin might have surprised me. He awoke such violent within me. Dark and contemptable things. He gave me a new understanding of the words "hate" and "loathing." And right now, I used those emotions to empower me.

"It's too bad I need you dead," he continued, oblivious to the fury broiling within me. "You were the first human-born I turned after all. It forges a bond, wouldn't you say?"

I ground my teeth together to keep from lashing out. More than a year ago, this shitgibbon had stalked me through the house and fed on my terror before ripping into me with his teeth and claws, leaving me for dead in a pool of my own blood.

"Don't flatter yourself," I grumbled.

"Oh, come on now. Don't tell me you don't like this new life of yours. I've had my share of humans" —I shivered at the delight in his voice—"but you, I'll never forget. Sweet little thing. So meek. So scared. And then to learn you survived…"

"You really enjoy the sound of your own voice, don't you?"

Corbin's eyes flashed yellow—a sign I'd angered him.

I inched another step backward, my steps matched by Corbin's buddies. The one whose nose I'd likely broken stood behind me, his breath stirring the hair at the back of my neck. He didn't touch me again, so he'd at least learned that lesson.

My gaze darted between the two in front of me. I stepped to the side until the third entered my periphery, his face stained with blood. I contemplated shouting for help. But that meant dragging some innocent bystander into this—and I loathed the thought of that. I was well and truly up shit creek—and man, my swearing had really increased lately. The things Corbin brought out of me...

I contemplated my options. The one lesson I'd received from Cole had focused primarily on fighting a single person. He'd been more focused on the challenges coming up as opposed to an ambush. Truthfully, I don't think either of us had envisioned this scenario.

"I truly am sorry about this," Corbin said. "But I can't have another alpha in my territory."

My brows shot upward. "*Your* territory?"

"Well, soon-to-be. Once I rid Mississippi of you,

your mate, and that second of yours, this territory will be mine for the taking. And by then, I'll have enough of my own pack members to take yours without a fight."

A brittle laugh slipped past my lips. "Good luck with that."

His eyes darkened at the sound of my laughter. "I'm sick of being forced to follow weak alphas. My former alpha *gave* us to the Vampire Queen to use at her whim without so much as a fight. Because he feared she would kill him. She would have. But a true alpha would have died fighting before he handed his people over to a monster like her."

"And Reggie?" I demanded. "What reason did you have for killing him?"

"He was useless and in my way," Corbin said, sighing. "You know that more than anyone. He couldn't even be bothered to teach you how to be a proper werewolf. For months I watched. He was a waste of air. A problem I remedied."

I forced myself to breathe, to remain calm. "And me?"

Corbin cocked his head. "You are an anomaly. As a human-born, you were weak. But, thanks to me, here you stand, stronger than ever, ready to fight for a pack you don't even want. I admire that. Alas, you're also standing in my way."

"And what about Daniel and Brenda?" I pressed. "They weren't alphas. They were innocent, like me."

"They were experiments," he said. "To see if I could turn other human-borns, as you already know."

"And Isabelle?"

His lip curled at the mention of Sam's sister. "She was revenge."

For his lackey I'd killed. This man truly was sick.

"And Laini?"

Corbin's smile widened, his eyes twinkling with amusement. "Ah, she tasted almost as sweet as you. Hopefully she will be the first of my new pack. If she survives the change, that is. We'll soon find out."

His implication hit me hard. He'd changed her already—or attempted to. I only prayed she survived.

"Well, I hate to disappoint you," I said, "but I don't plan on going anywhere."

Corbin nodded, then lifted his hand in the air. "You'll fight. But you'll also lose."

Before I could utter a response, Corbin snapped his fingers, signaling for his men to attack.

I was so screwed.

CHAPTER
TEN

A pair of meaty arms swung near my head.

I ducked and slammed my elbow back into my attacker's gut before whirling out of reach. A sharp exhalation told me I'd landed my hit, but I didn't stop to glance back at him. So far, this guy was having a bad day, what with his newly broken nose and bruised sternum.

The second guy charged me, his face a mask of determination. I side-stepped out of the way, then gave him a shove as he stumbled past me. He tumbled to the ground, his hands and knees scraping against the cement path.

Corbin, it seemed, was determined to hang back and let this play out. Right now, that worked to my benefit. The odds of fighting off two were certainly better than three.

His two lackeys picked themselves up and turned to face me. Rage burned in their eyes, and I knew if they got their hands on me, I was done for. Goal number one right now was to keep that from happening. I just needed to keep them off-balance and give myself enough of an opening that I could run back to the house. The park wasn't far, only a couple miles. I could run that far. The only question was if I could run *fast* enough to outpace them.

"Enough of this," Corbin snapped. "Take care of her already. It's getting light out."

He wasn't wrong. Already, sunlight filtered through the trees, burning away the lingering darkness. And pretty soon, people would be venturing into the park for their morning walks or heading to their jobs.

One of his men swiped at me, his fingers now long, sharp claws.

I gasped and jumped back as a lick of pain burned my flesh. My gaze dropped momentarily to inspect the damage. Blood seeped down my stomach, soaking into the newly tattered remains of my shirt.

Shit.

Not a great start. If these guys could partially

shift their limbs, I was done for. That was a talent I hadn't mastered yet. Fighting with fists I could handle, but their claws would just slowly bleed me out until nothing remained.

I stared at my bare hands and cursed. I was essentially weaponless.

Sensing my despair, Corbin chuckled and strode toward me. "Don't worry, Lucy. You did better than I expected. I'll make sure to pass that along to Sam."

Unbridled fury rose within me, and I stared at my hands, silently begging them to change. I remembered how they'd burned last night, how they'd ached to change. Maybe that meant I could do it. I just needed to focus. I concentrated on that thought, and *willed* them to comply. A tingle spread through my fingers, then right before my eyes, my hands shifted, my nails growing into sharp claws that glinted in the morning light. With a devilish grin, I lifted my head and caught Corbin's stare.

His stunned gaze landed on my hands, and he danced backward, beyond my reach.

This was a game changer.

Even the other two knew it, judging by how they hung back.

I took advantage of the distraction and started moving backward. My feet came silently down on the sidewalk as I stole step after step. If I turned and bolted, they'd give chase, but running had to be better than standing here and letting them carve me up.

"You never cease to amaze me," Corbin muttered. "Tell you what. Renounce the Mississippi Pack and go home with Sam. We'll forget each other exists, and just go on our merry little ways."

Laughter erupted from my lips. "You can't be serious."

"Deadly. Do the math here, sweetheart."

I glowered at him.

"Three against one. Sure, you might stand a small chance of taking one of us out. But what about the other two? I'm sure you'd rather go home to Sam right now, wouldn't you?"

I would. But I also wanted Corbin dead. And this seemed like the best chance I was ever going to get. Waiting to get him alone wasn't an option, not with his lackeys likely following him everywhere. With this new talent of mine, I felt like I might stand a chance.

No, I couldn't let myself get too cocky. Being able to shift my hands didn't give me the advantage. One of Anna's lessons had been to never underestimate your opponent, but also to never overestimate yourself. At the time, I hadn't given much thought to that, but now I understood. The adrenaline coursing through my veins made me feel like I could handle anything. Including fighting off three grown men. Even if I were taller and a hundred pounds heavier, I still wouldn't stand a chance. Three against one were not survivable odds.

"Tell *you* what," I said, parroting Corbin's words. "How about you three just go on your merry little way, and *I'll* let *you* go."

The corner of Corbin's mouth ticked upward. "I like your confidence."

I briefly considered his earlier offer. There was a part of me that would *love* to hand the pack over and return home to New Orleans with Sam. That was where we belonged. They were my pack, my family. The Mississippi Pack was something I'd been chained to.

The other part of me knew I could never abandon them like that. I couldn't allow someone like Corbin to take control of them. No, I wouldn't back down. I wouldn't relinquish the Mississippi Pack. And I absolutely wouldn't allow Corbin to hurt anyone else.

My silence must have been answer enough for

him. "Very well," Corbin said. "We'll make it quick for you."

Fear blossomed and my heart kicked into overdrive. Corbin's men bolted forward, their movements in perfect synchronicity.

This time, I screamed as I bolted backward. Time to bring awareness to this situation. Shocked by my outburst, one of the men stumbled. But the other's arms closed around me and together, we toppled to the ground. Pain lanced my side and my inner thigh the instant we hit the pavement.

Thankfully, Cole had shown me a few ground moves. I locked my trembling legs around my attacker's waist and flipped him over. Once I had him pinned, I struck, slamming the heel of my palm into his nose. The crunch of cartilage reverberated up my arm, but I didn't stop to take in the damage. Instead, I rolled off him and leapt to my feet, then kicked him square in the jaw. His head whipped to the side, blood flying from his lips.

Footsteps thundered behind me, and I whirled around. The other guy barreled toward me, and before I knew it, he'd rammed his shoulder into my gut and wrapped his arms around my waist. My lungs contracted, but I couldn't let something as trivial as *breathing* stop me. Before he could take me to the ground, I gripped his head between my hands —exactly as Cole had shown me—and cranked his neck. The guy let out a shout, but the force of my hands set off his balance and had him staggering to the side. Once his arms slipped from my waist, I centered myself and threw a sharp jab, aiming for his throat. The instant my knuckles connected, his eyes widened, and he released a choking breath as he dropped to a knee.

Perfect. Just where I wanted him.

Cupping the back of his head, I forced it down just as I snapped up my knee. The two came together in an explosive show of blood that stained the cement. I released him and turned to find myself facing off against Corbin.

Never in a million years would I believe I could have done this. Yes, I'd fought before, and Anna and Cole were training me, but I hadn't ever thought I'd win this fight. And now, only Corbin and I remained.

Corbin eyed his two men, disgust twisting his features. Then he lifted his head and stared at me. This time, he didn't utter a word. Guess the time for talking had passed. Instead, he attacked. Silent, and impossibly fast. Faster than the other two.

He was a flurry of movement, his hands lashing

out in an endless assault. I managed to block a few before the first connected. Then the second. And the third. Until the next thing I knew, I was laying on my back, a battered mess, staring up at the canopy of trees.

Every inch of me hurt and breathing became a lesson in agony. Punctured lung for sure. A few broken ribs, definitely. I couldn't focus on those, though. Not right now. Not with Corbin looming over me.

Through swollen eyes, I watched as his fingers extended into claws.

Sam had once said we could heal all wounds made by teeth and claws. But I had to guess there was a limit to that. If Corbin ripped out my throat, would I heal? Survey said... Unlikely.

Pick yourself up. Fight back. Don't let him win.

Cole had drummed that into me during our training session. More than once, I'd ended up in this position, with him standing over me. He'd shown me how to fight back in this position. How to lure my opponent in, give them a false sense of security. I didn't close my eyes—I wasn't sure they'd open again if I did—but I continued staring at the trees, counting the many branches and leaves.

Corbin stood over me, a sickening grin spreading across his face.

I waited for him to make his move, and when he lifted his arm, I mustered every ounce of strength I had left and struck. My foot connected with his knee, and satisfaction welled within me when I heard an audible pop echo through the woods.

Corbin cried out as he stumbled backward. I moved then, before he found his balance. I scraped myself off the ground and punched the inside of his second knee. Another *pop* and cry. I watched, a fresh surge of adrenaline coursing through my veins, as Corbin slammed down onto his dislocated knees. They bent inward at an awkward angle, and I took great joy in every muffled cry he uttered.

Panting, I gathered whatever reserves I had left, and managed a spinning kick. This kick had always been my sloppiest while training. But this morning, it came to me a bit more naturally, and I rejoiced when my heel connected with Corbin's face. His head whipped back, and I heard another crunch of bone. Corbin dropped to the ground like a sack of potatoes, his eyes closed and neck angled oddly. I knew it was possible for me to break someone's neck, just like I also knew it wouldn't kill him. A human, yes. But not a werewolf. He'd heal. And wake up pissed as hell.

I glanced around, dismayed to find Corbin's lackeys picking themselves up off the pavement. Crap! I needed to go. Now. If those two were back in the game... I'd lose. Every inch of me hurt and shook with the strain of merely standing. I didn't have it in me to keep fighting.

Cursing, I did the only thing I could.

I fled.

Yes, that meant letting Corbin live, but what choice did I have? Running meant I'd live to see another day. Staying meant dying. The choice was simple, no matter how much it pissed me off.

I hobbled out of the park. I needed to get home as quickly as possible. I'd barely rounded the first corner when I heard a human scream after she'd stumbled across Corbin and his men. If I'd waited any longer, I would have been caught at the scene.

I pushed forward, every step pure torture. I'd definitely broken something in my ankle—probably from the spinning kick. My heart pounded, my breaths coming hard and fast, sawing in and out of my damaged lungs. My chest felt like it might explode, it was so tight. I couldn't stop though. No matter what. If I did, I might not be able to start again. My legs grew weaker with every passing minute, my body heavier. It wasn't until I found myself leaning against a car that I realized I might have a concussion. I didn't remember stopping.

"Hey!" a voice shouted. "Hey, lady! Are you okay?"

Hands came down on my shoulders, and I whimpered. The only thing that kept me from lashing out was the distinct scent wafting off them. Human. Not werewolf.

"Jesus!" someone shouted. "Hey, lady, can you hear me?"

Movement blurred in front of my eyes, but I couldn't make it out. It took me a few moments to realize someone was waving a hand, trying to get my attention. But the adrenaline had long since worn off now, and I could hardly think, let alone focus.

"I think she's in shock," the first said. "She's shaking. My god. Her teeth are chattering."

Ah. Maybe that was why my jaw hurt. Or maybe Corbin had hit me. I vaguely remembered someone landing a punch.

"Call an ambulance."

"N-No," I stuttered. "No ambulance. Just... take me... home."

"Don't listen to her. She clearly needs a hospital."

I blinked and managed to focus, my gaze

narrowing on the people standing in front of me. Two males. Both wearing distressed expressions.

I cleared my throat and shook my head, fighting back a wince. "I'm fine. I just need to go home. My... husband is there."

"Your husband?" They shared a look. "Did he do this to you?"

A weak smile curved my lips. When I tasted blood, I realized my bottom lip was split in two. "No. Muggers. In the woods."

"Jesus," the second guy whispered. "You're lucky to be standing. We should call the cops."

I nodded. "I will. Just take me home, please."

They shared another look, then finally the first nodded. "Where's home?"

I rattled off the address, then pushed off the car and straightened. I needed to assure them I was fine. Werewolves couldn't go to hospitals, but they didn't know that. They were just two nice citizens taking care of a battered woman.

"Really," I said, running a trembling hand through my mussed hair. "I'm fine, I promise. Once I get home, I'll have my husband call the police."

"You sure?"

I nodded, then grit my teeth when a flash of pain struck like lightning in my head.

"Your place isn't too far from here," one said. "A few houses down."

Distantly, I was aware of someone folding me into the backseat of their car. I felt the seat cushion beneath my head and I closed my eyes, allowing myself to relax for the first time in what felt like hours.

They weren't kidding about only being a few houses away. They'd barely started the car before they'd pulled up in front of my place.

"Lucy!" a familiar voice shouted.

My wolf's presence flickered weakly in my head, responding to the sound of Sam's shout.

The car's back door flew open, and hands gathered me. Warm, strong hands. Hands I would know even if I were dead.

Sam lifted me out of the car and tucked me into his chest, his steady heartbeat soothing to my ears. I laid my head against his chest and sighed. Pain still ravaged me, but in his arms, I felt safe.

"What the hell happened?" he shouted, his words edged with a growl.

"It's okay, Sam," I whispered. "I'm okay."

"She said she was mugged. I told her we should call an ambulance and the police but she wouldn't let us."

Sam's arms tightened around me. "I'll call them immediately."

"Oh, good," one of my rescuers said. "I think that's for the best."

"Thank you so much for bringing her home." A gentle kiss feathered my brow.

"Sure thing, mister. You really should get her to the hospital."

"I will."

I could smell the humans' relief as they retreated to their car. I was someone else's problem now. They'd done their heroic duty and could return to their lives, gushing to everyone about the woman they'd saved this morning. I would have laughed if my chest didn't hurt so much.

When the car pulled away from the curb, Sam pulled me tighter against his chest. "Lucy?"

I hummed a nonverbal response, then sank into the awaiting darkness.

CHAPTER
ELEVEN

CONSCIOUSNESS RETURNED TO ME DROP BY DROP, like water filling a bucket. I first became aware of the dull ache in my body, but compared to past injuries, it didn't seem too bad. Some pain, some tenderness, but all in all, I'd suffered far worse. Then came the sound of soft voices speaking in low undertones. Surprisingly—or rather, *un*surprisingly—they were discussing me.

"She shouldn't have been out there alone!" a gravelly voice suddenly shouted.

Cole, I realized. Guess I should have expected that. Sam must have called him.

"You think I don't know that?" Sam snapped. I knew that tone well. I called it his "pissed-off alpha voice."

"How did this even happen?" Cole demanded.

Sam's low, drawn-out sigh made me want to reach out to him. But my arms seemed rather content resting on the mattress right now. Just like how my eyes didn't want to open. I knew I should let them know I was awake and eavesdropping on their conversation, but doing so required energy. And I wanted to lay here and rest a few more minutes before I returned to reality and gave them a rundown of everything that'd happened.

"I have a right to know," Cole pushed. "I'm her second, and—"

"Lucy had already left by the time I woke up," Sam replied, his exasperated tone almost making me smile. I could tell Sam's nerves were frayed—understandably so. It wasn't every day someone's mate turned up half-dead on their porch. Not to mention that Sam didn't particularly like Cole. "Anna and Vlad were dead to the world, and Lucy had left her phone behind. I didn't know where she'd gone."

"You could have tracked her!" Cole snapped.

Sam's deep growl lifted the hairs on my arms. Regardless of Cole's position in my pack, Sam wouldn't take well to someone yelling at him.

Especially considering he was far more dominant than Cole.

"I'm. Aware," Sam uttered, his tone taking on a dangerous edge. "I was on my way out the door when the car pulled up with her inside."

Cole bit out a few choice words, then took to pacing the length of the bedroom. "This is ridiculous. If you can't protect her, then maybe she should be with someone who—"

Sam lashed out with a savage snarl, one that had my gut clenching. Cole fell quiet, but I caught the distinct sound of him grinding his teeth.

"Allow me to make this *perfectly* clear," Sam intonated. He didn't sound like himself anymore, his voice edged with his wolf. "Try to take Lucy from me, and I'll eviscerate you."

When Cole didn't respond, Sam moved across the room, his booted feet slowly thumping on the floor. "Lucy is *my* mate. You may want me gone, but I'm not going anywhere. And if you keep pushing this issue, I'll rip you into pieces so small, your family won't be able to identify you. We may be on the same side here, but I do not take well to people trying to take from me the ones I love."

Sam's proclamation had my breath hitching in

my throat. For a moment, I feared they'd hear me, but they were so caught up in their testosterone-laden argument that both remained utterly oblivious to me. Funny, considering I was their topic of discussion.

"Noted," Cole responded, his tone dry. "But it's clear Lucy is in danger. Corbin obviously wants her dead—"

"She held her own against him," Sam argued. "How about instead of coddling her, we congratulate her. We can't wrap her in bubble wrap and lock her in a padded room somewhere. Lucy is strong. Stronger than even she knows. She can handle this."

Pride surged within me.

"If Lucy were any other alpha, this wouldn't be a concern. She'd be able to kill Corbin on sight."

This time, Sam laughed. "That's bullshit and you know it. Need I remind you, Corbin slaughtered your alpha already, and he nearly killed me. The only reason I'm here is because Lucy interfered. She not only survived the attack, but also fought back. Don't discount her because she's a woman."

Tears filled my closed eyes, my lashes growing damp. If I didn't already love Sam, that little speech would have thrown me over the edge.

"I don't give a shit that she's a woman. I care that she's an inexperienced alpha. We need to up her training. She won't survive another fight like that. Corbin will be ready. You saw the same scene I did."

Ah, so they'd gone to the park in search of Corbin and his men then.

"And just like you, I smelled an equal amount of Corbin's blood to Lucy's. She hurt him, Cole. *And* two other werewolves. She's incredible."

"Look at her." Cole's voice grew rough. "She's practically comatose."

"But she's *alive*. And made it back home," Sam continued. "Does it hurt me to see her this way? Yes. It fucking kills me. But I'm also proud as fuck that she was able to handle this. She's been training with Anna for one month, and completed one session with you. That's it. She's going to make one hell of a powerful alpha, and Corbin knows it. Let's stop focusing on her weaknesses and focus on her strengths."

Cole groaned. "We have less than an hour until the pack meeting. They can't see her like this."

"I disagree. We absolutely should let them see her like this. Let them see what Corbin is capable of. But even more so, let them see that Lucy is willing to *fight* him, for the pack, for us. Give her a chance to be the alpha you want her to be."

Hearing Sam talk about me, about the faith he

had that I could handle this, made me feel strong. It was one thing to believe in yourself, but to hear that others believed in you... I felt so powerful in this moment—even while laying on my back. I also knew I never wanted to disappoint him—or me. I wanted to *be* this person he spoke of. She sounded immensely strong and capable.

It was time to stop doubting myself. Reggie had named me his heir, and regardless of whether I remained the Mississippi Pack alpha, that didn't change who I was. Or who I wanted to be. My whole life, I'd lived in Anna's shadow. I'd let her lead and merely trailed behind her like a puppy. I didn't want to be that girl anymore.

So, I wouldn't.

The first step was to stop laying here, pretending to be unconscious. They could discuss my future all they wanted, but I would be a part of that conversation. I needed to take control of it. Because only I could decide what kind of future I had.

I blinked open my eyes and stared up at the bedroom ceiling. Pock marks marred the imperfect stucco, and yet, the ceiling still managed to hold up the upper floor, reminding me that things didn't need to be perfect to get the job done. Flaws and all, I could be the alpha everyone wanted me to be. The alpha *I* wanted to be.

With a quiet breath, I catalogued my injuries. Even now, I could feel them pulsing beneath my skin. The bruises and fractures created a litany of ouchies, but none were serious. Upside: it wouldn't take me long to fully recuperate. Downside: I couldn't use this attack to delay the upcoming pack challenges. *The Code* specifically emphasized only life-threatening injuries.

I wrapped one arm around my aching ribs, then pushed up from the mattress with the other. The second I moved, both Sam and Cole whirled around to face me. Relief softened Sam's hard expression, his eyes flickering with warmth as his gaze raked me over. An instant later, he stood next to my bed and offered me his hand. I slid my fingers over his palm, reveling in the feel of his roughened skin.

"Luce..." he murmured as he helped me to my feet.

I straightened, my eyes fluttering shut as I worked out the kinks in my body. I'd be tender for the next few days, but what else was new? That seemed to be my life right now.

Sam's arms came around my waist, gentle and loose, so as not to hurt me. I sank into his embrace and breathed him in for a moment before easing out of his grip and approaching Cole.

"What have I missed?"

My second stared at me, his expression inscrutable. For a moment, I thought he intended to scold me, but he must have seen something in my face. Something that I hope convinced him not to piss me off.

"We cleared the scene as best we could," Cole reported. "By the time we arrived, Corbin and his two men were gone."

I raised a brow. "How did you know there were three of them?"

Cole clucked his tongue. "We smelled them, obviously."

"Obviously," I muttered to myself. "Could you track them?"

"We followed the blood trails as far as we could. But once we reached the road, the trails vanished."

"Suggesting someone picked them up, since I suspect they followed me to the park."

Cole nodded. "Jorge is looking for nearby security cameras. Hopefully he finds something. A license plate, make and model, anything."

Hope bloomed within. Hopefully he found

something—*anything*—that could lead us to Corbin. And Laini.

I felt Sam's presence approach me from behind, and smiled when he pressed his body against my back, offering silent comfort. "Can you tell us what happened?"

I nodded. Withholding information wouldn't help us find Corbin. So, I quickly filled in the blanks for them, including my suspicions that he'd already changed Laini and my new ability to grow claws. The story didn't sound too fantastical when I told it, but both men seemed equally awestruck.

"I'm impressed you were able to fend them off on your own," Cole said.

Though it pleased me to hear his approval, I merely shrugged. I didn't *need* his approval—or so I kept telling myself. "Thanks to your lesson."

"Then I expect to see you again tomorrow."

I winced at the thought. Even my bruises sobbed. "Tomorrow? Seriously?"

He waved a dismissive hand. "You'll be much improved by tomorrow. Besides, it teaches another critical lesson."

"Which is?"

"Learning to fight while injured. Both Bryn and Marcus intend to challenge you. And guess what, they'll do it on the same night. You'll need to know how to defend yourself even with broken bones."

I groaned and dropped my head against Sam's chest. "Have I mentioned how exhausting it is being a werewolf?"

"Once or twice." Sam chuckled, the comforting sound rumbling against my back. But his voice took a darker tone when he continued, "As much as I hate to admit it, Cole's right. However, that won't stop me from ripping him to shreds if he hurts you unnecessarily. Just to *make a point.*"

Lovely. Two against one. And here I thought Sam might side with me. The traitor.

"Tell me about how Corbin changes the human-borns," Cole said, interrupting my thoughts. "You've seen it twice now?"

"Three," I said, my voice barely more than a whisper. I cleared my throat. "Four, if you include me."

"Right..." Chagrin colored Cole's cheeks, as though he'd forgotten I'd also once been one of Corbin's victims. "Still, if you could tell me a little about it, that'd be helpful. So we know what to expect."

"There's not much to say," I said. "It's a brutal process. Or at least Corbin's methods are brutal. For all I know, it might only take a bite for someone born of a werewolf parent to turn. But Corbin takes pleasure in the hunt. Daniel, Brenda, and I were all savagely attacked and left for dead." I left Izzy out of this. While her injuries might have resulted in her changing, she'd died. And bringing her up would only harm Sam. "It could be that the body needs to be near death for a human-born's werewolf gene to activate, similarly to vampires. It might also be completely unnecessary. I'm not a geneticist, so I have no idea."

"I think the severity of the attack is necessary." Sam's arms tightened around my waist. "In our pack, the human-born grow up among the wolf-born. We've had minor accidents. Little nips and scratches here and there. No human-born has ever turned before. My father and I were talking about it, and we're picturing it more like an infection. A single nip might not be enough to overwhelm the body, but injuries like what Lucy, Daniel, and Brenda sustained might be the key."

I shivered. That wasn't something I ever wanted another person to go through.

"So if Corbin has changed Laini…"

"Then he's already harmed her," I said, gentling my voice.

Cole's hands fisted at his sides and his jaw tightened. From what I understood, he didn't even know the human-born woman, seeing as how she belonged to the outer circle. But he was my second, and as such, he presumably felt an intrinsic desire to protect those weaker than him. I knew I did. And right now, the thought of Laini, injured and possibly dying, set off every alarm bell in my head.

"Tell me about the fourth one, the one who died," Cole ground out.

My hands immediately covered Sam's, and I gave a reassuring squeeze. "Sam's sister, Isabelle."

Cole paled. "I'm sorry, I didn't know."

Sam didn't speak. So I pressed forward. "Isabelle sadly never recovered. By the time Sam's pack reached the house, her heart had already stopped beating. With myself and the other two who survived, our hearts did stop, or so Anna tells me, but they immediately restarted. I suspect it has something to do with our human lives ending, and our werewolf lives starting."

"So it isn't guaranteed that a person will change," Cole mused.

"No. But the sample size is small currently. It isn't like we've done extensive research on this," Sam said. "I know some human-borns who would take the risk, though."

Cole nodded. "I can also think of a few who would volunteer. But let's focus on finding Corbin and Laini."

"And we only have"—I spared another glance at the bedroom clock—"half an hour left until the pack meeting."

Cole gave another slow nod. "I intend to check in with Jorge and see what he's managed to find. I'll let you know if I learn anything important."

"Not just important," I clarified. "I want to be informed of everything."

Cole looked as though he intended to argue, but before he could utter a word, I summoned my best alpha stare—learned from Adrien—and held up a hand. "Don't argue with me. Just do as I say."

Blinking, Cole eventually nodded. "Yes, alpha."

I gestured for Cole to leave. The instant he did, I slumped back against Sam and sighed. My entire body trembled from exhaustion, but I'd held it all together in front of Cole.

Strong arms swept me up, and I gasped, my arms immediately slipping around Sam's neck. "What are you doing?"

Sam's mouth pulled into a smile, the sort he reserved for me and me alone. "Well, we may be short on time, but at the very least, we should wash all the dirt and blood off you. Don't want you scaring the civilians."

I shook my head. "I don't have time for that, I need to—"

"Lucy." His gaze cut through me. "Don't argue with me. Just do as I say."

Okay. I couldn't help but burst out laughing. If I'd sounded anywhere near as ridiculous as he did, it was a wonder Cole had bothered listening. "Alright, guess I'm washing up then."

But first, I needed to plug in my darn phone.

CHAPTER
TWELVE

Sam sat me on the edge of the tub before returning to the sink and turning on the taps. The sound of running water soothed me, and I found my eyes drifting closed as I took a moment to breathe. Moments like these didn't come too often.

I jumped, my eyes flying open, when a warm washcloth touched my face.

Sam crouched before me. "Sorry," he murmured. "Didn't mean to startle you."

I chuckled. "Guess I'm a bit on edge."

"Understandably."

With careful strokes, Sam continued wiping my face, pausing every few moments to rinse the cloth. I didn't need to look at the sink to know the water had turned a murky brown. Dirt and blood didn't make a pretty color.

"You really scared me," Sam admitted, his voice gruff.

My gaze shifted to his, but I didn't utter a word.

"When that car pulled up, and I saw you slumped in the back seat..." He shuddered. "I thought I knew fear when Corbin stabbed you. But today..." He blew out a breath and rested his forehead against mine. "You really need to stop frightening me like this."

A breathless chuckle slipped past my lips. "If it helps, I definitely don't intend for these things to happen."

"Yeah, that scares me more."

My smile faded as I reached up and cupped Sam's cheeks. "I love you. More than anything."

His face softened and the fear eased from his expression. "Lucy, you are everything to me. I don't know what I would do if I lost you. It's like I can't breathe without you."

"I'm not going anywhere," I promised, my thumbs caressing his face.

He nodded and released a deep sigh. When he leaned back, I lowered my hands into my lap drew my own breath, centering myself.

Sam lifted his hand and returned to cleaning my face. "How are you feeling?"

"Tired. Frustrated. Angry. Sad. It's all a jumble up here," I said, tapping my head. I winced, immediately regretting all my life's decisions. My entire body throbbed with pain, so I hadn't really noticed the headache until now. Distantly, I remembered Corbin landing a few good swats that had likely jumbled my poor little brain.

"We'll find him," Sam assured me. "I don't doubt that in the slightest."

Oh, but I did. If Corbin could outmaneuver Sam's father, he could undoubtedly outsmart me. Adrien was the epitome of an alpha. If he'd failed to take out Corbin, what made me think I would succeed?

Sam gently brushed a strand of hair off my face and tsked under his breath. "Stop questioning yourself."

Heat flamed my cheeks. "How did you know what I was thinking?"

"Please. I can always tell what you're thinking just from the look on your face. You wear your emotions on your sleeve."

"Great. Something else I'll need to change."

"Change?" He lifted a brow. "Why would you need to change anything?"

"Alphas can't show their emotions. That would be considered a weakness."

Sam chuckled under his breath, then rinsed the cloth once more before getting to work on my neck. I could feel the grime abrading my skin as he washed me. "It's only a weakness if you let it be one. Every alpha leads in their own way, and only you can choose your method. Don't let Cole make you into something you aren't. You saw how compassionate and caring my father is. Our pack doesn't consider that a weakness. In fact, we consider it a strength."

I considered Sam's words with a slow nod.

"Listen." He placed the cloth on the bathroom counter, then handed me a brush to comb out my rat's nest. "Being an alpha isn't just about being the most powerful or ruthless. Alphas need to be equal parts strong and sympathetic. They lead by example. By molding themselves into what they believe is the best version of themselves, and hope that the pack does the same. A pack is only as strong as its weakest member."

"Yes, Yoda," I teased.

Sam snickered. "I'm serious. I know it sounds a little out there, but you have to keep in mind we aren't human, nor do we function like one. We're a seamless blend of man and animal. And animals don't play by human rules. You do whatever it takes to be the best alpha you can be."

I took a moment to absorb Sam's words, all while tonguing a small cut on the inside of my cheek. I'd been so concerned about becoming a strong leader that I hadn't given much thought as to the leader I wanted to be. I didn't want to be a totalitarian. Nor did I want to lead through brute strength. No, I wanted my pack to respect and admire me, like the New Orleans pack did Adrien. He'd earned it, busting his ass off to be worthy of their trust.

That was the kind of leader I wanted to be.

With a renewed purpose, I stood and walked toward the sink. Toward the *mirror*. I hadn't looked yet since waking, so I wasn't sure what to expect. But whatever my reflection held, I could handle it.

At first glance, I winced, then remembered werewolves healed fast. The bruises wouldn't last. The split lip would seal. The scrapes on my cheeks would fade.

I gripped the brush and slowly started easing it through my hair, careful of my throbbing skull. Then I gathered it into a loose knot and secured it at the base of my neck. The chosen hairstyle seemed to emphasize my injuries, and for a moment, I contemplated releasing my hair to give me something to hide behind.

No.

I was done hiding. Done playing in shadows.

As Sam had suggested to Cole, these injuries could help. Let the pack see that I was willing to stand up to Corbin and fight for them. Not only because I could, but because I *wanted* to protect them. These marks spoke better than anything I could possibly say to them.

"Ready?" Sam asked.

I squared my shoulders and blew out a long breath. Honestly, I had no idea if I was ready. I hadn't seen the pack since Reggie's funeral, and even then, I hadn't been able to touch base with them all. I probably should have called a meeting afterward, to discuss our future, but I'd been so caught up in my own drama that I hadn't thought of them. I couldn't even imagine what they thought of me. Here I was, a newly turned werewolf forced upon them. Someone they hadn't known until a year ago, and now I was their leader. All because their former alpha had named me his heir. To them, I was nothing more than Reggie's illegitimate daughter. I hadn't earned this position.

But I would.

"Luce?" Sam said, his hand brushing against mine.

I shook myself out and nodded. "I'm ready."

Or as ready as I was going to be. It was a good thing too, because right at that moment, the doorbell rang. The first pack member had arrived.

Time to put my game face on.

THIRTY PEOPLE NEVER SOUNDS LIKE MUCH, until you try cramming them into a single house. The poor living room was bursting at the seams, and the kitchen had grown so cramped, it was hard to breathe. The backyard fared a little better. At least people weren't sitting in each other's laps. The hard part was going to be figuring how to speak to everyone at once.

Thankfully, someone far more skilled in technology than me stepped up to help. Apparently, it was common in medium to larger sized packs for the alpha to be "miked," while everyone else wore earpieces. Kept nosy neighbors from overhearing talk that centered around werewolves. Clearly, I still had a lot to learn. But for now, the pack had the required technology to make this meeting possible.

I stood at the head of the living room and eyed the people surrounding me. The more dominant members had claimed the closest spots, while the lower-ranked members hovered in the kitchen, and the human-borns stood in the backyard. Some sort of hierarchy I knew nothing about. But I left them to it. That wasn't a fight I wanted to take on today. Not when Laini's family sat on the nearest couch to me, their despair so palpable, I could taste it.

To my left stood Cole, and to my right Sam. After we'd cleaned me up, I'd asked him to attend the meeting. I didn't care what Cole said or what the pack thought, Sam was my mate. And even more so, he had personal knowledge of Corbin. He was an asset, regardless of their discomfort with him.

"Very well, let's get started," I said, calling the meeting to order. I took another gander at the room, trying to recall as many names as possible. Sadly, I knew less than a third. Cole had been right when he'd called me an outsider. It was no wonder this pack wanted nothing to do with me.

I still hadn't decided yet as to whether I would stay in Jackson or return home. Regardless, I had a role to play here, one that required me to learn more about these people. I couldn't brush them aside as nameless faces anymore.

"As I'm sure everyone already knows, I'm Lucy Williams—Reginald Hayes' biological daughter. But there may be some who don't know that I was human-born."

No one so much as batted an eyelash in the living room, but I heard a smattering of whispers from the kitchen. Guess some people hadn't heard that tidbit of information about me.

"Reginald named me his heir before passing, which means after his death, I became your alpha."

"We know this already," someone growled.

My gaze shot in his direction, only to find a bearded, bushy-haired redhead. He stood next to the grandfather clock, his massive fists balanced on his broad hips. Give the man a kilt, and he would have reminded me of a Scottish Highland Games competitor.

Cole leaned in and whispered in my ear, "That's Marcus."

Ah. Well, damn. The man was built like a tree trunk. Just my luck.

I continued. "What you may not know is that last night, around eight p.m., a werewolf named Corbin abducted one of our pack mates." I made sure to emphasize the word *our*. I did notice a few sneers and scoffs, though. "I've come up against this man in the past. As you all know, he is the one who murdered Reginald, and turned me."

This time, even Marcus' eyes widened. Aha. Something he hadn't known then.

"Before Corbin murdered Reginald, he attacked and seriously injured two New Orleans' pack members, and killed a third."

Their expressions quickly morphed from surprise to grief. Werewolves were an interesting breed. They willingly challenged and killed each other, but when one died, they all grieved.

"Corbin is interested in one thing and one thing only: to run his own pack. He left his former pack in England in search of his own territory, and has apparently set his sights on Mississippi."

"He can't have it!" someone shouted from the back.

"No, he can't," I agreed. "This is *our* territory, and I refuse to let him take it or harm our pack. He's abducting human-borns with the intention of forcibly turning them into werewolves and creating his own pack. We can't allow this."

Unease swept through the crowd.

"Laini went missing last night, and this morning,

I had a small run-in with Corbin and two of his followers." I gestured to my face, and those surrounding me growled.

Laini's mother lifted her head, her tear-stained cheeks ripping apart my heart. I couldn't imagine the thoughts going through her head, the fears that Corbin had committed the same acts on her daughter.

"While I was able to injure the three of them, I wasn't able to finish Corbin off, and for that, I apologize. I didn't make that choice lightly, but it was a choice I had to make for my own survival. I assure you, next time he won't be so lucky. Not only will we stop him, but kill him. No one attacks our people and gets away with it."

I slowly approached Laini's family and placed a hand on her mother's shoulder. I hadn't yet told them the news that Laini had been attacked. That seemed best to discuss in private. But from the desolate expressions on their faces, it seemed they'd already come to the conclusion.

"I've asked Dominic to pair every human-born member with a wolf-born. This is to protect all of our people. Corbin went after Laini because she was alone and didn't present a threat." I squeezed her mother's shoulder. "So, until further notice, every human-born must remain with their assigned wolf-born counterpart. We don't want to lose *any* more of our people. I would also recommend everyone join into larger groups, preferably four to six people if you can. I won't force that on anyone, though. I do understand that you need to keep living your lives. However, this morning, Corbin wasn't alone. He had two other werewolves with him. It's safe to assume he'll continue in that fashion, attempting to outnumber you. Be smarter. Take precautions. Travel in groups."

The majority nodded their agreement. I only hoped those in the kitchen and yard felt the same way.

"I also ask that each group take a section of the city to search for Corbin and Laini. Cole has informed me that Corbin's scent was found inside Laini's car, so we can use that to hopefully track him down. We also have Jorge going through records and security camera feeds with the hope of finding Corbin's location. Anything that can help us track the bastard down."

"What about the police?" Laini's mother asked, her voice little more than a whisper.

"We can't involve the police in this matter. It would put the entire werewolf community at risk of exposure," I said, maintaining an even voice so all could hear. "We have to handle this ourselves."

I turned back to face the group and noticed a few displeased faces. "Listen, I know I'm not who you want as your alpha. But I promise you, I'll do everything in my power to not only put an end to this madness, but also find Laini. Regardless of the circumstances that brought me here, I do believe I can be a good alpha. And I intend to prove that to you all. In the meantime, let's focus on finding Laini and keeping all of our people safe. If anyone finds anything regarding Corbin or Laini, report to me immediately. It doesn't matter what time it is. I will be available twenty-four-seven."

"What about the full moon?" someone in the back asked.

I scanned the crowd, but I couldn't pick out the face. "What about it?"

A throat cleared, and the crowd parted as someone moved toward me. When Bryn stepped into view, I bit back a groan. She was the last thing I needed right now.

"You're protected right now, but once the full moon hits, anyone within the pack is permitted to challenge you."

I fought to school my expression. "I don't intend

to hide behind these recent events to protect myself. If a pack member chooses to prioritize challenging me over looking for Laini or hunting down Corbin, then I'll answer it."

If I wasn't mistaken, I caught a flash of something in Marcus' eyes. Surprise, and maybe even a hint of approval.

"That said, finding Laini and tracking down Corbin should take precedence. All I ask is that everyone consider what's best for the pack. If you feel that isn't me, by all means, you have the right to challenge me."

Bryn lifted her chin, narrowing her eyes to dangerous slits. Somehow, I knew there'd be no swaying her from this.

"Until that day, though, let's focus on Laini and Corbin. Remember to check in with Dominic to find your partner, but also try to remain in larger groups, for your own safety. If anyone comes across Corbin, report him to me immediately, but do not try to take him on by yourself. Other than that, this meeting is adjourned." I reached up and removed my mike, effectively ending the connection.

It took time for the crowd to disperse. They lingered, their gazes locked on me, as though waiting for me to say something more. When I didn't, they turned to their neighbors and began chatting, their animated body language telling me more than my ears could hear, not with that many voices talking at once.

"Good job," Cole said. "You hit them hard with that little speech of yours. I have a feeling you may have won Marcus over. He's not as dominant as he sometimes thinks he is, but he does have strong protective instincts. Bryn however..."

"Is going to be a problem," I acknowledged. But then, I hadn't expected anything less. "She was Reggie's significant other, or whatever that passed for in his life. Maybe she feels robbed, maybe she's grieving. Either way, she's lashing out, and I'm the easiest target."

Cole nodded. "Maybe try talking to her, see if you can reason with her. This isn't the time for unwarranted dominance fights."

I considered his suggestion. It couldn't hurt to try. Delaying any challenge fights would certainly work in my benefit, allowing me to focus more on Corbin and Laini.

I patted Cole on the shoulder and muttered a quick thanks. Before I could say anything else, someone called Cole's name, pulling his attention away from me. I'd started turning toward Sam when

I noticed a shorter woman breaking away from the crowd and heading toward me. I braced myself and pasted what I hoped was a welcoming smile on my face, not entirely sure what to expect.

She came to a stop in front of me, her scent oddly familiar, as though I'd smelled it before but couldn't place it. We must have met during my time here, and I'd somehow forgotten her.

"Hello," I hedged, not sure what to say.

The woman peered up at me with eyes as green as emeralds. I frowned as I took them in. It wasn't often I met someone with green eyes. Especially not ones as bright as hers. As bright as mine.

"Hello, alpha," she said, her voice light and lilting. "I wanted to introduce myself to you."

Okay, so we'd never actually met before then. I released a quiet breath, then offered my hand. She took it, her fingers gliding against mine before she gave them a small squeeze.

"My name is Olivia. I'm your sister."

CHAPTER
THIRTEEN

My whoozit-what-now?

I blinked once, twice, and then a third time, unsure I'd heard this woman correctly. Had she really just said she was my sister? I didn't have any sisters. My mom and dad had always told me "one and done" whenever I'd pestered them for a sibling. And then I'd met Anna, and she'd filled that gaping void for me. Unless—

I froze.

Unless.

Ah, good ole Reggie. Because, of course, Reggie. The man had humped more women than a seaman on shore duty. He'd even told me he had other children out there. I just hadn't given it too much thought. And I'd certainly never asked to meet one, nor had I assumed I'd stumble across one in my own pack. Especially considering he'd assured me they were all human-born. But Olivia was as much a wolf as I was. Which didn't line up with what I knew.

If I had a sister within my *own* pack, why had no one—including Reggie—told me? Why keep it a secret? I knew the pack didn't trust me, but that didn't mean they could hide things from me. Especially something as important as this.

When I didn't immediately respond, Olivia cocked her head and frowned.

"Right," I said more to myself, then pushed away my rattled thoughts. "Sister?"

A faint smile pulled at her lips. "Half, of course. Reginald was my biological father."

"Reggie," I murmured, shaking my head. Honestly, I was a tad surprised I hadn't seen this moment coming. The man had been a walking horn dog with only one goal in mind. Guess he'd gotten what he'd wanted after all: two werewolf children.

"It was a little strange for me too," Olivia said, "learning about him, about all this, and you."

"When..." I gave my head another little shake. "When were you—"

"Turned into a werewolf?"

I nodded, my mouth going dry. I hated asking

this question—knew how it affected me whenever someone asked. No one liked being asked about their past trauma, and it felt almost rude for me to prod. And yet I couldn't help but ask.

"Eight months ago," she said. "Reginald approached me, told me he could turn me if that was what I wanted."

My jaw gaped. "*Reggie* did this to you?" Her own father?

Olivia's brow wrinkled, and her gaze shot from me to Sam, who I suddenly realized was looming behind me. "Wasn't that how you were changed?"

Mouth still parched, I shook my head. "No, no that wasn't how I was changed. I can't believe Reggie would do something like that—"

"I agreed to it," Olivia said, her frown deepening.

That blew my mind. I knew some people would want this, but to allow your own father to nearly kill you... And why hadn't Reggie mentioned this to me? Eight months ago, I'd been living here, with him. Sure, he'd often go off on his own, and I may have been a bit sulky and dealing with all that'd happened, but I'd like to think he would have told me he'd done something like this. Introduce us, even.

"Does the pack know you're his daughter?" I asked, my chin gesturing to those surrounding us.

She rolled her eyes. "Oh yeah, he was quite pleased another of his children had successfully made the change. He announced it at my first pack meeting."

A pack meeting I wouldn't have been at. I hadn't attended any while here, too lost in my own problems to bother.

With a heavy breath, I scrubbed my hands down my face, and nodded. "Well, it's good to meet you, Olivia. I can't believe I have a sister. I'm not sure my brain is ready to process this right now."

She giggled—a soft, wholesome sound that made me smile. It made me curious. Was I younger or older? Did she have a family? Over the course of a year, I'd gone from my mom and dad, to suddenly having two dads—if I counted Reggie—to finding my mate and his pack, and now a sister. There was so much I needed to ask her. It also made me wonder, if she was older, did that make her his actual heir? Or would it still be me since Reggie had named me? Ugh, when did things become so complicated?

Another quiet thought pressed at the back of my mind: could she be alpha?

Was Olivia the answer to all my problems? Could I give her the pack and return home? Was she worthy? My skin buzzed with excitement at the thought. As Reggie's other child, maybe the pack would accept her. She'd need training, but so did I. Really, all I had on her was a month of learning how to fight. Olivia could easily pick that up in no time.

"Tell me about yourself," I said, hoping I didn't sound *too* eager.

"Not much to tell," she chuckled, her cheeks pinking. "I'm twenty-three—"

Younger, then. Damn. Not that I held that against her. But I might have gotten my hopes up.

"I just graduated college a year ago, with a degree in English Lit. I'm engaged to my high school sweetheart, and we own our own place here in town. All quite boring, actually."

"Nah, nothing boring about you," I said. "What about your parents?"

She shrugged. "Mom's gone now—cancer." A lifetime of pain flickered behind her eyes. "Dad— well, my stepdad—works for the local paper mill. He paid my way through college, all the while knowing he isn't my father."

I instinctively reached for her hand. "He *is* your father. Just because Reggie showed up and claimed a blood relation to you doesn't mean anything."

A grateful smile touched her lips before fading. "When Reginald showed up, I"—she drew a deep breath and steadied herself—"I couldn't help but think of my mom. It was breast cancer that took her from us."

I squeezed Olivia's hand.

"My fiancé and I paid to test my genetics, and well..." She shrugged, but the sadness in her eyes told me everything I needed to know. "Obviously, nothing's guaranteed. But when Reginald found me and made his offer, all I could think about was this could keep it from happening to me. Keep me from dying. My stepfather fell apart after my mother's death. He's still not the man he used to be. It's as though his grief destroyed him. I didn't want that life for my fiancé. So, I said yes."

I didn't know this woman, but that didn't stop me from pulling her into a hug. She paused for a moment before her arms tentatively closed around me, hugging me back.

"What's your fiancé's name?" I asked.

"Christopher," she said, and I could hear the smile in her voice.

We parted, and I brushed a stray tear away from her cheek. I couldn't imagine the loss and grief she must have felt. I'd experienced my own when I'd first been turned into a werewolf. But losing my mother was something I couldn't even fathom.

"Does Christopher know about any of this?" I asked. "About what you agreed to?"

"No." Her voice came out firm. "And he never will. I don't want him to know anything about this. He knows about vampires, obviously, but this... this is different, seeing as how it affects me. To him, vampires are monsters. I can't imagine how he'd react to werewolves."

"My best friend is a vampire," I told her, a bit defensively. "So's her husband. I certainly wouldn't call them monsters."

Surprise flickered in Olivia's eyes before color flamed in her cheeks. "I'm so sorry, I didn't mean it that way. I just meant—"

I chuckled and waved a dismissive hand. "Don't worry about it. I've thought the same thing a time or two in the last few years."

Olivia chewed on her bottom lip before asking, "Is your best friend really a vampire?"

"Yup. Anna. I've known her pretty much my whole life. She was turned almost two years ago. She's married now, to Dracula if you can believe it."

Olivia's eyes shot so comically wide, I couldn't help but snicker. That never got old.

"And speaking of mates," I said. "I should introduce you to mine."

I glanced over my shoulder and smiled up at Sam. He'd kept quiet this entire time, but he'd remained, a silent presence at my back. "Olivia, meet Sam, my mate. Sam, this is Olivia. My sister."

"Pleasure," he said, his voice a deep rumble.

Olivia's mouth parted into a soft *o* as she stared at him. I bit back a laugh, completely understanding her reaction. Sam was a breathtaking sort of guy. His height alone made a girl look twice.

"Wow," she whispered. Then she shook her head and dropped her gaze. "Sorry, I just mean, you're *tall*."

Sam's chuckle warmed my stomach. I instinctively leaned into him and reveled in the feel of his hard body pressed against mine.

"I hate to ask you this, Olivia, but has Reggie done this with anyone else? Do you know?"

She shook her head, her expression sobering. "Not that I know of. He never mentioned anyone else to me. And he did tell me about you. He said I was the first one he reached out to since I lived the closest. Made me feel all warm and fuzzy inside, you know?"

I nodded, hating my sperm donor all the more. Nothing like telling your child that the only reason you'd reached out to them was because of close proximity. The man certainly wouldn't have won any father-of-the-year awards.

I also had to acknowledge that Reggie might have done this to others without even telling Olivia. Knowing Reggie, the instant he'd learned it was possible, he would have sought out every one of his children. I suddenly had the terrifying image of a busload of new werewolves arriving at the house in search of him.

Shuddering, I banished that image from my head. I had enough problems without borrowing more. For now, it was just me and Olivia. And that was plenty.

"So, if Christopher doesn't know about any of this, what have you done to keep your wolf a secret? How do you shift?"

Olivia bit her lip again and dropped her gaze. "Um, well, I've only shifted a couple times during pack meetings. They're helping me learn how to control myself."

I was glad to hear that. I certainly hadn't taken advantage of that during my year here.

"Anyway," Olivia said, interrupting my thoughts. "I just thought I should introduce myself. When you returned to Jackson and didn't seek me out, I wondered why."

"I'm so sorry. No one told me about you. I had no idea." A genuine smile spread across my face. "But I do now, and I definitely want to get to know you. Once this whole situation is handled, you and I can spend all the time in the world getting to know each other. For now, how about we take a look at the roster and see who you're paired up with."

"Yeah," Olivia murmured.

"Why don't you two go take care of that," Sam said, reminding me of his presence. "I'm going to take a step back, let the pack converse without feeling invaded upon by my presence."

"Thank you," I murmured, grateful for the space he offered.

Sam leaned in and brushed a kiss across my brow before retreating to our bedroom. On the upside, no one had started a fight with him, but on the downside, I could tell he felt a little put off. While no one had questioned his presence, they also hadn't welcomed him. Not that they'd entirely welcomed me. I made a mental note to work on that, then led Olivia into the kitchen.

Tacked to the wall next to the fridge was a massive list. Olivia and I came to a stop in front of it, and I began perusing the names. When her name jumped out at me, I tapped it. "Scotia. Know her?"

Olivia shook her head. "I've only met a few human-borns. Scotia wasn't one of them."

"Alright, then we do this the old-fashioned way."

I pulled Olivia into the backyard and grabbed a chair from the nearby patio table. One hop up, and now I could see above the thrumming crowd.

"Scotia?" I called. "Is there a Scotia here?"

Slowly, a small hand rose near the back of the crowd. I pointed Olivia in her direction and watched as the two girls came together in the middle of the yard. Once I saw them start chatting, I hopped back down and returned inside.

"Alpha," a gruff voice rose at my side.

From the corner of my eye, I caught sight of the red bushy beard and immediately knew who'd addressed me. "Marcus."

His gaze swept my length, as though appraising me. It wasn't sexual, but it was certainly predatory. A wolf eyeing up another wolf. Then, with a sly grin more worthy of a fox, Marcus said, "I've decided not to challenge you."

Surprise had my mouth falling open, but I soon clicked it shut and gathered my wits. "You have?"

He nodded, then gestured to my battered face. "Corbin did that?"

"Mhmm."

"Then I look forward to returning the favor."

Rendered speechless, I simply stared at the burly wolf. Sam had suggested this might happen, that Marcus and Bryn might change their minds about challenging me if they saw I cared enough to fight. My face told a story my words hadn't. And Marcus seemed content now. As though my bruises had satiated his desire to claim the pack.

Werewolves were... weird creatures.

"I look forward to seeing you pound his face in," I said. Seemed the best response. Give the wolf what he wanted, especially considering it was the same thing I wanted. "But I will be the one to finish him."

"So long as I can rough him up a bit first," Marcus demanded in a booming voice.

I contemplated his request. I knew I couldn't allow him to dictate *anything* to me. So, instead, I offered a compromise. "Tell you what, if your team finds Corbin first, you can beat the snot out of him as much as you want. But you bring him to me alive."

"Deal," Marcus said, grinning. And oh yeah, that was a predator staring out of his eyes.

Without another word, Marcus vanished back into the crowd. I'd barely made it three steps when another shadow darted into my path. My head immediately rose, and I bit back a curse at the sight of Bryn.

"You might have convinced everyone that you're Little Miss Perfect, but I know better," she hissed.

Honestly, I had no idea how to even respond to that. So, I merely nodded. "Sounds good, Bryn." I moved to brush past her, but Bryn's clawed hand encircled my arm, yanking me to a stop.

My wolf woke inside my head and shot to her feet, sensing the threat. No one else had noticed, but we sure had. My gaze dropped to Bryn's hand, then slowly rose to her face. I gave her a cold assessment, then grabbed her hand with my free one and squeezed. It didn't take long for Bryn to suck in a sharp breath and release me.

"Touch me again, and I'll skin you alive," I said in a deceptively calm voice.

Bryn's eyes flickered briefly before they slitted to a glare. "I'm going to destroy you on the full moon."

I slowly leaned forward, getting so close we shared breath. I didn't utter a word, but I let my wolf out, felt my beast fill my senses. I'd tested this on Anna once, and she'd said if she'd been human, she would have shat herself. She'd said it was the most terrifying experience she'd ever had, and she'd faced the Vampire Queen.

Bryn seemed to share that opinion.

Her face blanched, and she fell back a step. As though realizing what she'd just done, she lifted her chin, snarled, and stormed off.

Rubbing my brow, I returned to the living room and glanced around. Everyone mingled about as though this were nothing more than a common get-together now. But I just wanted them out so I could sleep. And shower. And eat. But maybe not in that order.

I activated the mic and called out, "If I could have your attention."

Every last wolf turned to face me.

"Everyone has been paired up, so it's time to get out there and start searching. We need to find Laini. Jorge and Cole have broken the city up into sections. Find yours and get to work." When no one moved, I sighed and pinched my brow. "Now, please."

That got them moving.

One by one, the pack filtered out of my house, until I finally stood alone in my living room.

Eyes closed, I released a slow breath. Quiet at last.

"Alpha?"

Or not.

My eyes flashed open, and I turned to find a

medium-height werewolf standing in my kitchen, a laptop tucked under his arm.

"I'm Jorge," he told me, his voice slightly accented. "Cole asked me to remain behind so we can go over what I've found."

Right. Nodding, I gestured toward the kitchen table. "Have a seat."

No rest for the wicked and all that. I only hoped I could stay awake long enough to learn something important.

CHAPTER
FOURTEEN

I COLLAPSED INTO A KITCHEN CHAIR AND released a long, slow breath. I was so tired, my eyes felt like sandpaper. It didn't help that my body ached all over either. I'd managed to ignore it during the pack meeting, but now every bruise, scrape, and broken bone seemed to flare to life all at once, reminding me of the beating I'd taken earlier this morning. Thankfully, everything would heal. But a little sleep would help me heal faster. Protein, too. Not that I had an opportunity for either right now.

I lifted my legs onto a nearby chair and had just begun kneading my thighs when Sam appeared, his shadow looming over me. Without a word, he lifted my legs from the chair, sat, and placed them in his lap. Then he set to work, his fingers massaging the inner arch of my feet. I practically melted into the chair, my head tipping back as I moaned. Relief spread up my legs and for one blissful moment, my body sighed contentedly.

Cole and Jorge took their own seats across from us, and Jorge opened his laptop. The two shot me matching amused glances before Jorge turned back to his screen. Honestly, I didn't care what this looked like to them. A girl deserved a little pain relief, right?

"Okay, courtesy of Sam's father, we received their file on Corbin. Here's what they learned," Jorge began. "Corbin Brown, aged thirty-six, Caucasian, former member of the England Pack, and a British National. Defected from his pack approximately one year ago and left the country, arriving here shortly after. He has a colorful history with the MPS—Metropolitan Police Services. Theft, disturbing the peace, a few assault charges..." Jorge's eyes skimmed the screen as he read off Corbin's dossier. "All of it came to a stop, though, when he joined the England Pack. When I reached out to the England Pack alpha, he mentioned that Corbin had transferred from a smaller auxiliary pack located in northern England, one that disbanded when this alpha took over. He described Corbin as argumentative, temperamental, and someone who struggles with authority figures."

"Check, check, and check," I muttered. That fit everything I knew about him. "Was anyone able to track down anything that might help us locate him now? A property, license plate number, video feed of him taking Laini? Anything that might help."

Jorge offered a grim smile. "Unfortunately, I wasn't able to dig up much. There weren't any cameras on the road where Laini was taken. Now, there *were* cameras near the park where he attacked you, but whoever picked him and his men up kept their vehicle out of sight."

I sighed.

"I did find one thing. It might be nothing. Or it could be everything. I found three recent property purchases in the nearby area, all under the name Evan Brown."

"Okay..." I hedged, wondering how that was relevant.

"Corbin's middle name is Evan," Jorge stated.

My eyes widened. Could this be a connection? Brown was a popular surname. This Evan Brown could be someone else entirely. But to learn that Corbin shared two names with this person... surely it couldn't be purely coincidental?

"You think they're the same person?"

"It's hard to say. Usually there's paper trails we can track, but from what it looks like, these sales were all done privately, and paid for in cash. Lump sums like that can be tracked, if you know how, but hacking into that kind of information..." Jorge trailed off.

I nodded. We had to be careful here. We couldn't draw attention to us, and if Jorge went hacking into banks, well, who knew what hell that would rain down on us.

"With private sales like that, Corbin could give any name to place on the deed, and the previous owner wouldn't care. They see the cash—"

"And they take it and run," Sam supplied.

"Okay. Not ideal, but it's a start. We can check out these locations, see if we can pick up on any familiar scents." It was better than nothing, that was for sure. "Were you able to find anything else?"

"We do have a contact in the local PD," Jorge said. "Someone the pack has worked with in the past. He knows what we are and keeps it a secret. He has a distant family member who belongs to a pack in Texas. I asked him to look into Laini's abduction."

Excitement thrummed in my veins. I pulled my

feet from Sam's lap and sat up, my attention locked on Jorge. "Tell me you found something."

"There was one call made to the local PD about a possible disturbance around the time Laini was taken. The person reporting it, unfortunately, was drunk. So the report wasn't taken seriously, and no one followed up on it."

I slumped back in disappointment. Maybe it was a good thing the police weren't involved, but I'd hoped for something. Anything.

"However," Jorge continued, "there's a house about a mile up the road that has security cameras in their front yard, and they gave me permission to look at their feeds."

My pulse quickened, sweeping away the disappointment.

"The feed captured what we think was Corbin's vehicle. It lined up timeline wise. And we were able to catch the last four numbers of the license plate as they sped by."

Okay, that was something. Not great. The full license plate would have been better. But this was progress. "But you have a description of the vehicle then," I said, excitement raising my voice.

"Yes. We do. And with the help of our PD

contact, we can use the description and the last four digits to hopefully narrow down the vehicle."

It took every ounce of restraint in me not to fist pump the air. Finally—*finally*—we were getting somewhere! We were closing in on this bastard, and when we did—oh, I would take great pleasure in unaliving him.

"This is all great," I said.

"Don't get too excited," Cole interrupted, completely killing my hard-on. "This Evan Brown could be someone else entirely, and the vehicle might not lead us anywhere."

I unleashed an annoyed glare on him. "Thank you, Mr. Grumpy-Pants. I choose to remain positive."

The three men chuckled.

"Fair enough," Cole said.

"Between the video feed, the vehicle description, the real estate, and our people combing the city, I feel good about our chances of finding him."

"My father has kept his people on Corbin's trail too," Sam said. "They're trying to track down any credit cards he might be using, cell phones, anything trackable. So far, they haven't had any luck, but they aren't giving up."

I hadn't realized Adrien had been doing that for us, but it didn't surprise me. A smile rose to my lips.

"He likely ditched the cards and phone," Cole said. "Those are too easily tracked."

"But my father intends to continue pursuing those paths for us, just in case something pops up," Sam said. "He wants to help us any way he can."

I reached out and touched Sam's hand. "Thank him for me."

A quick nod.

"In other news, Marcus retracted his challenge," I said. "He just wants a piece of Corbin, which I assured him he could have *if* his team finds him first, and delivers him to me alive."

Cole chuckled. "That should keep him motivated. What about Bryn?"

"I don't think I'll be so lucky with her. She's really taking it personally. And speaking of personally"—I leaned against the kitchen table and unleashed my most alpha stare on Cole—"why the hell didn't you tell me I have a sister?"

Cole blinked. "Was I supposed to?"

Rough laughter slipped past my lips. "Uh, yes? That's something I would have liked to know."

"Wait... you didn't know you had a sister?" Cole and Jorge shared a surprised glance. "Like, at all?"

I huffed out a flabbergasted breath. "No, I didn't know about Olivia until she introduced herself tonight."

The two men sat silently. "Reginald never told you?"

"What part of 'No, I didn't know' don't you understand?"

Cole lifted his hands, then shrugged. "Maybe he thought you wouldn't like her? I don't know. I rarely understood Reginald's motives. Huh. I honestly had no idea that you two hadn't met. What'd you think of her?"

"She seemed nice." I really didn't have much more to say than that. Not yet, anyway. "A little shy? Anyway, I told her we'd get to know each other once we've handled Corbin. She mentioned that the pack has been helping her learn to shift. I'd like to help her with that too. You know, since our experiences differ from your guys'."

"You have your hands full right now," Cole countered. "Let's not worry about teaching your sister to shift just yet. She's not a human-born anymore, so she's in no danger of Corbin targeting her. And she's gone eight months so far without any shifting troubles. Let's focus on finding Corbin and Laini and your upcoming fight with Bryn."

I grumbled under my breath, unhappy with Cole's assessment. But I couldn't argue with it either. Everything he'd said made perfect sense. But if he thought I was going to ignore my sister, he had another thing coming to him. I hadn't mentioned to him that I'd been practicing shifting—something I needed to continue doing. If I invited my sister along, no harm, no foul, right? Two birds, one stone and all that. She needed the help as much as I did, considering she was engaged to a human. The last thing we needed was her losing control and harming him.

"Alright." I pushed to my feet, groaning softly. "Let's wrap this up. We have three locations to check out. Sam and I will take one. You and Dominic can take a second. And then I'll let you assign the third to whoever you feel is most competent."

"Davis and Lee will suffice," Cole said.

"Good. If anyone finds anything, call it in," I said. "No playing hero. If someone finds Laini or Corbin, we'll handle this as a pack."

Cole nodded, relief softening his face. I almost laughed at the expression. No way I intended to play the hero, and sweep in and kill Corbin without any help at all. I'd gone up against Corbin twice. The first had nearly killed me, the second I'd held my own but just barely. I didn't need any more near-death experiences. We went in as a team. Yes, I'd be the one to kill him, but I'd have backup there to help.

"You also need to rest," Sam said, his fingers grazing my back in a reassuring touch.

Yes, that was also on my to-do list. My bones practically ached to lay down somewhere and sleep for a week.

"I'll sleep after we check out our location," I assured him. "Jorge, can you text the address to me?"

With a quick nod, Jorge did exactly that, my phone pinging with the update.

"Alright team, let's do this."

All three gazes swung toward me.

"What?" I asked. "You expecting me to do a cheer? Anna was the cheerleader, not me."

Listening to their chuckles, I headed to my bedroom to change into something a tad more suitable for hunting werewolves.

Like Kevlar.

CHAPTER
FIFTEEN

SAM STARED AT ME, HIS EXPRESSION incredulous and rather comical. His wide-eyed, unblinking stare had me pressing my lips together to keep from laughing. In all fairness, I did make for quite the sight. But, for once, it was nice not to have to wear workout gear.

"Okay, what?" I asked, my voice barely above a whisper, just in case.

He only shook his head, then wisely directed his gaze forward. "Nothing."

"Doesn't seem like nothing. You're staring at me like you've never seen me before."

"Um-hmm."

"*Um-hmm?*" I replied, shooting him my own

dubious stare. "What does *um-hmm* mean? It's not even a word."

"Sure it is," he countered.

"Use it in a sentence," I whispered back.

"Um-hmm," he repeated, nodding his head, as though that would give me any sort of clarification.

Chuckling under my breath, I tipped back my ball cap—the one I'd looped my ponytail through—and winked at Sam. The hat had been a gift from Anna a few weeks back. A sort of *thank you for not dying* gift, she'd said. She'd found it hilarious when she'd stumbled across it online and immediately ordered it for me. A hat with bleeding fangs that read *Camp Bite Me.* When I'd asked why she hadn't bought it for herself, she'd said no one cool wore ball caps at night.

Today, I'd paired it with a t-shirt designed with a vampire-inspired llama—cape and all. Beneath it scrawled the word *Dracullama.* The second I'd spotted it, I knew I had to have it, just to mess with Battikins. He hadn't seen the shirt yet, but I had high hopes for tonight. Sometimes, we all needed a good laugh, and I couldn't wait to see the look on ole Drac's face when he rose from his coffin.

"Way to be discreet," Sam said, snorting.

I snickered and shook my head. We were out in

the boondocks surrounded by acres of woodland. Other than the beautifully curated house standing a few hundred feet away from us, we were the only ones for miles that my senses could pick up.

Still, we needed to proceed with caution, since we were hunting werewolves. They wouldn't be caught unaware here.

"I honestly don't see this being a place Corbin would purchase," I commented.

The entire estate was well-groomed and vibrantly green, while the nearby lake held a quiet charm. It didn't look like a place someone would hide after a kidnapping.

"I doubt he's living in a run-down shack," Sam said.

"Yeah, but look at this place. Jorge didn't say what it sold for, but it must have gone for millions. Do you honestly think Corbin has access to those sort of funds? And cash, no less? This sort of place requires loans. Loans means banks, which means identity checks. I just don't see this being a place Corbin would buy."

"We don't know his financial situation. For all we know, he might have purchased this place to throw us off his tracks."

"Or it belongs to an entirely different person

named Evan Brown, with no connection to any of this whatsoever."

"That too," Sam said. "But we won't know until we investigate."

Which meant, it was time to shift.

I removed my ball cap and winced when the sun blasted me in the face. But I couldn't remain dressed for the next part. Hunkering down behind a prickly bush, I quickly disrobed, then let my wolf take over. Thankfully, I'd thought about this in advance, and prior to leaving my house, I'd downed more than a few allergy pills. Sneezing wasn't conducive to hunting werewolves, so I needed to take precautions. I only hoped I'd given it enough time for the pills to kick in, but not too long that I'd metabolized them already.

A soft grunt rose from my lips as my body reshaped itself. Oddly, it felt almost good. Like stretching a cramped muscle after the beating I'd taken. I gave a relieved sigh as I settled onto four legs and shook out my fur.

When I didn't sneeze, I grinned and glanced over to find Sam towering next to me, his shoulder at level with my head. He gave me an approving nod—likely because I'd shifted three times faster than before, thanks to my practicing—and led us out from behind the bush. I followed behind him, my steps quiet and careful. The last thing we needed was to attract the owners, whoever they might be. I couldn't imagine them responding well to two wolves stalking their property.

Sam trotted toward the house. With every step, I strained my senses in an attempt to pick up on *anything*. But the only thing I could smell was the lake, and all I could hear were the waterfowl and the birds in the trees. It was almost eerily quiet otherwise. Which made me wonder if Corbin was, in fact, here.

We approached the front step, and that was when I heard it: a soft grunt. Almost like someone'd been struck. My head snapped up, and I unleashed a low growl. Another slap and cry.

Oh my god. *Laini!*

Was he hurting her?

I caught wind of a woman's soft cry, almost like a whimper, and I exploded. Rage unlike anything I'd ever experienced tore through me, like a tempest, spurring me toward the front door. I didn't have hands to grab the door handle with, but I didn't need one. I was a werewolf. In a fight, I'd win against the door.

Just before I could bust through the door, Sam

bolted in front of me and shook his head. Then, right before my eyes, he lifted a front paw and reshaped it into a human hand. I stared, awestruck, as he grew an opposable thumb, and simply opened the front door. I'd never seen him do this before, but it made sense. If one could partially shape their hand into claws, logic dictated that they'd be able to do the reverse. Huffing my approval, I watched as his paw reshaped into wolf-form and together, we hurried into the house.

Another slap, another cry, another groan.

My lips curled back, and I rushed forward, careful to keep my steps quiet. We couldn't alert anyone to our presence. I had to remember that. Had to keep my mind on the goal. Save Laini. Kill Corbin. If that meant sneaking up on the bastard and ripping out his throat, so be it. At least it would finally be finished.

We stalked toward the sounds, finding ourselves closing in on a bedroom. A plethora of scents surrounded us. So many, in fact, I couldn't narrow them all down. But I did pick up on the distinct smell of sweat, and something else. Something I couldn't place.

At the sound of a harder strike, I crouched low. Sam and I shared one final glance, both of us knowing the moment of truth had come upon us. Then, with a nod, we lunged into the room and... came crashing to a stop.

A sharp shriek practically ruptured my ear drums, but it was my eyes and my brain that would never recover from this. Never recover from the sight of a man and woman scrambling off a bed, her bare ass red with his handprint, and his, uh, *happily engorged doodle-dasher* bobbing between his legs.

For a moment, I was grateful I wasn't in human form. Nothing would have been able to hide the embarrassing flames heating my cheeks. But then I realized how strange this must look to the humans. How terrifying to see two humongous wolves prowling into their sex-den in the middle of the day.

Sam and I shared a look before we turned and bolted out of the house, back to our clothes in the nearby brush. We needed to reach them before the owner came dashing out in his birthday suit, shotgun in hand.

I dove into the bush, quickly shifted, and threw on my clothes with Sam only a breath behind me. Once changed, we ran to the car we'd stashed behind the nearby barn, and hurried inside. I cranked the ignition, but while my brain *screamed* at me to hurry, I took it slow. The humans would be looking for wolves, not us. And if I went tearing out of there like a bat out of hell, it would only attract attention. So even though my heart pounded in my chest, I slowly guided the car off the land.

The instant we hit the road, Sam and I burst out laughing until tears streamed down my cheeks.

"Trust us to stumble across *that*," I cried out, still laughing.

Sam wheezed for breath as he leaned over and tied his shoes. "I seriously thought we'd found him."

"Me too," I said, breathless. "I thought someone was being hit."

"Someone *was*," he joked. "Just not in the way we thought."

The sight of her handprinted ass would follow me to my grave. "I think it's safe to say there's another Evan Brown out there."

"And he's likely on the phone with the police right now, reporting two wolves for breaking and entering."

I choked on another laugh. "Well, at least we gave them a memory."

"They gave us one too," Sam chuckled.

"Here's hoping the others had better luck."

"I don't know. *Someone* certainly got lucky. Just wasn't us," he said, winking.

Scoffing under my breath, I swatted at Sam's arm, then guided the car home, my thoughts taking a more interesting turn as I pondered a little experimentation of our own.

SAM AND I ROLLED INTO THE HOUSE AROUND dinner time. Silence greeted us, telling me Cole and the others hadn't returned from checking out their properties yet. I grinned. For once, it was just me and Sam. Exhaustion weighed heavily on my shoulders, but that didn't stop me from looping my arms around his neck and stretching onto my tiptoes. Clearly reading my thoughts, Sam shucked off my ball cap, then hauled me up against the nearest wall and kissed the hell outta me.

I sucked in a surprised breath, shocked by his amorous response. Maybe the scene we'd stumbled across had awoken something within him, something naughty and *fun*.

My mouth immediately opened to him. Heat blossomed in my stomach the instant Sam's tongue stroked mine, lighting a flame within me. I clutched him tighter, my legs gripping his waist, my back pressed firmly against the wall.

I brushed aside all other thoughts and focused on Sam. We were alone, and I wanted him—that was all that mattered. Everything else could wait and give us this little gift of precious time together.

Sam braced his knee under my butt before his hands swept up to my face, cupping my cheeks and brushing back my hair. His mouth fed at mine, his kiss frenzied.

I couldn't help but chuckle against his mouth.

He paused, his eyes slowly opening as he murmured against my lips, "What's so funny?"

"You," I teased. "One might think you're a little hot and bothered? Did you like what you saw this afternoon?"

Sam chuckled, then leaned his forehead against mine and peered into my eyes. "I don't need to see two people fucking to get hot and bothered around you."

"You sweet talker you," I joked.

Sam stole another kiss, except this one was slow and purposeful. I melted into him, my body practically writhing against his—

"Ew, Lucy!" came Anna's voice.

I jerked against Sam, tearing my mouth from his. My head fell back against the wall, and I released a frustrated growl. "You've gotta be kidding me."

"Come on," Anna continued. "If you two wanna fuck, go to your room. I don't need to see this."

"We need to get our own place," Sam grumbled.

"This *is* my place," I countered before slowly sliding down the wall and returning to my own two feet.

"I can hear you, you know," Anna said.

I stole a peek over Sam's shoulder to find her standing in the middle of the living room, arms crossed over her chest, and wearing a slight scowl. As though I'd offended her with my last comment.

"Shouldn't you be sleeping or something? Curled up next to your undead husband?"

She rolled her eyes. "I'm not even going to bother answering that."

Yeah, yeah. It wasn't *my* fault that Anna woke much earlier than Vlad did, but apparently Sam and I were paying the price.

"And before you go all *Lucy* on me," she said, "you should know that you have visitors coming tonight."

A frown knotted my brow. "I do?"

Anna's sigh spoke volumes. She stalked toward me and grabbed my hand before slapping my cell phone into my palm. It hadn't yet been fully charged when we'd headed out to investigate Mr. Brown's house, and since Sam had a cell, I hadn't felt the need to bring mine. Guess I'd been wrong.

"If you bothered to take this thing with you, you'd know your mom and dad are arriving in a few hours," Anna said.

Alarm brought my head snapping up. "What? Why on Earth would they come here?"

"*Apparently*, someone hasn't been returning their calls." Anna eyed me. "I wonder who could be responsible for that."

I winced. Yeah. My bad.

"So, now they're driving all the way here to check on you. They left about three hours ago."

Meaning I had about two hours to get my shit together. Most people could make the drive in four, but my dad drove like an eighty-year-old man.

"It so isn't the best time for this," I muttered. Not with everything going on.

"No shit," Anna commented. "But it's too late now. So we'll just have to make the best of the situation."

I nodded, then glanced at Sam. Guess we were shelving those naughty plans of ours. Thankfully, Anna and I had a long-established routine for whenever our parental units came to visit.

"Alright. Well, let's get busy."

"Busy?" Sam asked, his attention drifting between me and Anna.

"Yeah, and sorry, but not in the fun way."

"There's a fun way?" he asked.

"You know, 'getting busy'," I said with air quotes.

Understanding dawned on Sam's face. "Ah. Then what do you mean?"

I jabbed a finger toward Anna. "Laundry?"

"You know it. Dishes are yours."

"Who gets garbage?"

"Sam does," Anna said, laughing. "He's part of this, whether he likes it or not."

I patted his shoulder reassuringly. "And dusting?"

"All yours, kiddo," Anna said.

"Fine, then you get the toilets."

"Oh, man!" Her groan echoed through the living room. I nearly burst out laughing. I would take dusting any day of the week over latrine duty.

"Sam can straighten up the guest room," I said.

"I can?"

The look of pure alarm on his face made me laugh. "Come on, you're part of the gang. That means helping to clean up before any parents arrive."

"Aren't you two adults?" Sam argued.

"Well, that one's immortal," I said, hiking a

thumb in Anna's direction. "Doesn't change anything though. Unless you wanna hear my mom complaining about my abhorrent housework skills, then time to get cracking."

Sam shook his head but without another word, he planted a kiss atop my head and immediately headed for the kitchen. A smile tugged at my lips. I'd always imagined me and Anna doing this until the day we died. Seeing as how she was a vampire, that part of the equation had been removed, but I rather enjoyed including Sam in our group. Now, if only we could get Vlad to help... I had to admit, I wouldn't mind watching the five-hundred-year-old scrub toilets. That would be a sight for sore eyes.

Laughing to myself, I trailed after Sam into the kitchen, ready to tackle a sink full of dirty dishes.

CHAPTER
SIXTEEN

WE WERE AT T-MINUS FIVE MINUTES UNTIL MY parent's arrival. I scrutinized the living room for any signs of dust or clutter. Nothing stood out to me. I couldn't believe this was how my night was ending though. Instead of hunting down Corbin, I was preparing to welcome my parents. At least I wasn't missing out on anything. Over the last two hours, all of the hunting parties had checked in. Sadly, none had caught a whiff of Corbin nor Laini around town. Nor had the other two properties panned out. Seemed our sexually adventurous Mr. Evan Brown enjoyed gobbling up real estate.

Which put us right back to square one. And didn't that annoy the ever-loving bejesus out of me.

Every time it felt like we were gaining ground, something happened to snatch it away.

I was exhausted. Mentally, physically, and any other way a girl could be exhausted. I just wanted to pop some popcorn, put on a movie, and relax. But I couldn't. I wouldn't even know how to relax right now. Instead, I paced the width of the house, my nerves all a-jitter, and stared at the clock.

My parents had called a few minutes back to announce their arrival. I'd answered this time, much to their relief. After a light scolding, my mother had proclaimed that they would be staying in the second guest room. At my place.

I had no idea what to say to that. I couldn't say no—they were my parents. But my house was starting to feel like a clown car with one too many people stuffed inside. Two vampires, two werewolves, and two humans. It sounded like the start of a bad joke. And a little like high school again. I mean... was I even allowed to live with my boyfriend-slash-mate in the same house as my parents? Weren't there rules about that? There'd certainly be no sexy shenanigans while sharing a roof with family.

I shuddered just thinking about it.

"Fretting isn't going to change anything," Anna said.

She sat on the four-seater couch, her legs stretched over Vlad's lap. He lifted his head, his gaze drifting over my shirt. A slight smile tugged at his lips, exposing the tips of his fangs, before he refocused on his book. His expression when he'd first seen *Dracullama* had made it all worth it.

"You'd be fretting too if your mom was coming to visit."

"I'd be casually dead for a few days if my mom was coming to visit," Anna retorted in a wry voice.

In all fairness, Anna's mother was, like, uber religious. When she first met Vlad, she'd worn a crucifix around her neck, laced their pizza with garlic, and decorated her front lawn with a Nativity Scene. I'd almost died when I'd seen it. My mother, on the other hand, was sugar and spice and all things nice—except when it came to werewolf politics. That brought out a rather shrewd side of her I'd never seen when younger. She hated all things werewolf, thanks to Reggie and his womanizing ways.

My stepfather, on the other hand, was often as chill as a chinchilla. Calm in the face of *all* the drama. And seeing as how his stepdaughter was a werewolf and her best friend a vampire, there was often quite a bit of drama.

The doorbell rang precisely thirty seconds later. I marched to the front door with Sam close on my heels. Anna and Vlad remained seated. She adored my mother, but she knew it was pointless to get up for at least the first ten minutes—during which, my mother would be fawning all over me.

I pulled open the door with a beaming smile, one that immediately dropped when my mother choked on a gasp.

"What on god's green earth happened to your face?"

Oh, damn! I'd forgotten about that, and I sure as heck couldn't tell her the truth. She'd never leave my side again if she thought I was in danger.

"I saved a baby from a runaway horse," I lied through my teeth.

My mother's face slackened, and her lips pressed into a grim line. "Lucy Adaline Williams, you may choose not to tell me something, but that doesn't mean you get to lie to me."

Oh damn. She went right for the middle name.

Anna snickered from the couch. "Hi, Mom!"

My mother hardly batted an eyelash as she turned to take in Anna and Vlad. Her eyes softened briefly as she basked in their marital bliss. "Hello, Anna, my love. Good to see you." Then she rounded back on me. "Well? Are you going to tell me what this"—she gestured to my face—"is all about?"

"Nope," I said, popping the *P*. It seemed safer to keep her in the dark.

Disapproval stamped her face before she stormed inside and dropped her bag on the floor. I knew the moment her gaze fell on Sam because her whole body tightened. "It better not have been you," she said, by way of greeting.

"Mom!"

"What?" She whirled around, her hand pressed to her chest. "I show up to find you lookin' all bruised and battered. I'm allowed to question your boyfriend."

"Sam isn't my boyfriend," I grumbled.

"Darlin', you know I don't believe in that mate nonsense."

Thanks, Reggie. "Whether or not you believe in it doesn't make it any less true, Mom. Just because Reggie lied to you doesn't mean Sam's lying to me."

Her jaw tightened. Reggie wasn't exactly a topic my mother enjoyed discussing. In fact, she'd deigned to tell me about him until I'd met Sam and brought him home. The second she'd realized what he was, she'd thrown him out on his ass, then proceeded to tell me the colorful story of how she met Reggie.

Ignoring my mom, I reached for my dad and hugged him tight. "Hey, Daddy."

"Hi, Princess." At least one of them was sane. "You're okay, right?"

"I'm fine," I assured him.

I lugged in the rest of their luggage—my god, how long were they planning on staying?—and closed the door. The instant I did, my mom descended, fretting over me like a mother hen, and introducing me to all new levels of hell. She nettled over everything, from the bruises on my face, to my weight, to my outfit. From the sound of her clucking tongue, she didn't approve of the *Dracullama* shirt.

"So, care to tell me why you haven't been answering your phone lately?"

"Come on, Mama, you know I've been busy."

"Too busy to talk to your mother?"

Youch. Another shot of motherly guilt straight to the heart. Right now, I was wondering if I wouldn't prefer Anna's mother's particular brand of crazy over my mom's over-protectiveness.

"You know, you really didn't need to come all this way," I said.

"How else could I get you to speak to me?" My

mother turned and planted her hands on her hips, studying Sam. "It better not be you keeping her from me."

Poor Sam blanched, his face slackening at my mother's words.

"Mom, leave Sam alone."

"Why? He's your *mate*, isn't he? Shouldn't I be allowed to talk to him?"

"Barbara," my father finally said, stepping in. "Leave the kids be, won'tcha? Come on, let's go get settled into the guest room. It's late and we've been driving all afternoon. We can spend time with them tomorrow."

I shot my father a grateful look, one my mother spotted with pursed lips.

For a moment, I expected her to go off again, spouting about how it was her right as a mother to demand answers. But before she could get fired up, my father took her hand and led her toward the hallway. A quick glance back had me pointing down the hallway and then holding up two fingers, indicating the second door. He nodded and latched onto a suitcase along the way. I had to admit, it frightened me that she'd packed more than one bag. One meant a weekend stay type thing. But she'd packed three. *Three*. Was she planning to stay for a few months? I couldn't handle that.

The moment their door clicked shut, I released a long breath and slumped into a nearby rocking chair. "Sweet baby Jesus, that woman..."

Sam stood next to the armrest and ran his fingers through my hair. "She loves you, that's all."

"She could nag a horse to death," I muttered.

Anna's shoulders shook with laughter. "What does that even mean?"

"I dunno, man. I'm tired, leave me alone."

Considering I hadn't slept in over thirty-six hours, I was impressed I was still standing. Well, sitting. And the rocking chair was calling my name, whispering all sorts of dirty thoughts into my head about going to sleep. *Just close your eyes*, it taunted, like some sort of seductive siren.

"Come on," Sam said. "Let's get you tucked into bed. You need some sleep if you're going to start fresh tomorrow."

"Start fresh," I repeated, snickering. "No one starts fresh."

"Okay," Sam murmured, clearly just appeasing me.

"Tomorrow, we need to find Corbin," I said. "We need to finish this."

"We will. But we can't do that if you're dead on your feet."

I nodded. "You coming to bed too?"

Sam's eyes twinkled. "Sure you want me to?"

Anna cleared her throat. "Need I remind you two that we have exceptional hearing. *And* Lucy's parents are here."

I burst out laughing. She sounded so dignified for someone who'd been screaming Vlad's name the night before last. "Maybe you should keep that in mind too," I said, reminding her of our previous discussion.

Vlad's head rose, and I choked on my laugh at the sight of his furrowed brows. "What does that mean?" he asked, his voice a bit stilted.

"Never mind her," Anna growled, eyes alight with the promise of retribution.

"*Oh, Vlad,*" I cried out, imitating Anna's high-pitched voice. "*Impale me harder.*"

"Lucy Adaline!" Anna shouted, also invoking the dreaded middle name. She reached for the couch cushion sitting innocently beside her and whipped it at my head.

I caught it and held it up in the air. "Thanks, girl."

"You're horrible, and I hope you choke on Sam's dick and die."

"It's certainly big enough," I shot back.

Stunned silence filled the room before Anna and I burst into shared laughter. The two men, on the other hand, didn't seem inclined to join.

"And on that note..." Sam said. He turned and vanished into our bedroom.

I was still laughing as I trailed after him. Laughter that soon died when I caught sight of my mother standing in her doorway, staring at me with wide, unblinking eyes. She'd clearly heard *everything*.

Heat warmed my cheeks, and I ducked into the room, all the while telling myself that had *not* just happened.

At seven in the morning, the sun was already shining into the kitchen. Squinting, I held up a hand to shield my eyes from the blinding glare. It was *way* too early to be this bright. I couldn't even believe I was awake. I'd meant to sleep in. Told myself I'd earned it. Deserved it. But the second the clock struck seven, my eyes flashed open, and I'd remembered. Cole. I was due to meet with him in an hour.

"Good morning," came a sharp voice from the kitchenette.

I blinked away any lingering sleep and muttered a good morning to my mother, who sat on a tall stool, cup of tea in hand. Guess she hadn't had any issues finding everything. Thank goodness.

"Why don't you have a cup of tea and sit with me," my mom said.

I groaned and tipped my head back. "Mom, seriously. It's seven in the morning. Couldn't you give it at least another hour before interrogating me."

A small smile flashed at me from behind her tea cup. "You never were a morning person."

"And yet, you continue to pester me before noon."

Her soft chuckle brought a smile to my own lips. My first this morning. My mother and I often sniped at one another, but there was no doubt that we loved each other.

"Your father is still asleep," she said.

"So's Sam."

"And Anna and Vlad are..."

"Dead," I said, finishing that sentence for her.

My mother paled, then cleared her throat and

lowered her mug to the table. "I'm not sure I'll ever get used to that."

I shrugged. "You do, eventually. But yeah, it's different."

Nodding, my mom picked up the cup and took another sip. "You look better."

Did I? I'd stumbled into the bathroom to relieve my bladder and brush my teeth, but I hadn't actually glanced in the mirror. My brain didn't function at its best this early. And most of the time, I avoided the vanity until I'd at least showered. Self-perseverance and all that.

"Sit, Lucy."

Ah, the mom-tone. One that never left room for arguing. I minced over to the table and dragged myself onto a free stool. Then I reached for the tea pot and poured myself my own mug. Maybe a little caffeine would help ease this conversation.

"I know you don't want me prying—"

"Then don't," I said.

"Lucy..." She shook her head. "I'm your mother. I'm always going to worry about you. When we visit, the last thing I expect to see is you looking like"—she waved a hand in my general direction—"this."

She wasn't going to let this go, clearly. "If you must know, I got into a fight."

"Well, that much is obvious," she muttered.

And people wondered where I learned my sarcasm from. Wait, no they didn't. They just thought it came from Anna. But I'd been exposed to sarcasm a long time before Anna entered the scene.

"With whom?"

"Corbin."

Her expression tightened. She knew *all* about him, thanks to his New Orleans shenanigans.

"And Cole."

She slowly arched a brow. "I don't know a Cole."

"He's my second," I told her. "He was Reggie's second too. A good guy. He's taken it upon himself to teach me how to fight werewolves. Anna's lessons weren't enough."

"Clearly, if your face is any indication."

"Gee, thanks, Mom."

She shrugged. "I'm not here to lie to you. You looked terrible last night. Less so this morning, thank goodness. So, what are you going to do about this Corbin fellow?"

"Oh, the usual. Track him down. Kick his ass. Then kill him."

She started at my words and stared at me, as though unsure she'd heard me correctly.

Instead of repeating them, I merely nodded. "He needs to die, Mom. He's hurt too many people."

"I just want you to be careful," she said. "This man's already stabbed you once. Can't you let the others take care of it? I'd hate to see you hurt again."

"I'll be okay. I can handle myself."

"We'll have to agree to disagree," she muttered.

"Hey, I may look bad, but I walked away from the fight. Corbin didn't."

My proclamation seemed to intrigue her. She appraised me from over the rim of her mug, her eyes sparking with something that looked awfully similar to pride. "Next time, finish the fight before he can do *that* to you."

I nodded. "That's the plan."

"Good girl. Your father and I won't stay too long, I promise. We just wanted to make sure you're well. But it sounds like you need to focus on this problem. We'll stay one more night, maybe two. And then head home."

Relief rounded my shoulders. "Thanks, Mom. I really appreciate that. And hey, once this is done, Sam and I can return home."

"You're planning to return to New Orleans then?"

"Hopefully," I said. Though, I paused afterward.

Was that still the plan? It had been when we'd first started this whole mess. But then Cole had entered the picture, and now I was wondering if I shouldn't stay.

I banished those thoughts and focused on my mother. Until we dealt with Corbin, there wasn't any point in thinking about anything else. Wherever Sam and I ended up, though, that would be home. And I couldn't wait for that moment to arrive.

CHAPTER
SEVENTEEN

THAT SUPPOSED "ONE NIGHT" SOON TURNED INTO two, then four, with no sign of my parents leaving. Every time I asked when they planned to return home, my mom would shrug and claim there was no rush.

No rush?

Who was she kidding? This was so *not* the right time for an extended visit. Did she not remember our lovely kitchen conversation? We had too much going on to sit back and visit. In fact, most days we were hardly home. Each morning began with me in the boxing ring with Cole while Sam played spectator and offered advice. Then we spent the rest of the day scouring the streets with the pack, with Anna and Vlad aiding the search after sunset. Every night, we returned home overheated, frustrated, and impatient, only to find my mom elbow-deep in the kitchen, preparing us a meal. Sam suspected they hadn't left yet because she wanted to offer us her support, feed us, and most importantly, ensure I was okay. I appreciated her concern—I did—but now wasn't the time.

Especially considering tonight was the full moon.

Thanks to their overbearing presence, I'd arranged to hold the meeting at Cole's. To keep my parents from attending. Not only were they not permitted, but I also didn't need my mom watching me fight—and possibly kill—someone. Unfortunately, Bryn showed no signs of changing her mind, which meant tomorrow, she would issue the challenge.

My nerves were already shot, but I had a feeling this fight would put me over the edge, and I didn't want my parents to see that.

"They need to leave," I muttered as Sam and I headed for our bedroom. It was half-past two in the morning, and my dogs were barking after hours of combing the city. There had to be a better way than this, but so far, no new information had cropped up to help narrow our search. How the police did this day in and day out, I'd never understand. Of course, they were formally trained, and we were just a pack of werewolves.

"Have you told her that?"

I glared at him. "Many, *many* times. But she's stubborn and refuses to listen."

Sam bumped my shoulder. "Sounds like someone else I know."

"Oh, ha, ha. Very funny. I'll have you know I get my stubbornness from Anna, thank you very much."

"I heard that!" Anna shot back from her room. She and Vlad had escorted us home and were now planning to head out in search of their own dinner. My mom might have been preparing meals for me and Sam, but she apparently drew a line in the sand when it came to blood. The vampires could fend for themselves, she'd said, before patting Anna on the head and giving her a quick kiss on the cheek.

Sam and I, on the other hand, were headed to bed. Tonight—seeing as how it was past midnight— was the big fight, but Cole insisted I still show for our morning session. Therefore, I needed to rest now. I couldn't imagine winning the fight on no sleep.

"Hopefully they leave this afternoon," I continued, my voice low.

My mother might not be a werewolf, but she

certainly had the ears of one, and she'd opted to stay up late tonight, waiting for our return. "If something goes wrong and I lose..."

"Hey." Sam clutched my hands in his and pulled me flush against his body. "You aren't going to lose."

"You don't know that. And I don't want them here for that, to see you guys come home without me..." My voice grew faint. I couldn't even imagine that scene. "Their presence is a distraction. Not to mention dangerous. We're in the middle of a crisis, and she's what, baking us muffins?"

"In all fairness, they were delicious muffins."

"Sam," I scoffed, though a faint smile tugged at my lips. Trust him to be thinking about food in a moment like this.

"You've got this," Sam said. He wrapped me in his arms and held me close. I sank into the embrace and rested my head against his chest, breathing in his scent. My parents weren't the only ones that worried me. There was also Sam, Anna, and Vlad. Anna and Vlad couldn't attend the meeting, seeing as how they were vampires. But Sam? Fear clamped around my heart at the thought of him *watching* me die. Of course, he utterly refused to leave. And Anna and Vlad had guilted him into keeping them informed at all times. They wanted a blow by blow.

It all stressed me the eff out.

I lifted my head from Sam's chest and gazed up at him, memorizing every little detail about him, just in case. "Promise me if it goes badly, you won't interfere, and you'll take care of my parents."

"You'll take care of them yourself—"

"Sam."

His mouth clicked shut, and his jaw tightened until a tic throbbed near his temple.

"Promise me," I repeated. "I need to know you'll take care of them." It was the only promise I could extract from him, and similar to the one I'd forced out of my mom and Anna, too. My mom loathed werewolves, but she wouldn't abandon Sam, not when she knew what he meant to me. And Anna would help. Worst case scenario, they'd all take care of each other. I couldn't ask for anything more than that.

Other than to win the fight.

I *could* ask for that.

"Fine," he growled. "But promise me you won't give up. You have a lot to live for."

A small smile teased my lips. I stretched on my toes and brushed a light kiss against his mouth. "Like you?"

"Hell yes, like me," he grumbled.

Before I could utter a response, Sam knocked my legs out from beneath me and tossed me onto the bed. I collapsed into the pillows, laughing. All my training, and I hadn't seen that move coming from a mile away. Not that I was complaining. Most girls enjoyed a good toss into the pillows. Especially when the one tossing them crawled on top after.

From the wicked twinkle in his eye, I suspected sleep wouldn't be had for another few hours. But what a way to spend what might be my last morning with him.

A SHRILL RING INVADED MY DREAMS AND dragged me out of my blissful sleep.

No, no, no, this wasn't happening. I didn't want to wake up. I just wanted to keep sleeping. I *needed* sleep. What didn't people understand about that?

Groaning, I snuggled closer to Sam, burying my face against his neck. I didn't know what time it was, but it had to be too early for friendly phone calls. Which meant, something bad had likely happened. It felt like I'd only been asleep for a few hours at most. My body definitely didn't *feel* rested, though Sam might have had something to do with that.

When the ringing didn't stop, I unleashed a low growl, then flopped onto my back. The noise came from my nightstand, right next to my head. Sam didn't seem disturbed, but I'd long since learned the man could sleep through a hurricane. Not me, though. I was the unfortunate one who woke at the slightest sound.

I rolled onto my side and snatched up my phone. It took a few tries for my damn fingers to swipe properly, but once I did, I pressed the phone to my ear and snapped, "What?"

Silence greeted me.

I pulled the phone away from my head and blinked, glaring at the name. Why on Earth was Cole calling me? I still had a few hours left until we'd planned to meet, so it couldn't have anything to do with that. "Cole, I know it's you. Why the hell are you calling me so early?"

"I knew you weren't a morning person, but damn."

I flopped onto my back and bit back a sharp reply. Snapping at him again likely wouldn't get the information out of him any faster. But I did envision breaking one—or three—of his fingers. "Tell me what you want so I can go back to sleep."

"I'm afraid there won't be any more sleep for you today."

My eyes slammed shut, and I pressed my head deep into the pillows. "What happened?"

"Another human-born," was all he said.

That had my eyes snapping open. I stared at the pockmarked ceiling, then cursed. "Who?"

"Lincoln."

I didn't know the man, but I recognized the name from the roster. A roster I'd made myself memorize.

"What happened?"

As though sensing the tension now coursing through my body, Sam rolled over, slung an arm around my waist, and pulled me up against him. As though even in his sleep, all he wanted to do was comfort me.

"He and Lee had just returned from their patrol and were getting some rest when a few of Corbin's men busted down the door and took Lincoln."

I released a slow breath. This was getting ridiculous. We'd paired our human-borns up with wolves, and even then, the wolves couldn't protect them.

"Where's Lee?"

Cole's hesitation spoke volumes. I shrugged off

Sam's arm and sat up in bed, the blankets gripped to my chest. "Cole. Where's Lee?"

"Dead," he croaked.

The room spun. Lee was dead? He was a dominant wolf, ranked fifth in the pack. Not to mention, he was Laini's brother. That poor family. My heart fractured for them. I couldn't imagine their pain right now.

"My god," I whispered. What the hell was happening? How was this even possible? I knew Corbin would recuperate, but I hadn't imagined it would be so quickly.

Guilt needled my chest. If I'd just killed Corbin, if I'd just said *eff it* and killed the bastard, this never would have happened. Cursing, I bent my knees up to my chest and rested my forehead against them. When had this become such a shitshow? Why did Corbin keep getting the upper hand? Why hadn't we handled this problem yet? What kind of alpha was I that I hadn't been able to get a grip on this? We needed to do better—*I* needed to do better. The pack relied on me, on the most dominant. And now, one was dead, and two human-borns missing.

"There's more," Cole said, his voice hoarse.

Oh hell. What else could there possibly be?

"We aren't the only pack reporting missing

human-borns," Cole continued. "I just got a call from one of the Alabama Pack members. It was against his alpha's wishes, so keep this intel between us. But he asked me to keep an eye out for a few of his people. They're missing three human-borns and four wolves."

My mouth parted in surprise. I honestly had no idea how to respond to that.

"Lucy?" Cole called over the line.

"Yeah. Yeah, I'm here. Just... trying to digest all this."

"I hear ya."

"Do you think Corbin took them?"

Cole's sigh carried across the line. "I truthfully don't know what to think. I mean, it'd be too coincidental for Alabama's human-borns to go missing for any other reason right now."

"And the four wolf-born?"

"He isn't sure if they're dead or alive. They just vanished."

Holy crap on a cracker. Had Corbin killed them and ditched their bodies? Except, I hadn't known him to be that careful in his actions. Usually he just let the bodies fall and left others to clean up his mess.

"What do you think happened?" I asked Cole. "What does your gut tell you?"

Another loud breath. "My gut tells me that he's abducting people from other packs as well. And if I'm right, then he's likely turned our human-borns."

"What about the missing wolf-borns?"

Cole's voice dropped an octave. "Either they're dead, or they've joined his side."

I sucked in a sharp breath. "Is that possible?"

"Sure. Why not? He's never been without supporters. He had someone with him in New Orleans when you first came up against him. Then yesterday in the park, he had two others with him. His former alpha never mentioned any other wolves defecting with him. So, where are these werewolves coming from? They aren't from our pack. They have to be coming from somewhere."

I shuddered at the thought. "He's recruiting."

"That would be my guess too. But how? It's not like he can put up wanted posters in public. And he isn't from America, so I doubt these are people he knows." Cole hummed quietly under his breath as he considered his own question. "He's likely accepting anyone in order to grow his numbers. I wouldn't be surprised if—" Cole broke off and mumbled something in the background.

"Cole?"

"One sec," he called back to me.

I rolled my eyes, but did as he said. When he didn't return after a few moments, I started drumming my fingers against the phone. Patience had always been a virtue of mine, but that didn't seem to be the case this morning. If he didn't get his ass back on the phone in the three seconds, I'd—

"Okay, Jorge found something."

Relief had my forgetting about my unspoken threats. "Like what?"

"He stumbled onto some sort of encrypted forum on the dark web."

"On the what?"

"The dark web," Cole repeated, as though that clarified things for me. "It's a subset of the internet, one that is intentionally kept hidden to keep anyone from stumbling onto it. Often, it's where the really bad shit happens."

"Criminal interwebbing," I mused.

Cole grunted, then I caught the sound of him clicking on a keyboard. "Okay, at first glance, it looks like a forum specifically dedicated to werewolves."

Damn, that didn't sound good. Werewolves were supposed to be a secret. If people knew about us, even if only on this dark web, how long would it take for word to spread?

"Jorge is going to work on breaking the

encryption. He thinks it'll take a day or two. If I had to wager a guess, I'd say this is where Corbin is recruiting people," Cole said.

Dread settled in the pit of my stomach. "If you're right..."

"Then the missing Alabama wolves might not be dead at all."

"They might be part of his new pack," I finished.

"And that's just the Alabama Pack that we know of. A lot of alphas don't like to share information with other packs. Wolves could be missing from other packs across the country, and we wouldn't know."

Meaning, Corbin's pack could be a hell of a lot larger than we were anticipating. It also meant they could have more resources than we expected.

"This is bad," I murmured more to myself than Cole.

"It certainly isn't good."

"Tell Jorge to keep working on that encryption," I ordered. "In the meantime, we need to reach out to all the other packs, see which are missing members."

"Lucy, that'll take forever. Do you know how many packs there are in the country?"

"It doesn't matter how long it takes, Cole. It's our responsibility. Not only do these alphas need to know what's going on so they can monitor their own packs, but they also need to know that this is all connected. How have you guys all survived so long without communicating with each other?"

"Each pack is independently managed," Cole said. "Their business isn't ours."

"Yeah, well I'm making it ours. We can't just ignore this. Corbin has become a threat to every pack in the country. They deserve to be made aware."

I could practically hear Cole pinching the bridge of his nose. "I know I should be proud you want to take up this mantel, and that you care enough to help the other packs. But right now, all I care about is ours. And this just adds more onto our already full plate."

"Then spread out the workload," I said. "We have an entire pack who want to help. Use them."

"Jesus, Lucy."

"Listen." My temper flared, and it took a moment for me to rein it back in. "We have a meeting tonight. We need to give them a progress update. We haven't been able to find Corbin, and now we have another abducted human-born and a dead wolf. They deserve to see us taking action. So stop fucking arguing with me, and do as I say."

At the sound of me cursing, Sam's eyes slowly

open. The instant he saw me on the phone, he frowned and sat up in bed, the blankets spilling into his lap. I saw the concern in his gaze, and I held up a finger.

"We need to find him, Cole." I glanced at the nearby clock and grimaced. Six in the morning. "I'll be at your place in two hours. I expect a progress report by then. And tell Jorge I want to know what's happening on that forum."

Cole grumbled an agreement right before I disconnected the call. Then I blew out a breath and leaned back against the headboard.

Sam twined his fingers through mine. "Rough morning?"

"Rough few months," I said, grimacing at the sound of my own voice. I sounded whiny, petulant. But Sam didn't hold it against me. I told him about Cole's call and everything I'd learned.

When I was finished, Sam raked his other hand through his hair and cursed. "You were right to insist we involve the other alphas. We have to put a stop to this, and they have a right to know what's going on."

I nodded, finding comfort in Sam's words. But it didn't stop the dread from gnawing at my chest. We *did* need to put a stop to this, and soon, before Corbin did it for us.

CHAPTER
EIGHTEEN

I BOUNCED ON MY TOES IN COLE'S BOXING RING, evading his jabs with some quick footwork. That was the lesson today, he'd told me. Not to hit back, but to stay on my toes and remain fluid. To dodge everything he threw at me, and be aware of my opponent's tells. An interesting lesson. My legs ached with the effort, but I found myself enjoying this session more than previous ones.

Cole snapped out a sharp jab. I dodged to the side, letting his fist skim past my nose, then returned to bouncing back and forth. I analyzed his every moment and finally noticed a small tell. He tended to fake in the opposite direction. So when it looked like he intended to go left, he actually went right.

Nailing that down made this task so much easier. I could read him like an open book.

"How many alphas have been contacted?" I asked, my voice a bit breathless, mixing business with my workout.

"Five currently," Cole replied, his left shoulder dropping, so I went right just in time to evade what would have been a devastating hook. "So far no one is missing any pack members."

"Good." I released a slow breath in an attempt to slow my pulse. "Continue reaching out."

"They could be lying, you know," Cole suggested.

I shrugged, all while tracking his movements. "Could be. But at least we've done the right thing by reaching out. What they do with that information is up to them." I ducked another quick jab. "What about Jorge? Was he able to crack the encryption?"

"Not as of yet." Cole's jaw tensed and his left foot twitched before his right swung out in a side kick.

I blocked the attack and danced back out of reach. If I wasn't mistaken, my second was starting to get frustrated. Not because I'd given him orders to contact the other alphas, but because he couldn't seem to land a single hit.

Biting back a grin, I kept my attention on him and leapt out of range just as he attempted a grab.

"Sneaky," I said, chuckling. "But I'm too quick for you."

Temper flared in his eyes. "Don't get cocky."

"I'm allowed to celebrate my wins," I told him.

"You haven't won yet." He lifted an arm and mopped his brow. He was expending more effort than I was. With every missed hit, he spent more energy than me. I hadn't even broken a sweat yet. And believe me, inside, I was crowing. Call it revenge for every bruise and sore muscle.

I wasn't sure how long we'd been at it, and I couldn't risk breaking focus to glance at the clock. Couldn't be much longer, though. Some of us had other things to do today. Like track down victims and kidnappers, all while preparing for tonight's pack meeting and highly anticipated challenge.

Cole feinted to the left, so I moved to the right. Except this time, he countered and snapped out a hard punch that caught me square in the sternum. My lungs compressed and I toppled to the ground, left staring up at the spinning ceiling and wondering if I'd ever breathe again.

Sam seated himself next to me and laid his hand

across my ribs, rubbing the exact spot where Cole's hit had connected.

"Log that away as another lesson," Cole grunted, plopping down on the other side of me and unwrapping his hands. "You can't get overconfident. And don't lose focus. What were you thinking about just now?"

I choked in a rasping gasp, then coughed. Once I could breathe again, I slowly sat up and choked out, "About all the things I have to do today."

Cole shot me a disappointed glare, then shook his head. "You must remain focused at all times. It didn't take long for me to figure out what was going on. I corrected my movements, and you didn't even notice. One hit. That's all it takes. One solid hit, and Bryn wins."

I nodded, properly chastised. Sam hopped to his feet and offered a hand, which I took. As he pulled me up, I glanced at Cole. "Do you think I stand a chance tonight?"

"Yes," he said, without hesitation. "Unfortunately, Bryn has no intentions of revoking her challenge, so tonight you'll have to fight. But you'll win."

"So confident," I murmured.

"Hey." Sam reached for my face and brushed

back my sweaty hair. "We're absolutely confident in you. You can do anything you put your mind to. And you *will* win tonight, because you don't know how to lose."

I wasn't too sure about that. I'd lost plenty of things throughout my life. My virginity, for one. My sanity, for another. But I understood what Sam was saying. I wouldn't lose, because I *couldn't* lose. Because losing meant abandoning everyone I loved—abandoning *him*. And that wasn't an acceptable scenario. I intended to live a long and happy life with Sam. And to do that, I had to win this fight. The math was simple.

As a team, we headed downstairs. Cole and I immediately checked our messages, only to find that nothing had changed in the hour and a half we'd been sparring. Laini and Lincoln were still missing, Corbin was still untraceable, and Jorge was still working on the dark net forum. Meanwhile, my pack was preparing for tonight's meeting, while I prepared for the fight.

When this was all over, I needed a vacation. Somewhere warm and sunny with a beach. But also quiet and comfortable, where Sam and I could relax all day, just listening to the waves hit the sand. That sounded like heaven.

"Why don't you head home," Cole suggested. "Your parents are still visiting?"

"Unfortunately. My mom seems to think she's needed here still. It's why we're holding the meeting at your place."

Cole contemplated that with a serious air. "Good call. I couldn't imagine having humans present, let alone the alpha's parents. That's just... weird."

I chuckled. It was an odd situation.

"Meeting starts at eight o'clock," Cole said. "Meet back here at seven-thirty."

I nodded, remembering this conversation from earlier.

"Once the pack arrives, we'll give everyone a status update, and then it'll be show time."

Another nod. If Bryn won tonight, she'd become the new alpha, which was why the fight had to happen first. To give the pack time to adjust to their new leader if I lost. If I won, Bryn's family would be given leave to mourn the loss of their family member. I still couldn't believe this fight had to end in a death. But as Cole had said the last time I'd questioned it, those were the rules. Well that may be, but they were stupid rules if you asked me.

"See you tonight," I said with a wave before heading for the front door.

Sam swung it open, and we walked out into the mid-day heat. Neither of us spoke until we were belted into the car. Sam fired up the engine, then turned toward me and cupped my face.

"You've got this," he said. "I believe in you."

My lip quivered. I liked the idea of being an alpha, but not if this was the cost. Constantly fighting for my life wasn't how I wanted to live. Maybe it was time to revert to my original plan and appoint a new alpha so I could step down.

Sam's hands fell away from my face. He gripped the steering wheel, and we pulled away from Cole's house. Neither of us spoke, but in my head was a cacophony I knew wouldn't shut up until after the fight tonight.

My parents insisted Sam and I spend the afternoon with them. Clearly, they were suffering from nerves as well because every time they thought I wasn't watching, they stared at me with such fearful expressions that made my breath catch. They didn't know all the details about tonight's meeting, but they knew enough to know my life was in danger.

"You *can't* come," I argued for the tenth time. "This is a *pack* meeting. Not a family get together. Only pack is allowed to attend. You two aren't even werewolves, for crying out loud."

And thank the lord for that. I couldn't handle my mother being there. Cole had preached about focus this morning, and my mother was the antithesis of that.

"I don't understand why—"

"Mom," I snapped. I bit back my wince. I hated using that tone with her, hated upsetting her on what might be my last day with them, but I couldn't relent on this. They weren't allowed to attend, and that was final. "I love you. I appreciate that you wanna come and support me. But the fact remains, you *can't*. Anna and Vlad won't be there either."

"But Sam can go?" she accused, her narrowed eyes darting to him.

"Sam is a werewolf and is welcome because he's my mate."

"And I'm your mother."

I sighed and dropped my head onto the table with a loud thump. I was twenty-seven for crying out loud. I shouldn't be having this argument with my mother. It wasn't like I was asking permission to be out past my curfew or something.

"Barbara," my father cautioned, his voice soft. "She's already explained this to us multiple times. You need to let it go."

"Let it go?" My mother whirled on him with an accusing stare. "You want to just let this go? She could die, Richard."

"We have to trust that she can handle this and will come back to us."

My mother choked, clearly feeling a little betrayed by her husband and daughter. Lifting my head from the table, I laid a comforting hand on my mother's shoulder and gave it a small squeeze, mindful of my strength.

"Cole and Anna have taught me well," I assured her. "I can hold my own against Cole, and he's my second. Which means he's stronger than Bryn."

My mother's muscles slackened, and she leaned back in her chair. "I hate this. I hate what happened to you. I hate that this is your life now. I just wanted a normal life for you. And when I found out about all this werewolf nonsense, I vowed to keep it from you. I didn't want you anywhere near all this insanity." She bit her lip and stared forlornly down the hall. "I know it's not your fault. But I truly do hate your life now."

Pain pricked my heart. "I know, Mom. But it's not all terrible. I have Sam."

"If that's the only good thing you can pick out from all of this, then that isn't a win," she said. "You know I think Sam is great—"

"Gee, thanks," he teased.

"—but he was born a werewolf. He was raised into this lifestyle. You weren't. You know what it means to be human and free from all this." She leaned forward and snatched my hand. "You could walk away from all of this right now. Just put it behind you."

I blinked, startled by this change of attitude. I hadn't realized how much my mother hated this for me.

"There are werewolves out there who do it all by themselves," she urged. "You don't need to be the alpha, or even part of this pack. And you certainly don't need to be the one who finds this Corbin fellow. Leave it to the others. Or hell, the police, even. They don't need to know he's a werewolf to handle this."

"Mom—"

"No, don't *Mom* me. I want you to really think about this Lucy. Think about what this life will do to you. You've been a werewolf for almost a year and a half, and in that time, you've already almost died once. Tonight marks the second."

Third, if we counted when Corbin first attacked me. But I didn't feel a need to bring *that* up. It would only reinforce her point. Instead, I argued with, "Only if I lose."

My mother's expression told me exactly how she thought tonight would end.

Anger bubbled under the surface, and I barked out a laugh. "Thanks for the vote of confidence, Mom."

"No, honey, it's not that I don't think you can win, it's just..." Her words trailed off, as though she couldn't think of how to fix this.

My head jerked in a sharp nod. "How about we end this conversation now before either of us says something we regret? After all, I might die tonight, and these might be your last words to me." Okay, so that was a low blow, but I hated that my mother didn't believe I'd win the fight. Everyone else did, so why couldn't she?

"Lucy's got this," Sam said, his voice quiet, but firm. As though he had no doubts whatsoever.

I turned to face him with a grateful smile.

"I've watched her fight Cole, and she survived

not one of Corbin's attacks, but two. Don't lose faith in her when we're so close."

I reached out and gripped Sam's hand. I'd certainly won the lottery the day Fate decided to make him my mate.

"Don't worry, Barbara," came Anna's voice as she strode into the kitchen, now awake at four thirty.

I immediately leapt to my feet and pulled all the curtains and blinds, lest she burst into flame right here in front of us.

"Vlad and I will be here with you tonight. We just need to pop out for some blood, but afterward, we'll keep each other company. And Sam will be keeping me apprised of the fight. We'll know the instant Lucy wins."

I shot her an equally grateful grin. I loved the way she'd worded that, as though she also had all the confidence in me.

"This is why you stayed, isn't it?" I asked, glancing at my dad. "Because of the fight?"

A sheepish smile pulled at his lips. "Like we'd leave you to face this alone."

I came up behind my dad and looped my arms around his neck, hauling him back for a hug. "Thank you."

"Sweetheart, you don't have to thank us. You

know how much we love you. Your mother just has trouble expressing it properly, sometimes."

Everyone laughed—except my mother. She glared at my father, then clucked under her breath and rose from her seat. "Well, if we aren't allowed to go, then I guess we'll remain behind with the vampires."

The way she said the word *vampires*, with such disgust, had me biting back a laugh. Even Anna seemed a little put off by it, her wide eyes tracking my mother as she stormed across the kitchen.

"We vampires make good company," Anna teased. "We'll keep them entertained."

"Thank you." My gaze zeroed in on Anna and I lifted a brow. I didn't need to speak my request out loud for Anna to get it. She merely nodded, then placed a delicate hand over her chest, silently vowing to watch over my parents should anything happen.

Neither Sam nor Anna would abandon my parents, and I loved them all the more for it. This here was my family. And I knew without a doubt, should the worst come to pass tonight, they'd all look out for and protect each other.

It was a realization that filled me with a sense of calm, even when facing my possible doom.

CHAPTER
NINETEEN

The moment had arrived.

I stood in Cole's living room, anxiously wringing my hands. Seven-thirty had come far quicker than I'd expected. Somehow it'd felt as though time had both flown by and dragged simultaneously. My father had convinced us to watch a movie together, and while there were certainly other things I could have done with my time, I couldn't deny his request. Not when I knew it might be the last time I saw my family. So I let them guilt me into watching some superhero movie. I couldn't even say which one—I hadn't been able to focus on the movie at all. I just kept thinking about tonight and what I was about to face.

My skin crawled and butterflies flapped in my stomach. Every time someone opened the door, I practically jumped out of my skin. The anticipation was horrid. I just wanted to get this over and done with, regardless of the outcome.

Sam and I had been the first to arrive, exactly as Cole had asked. He'd greeted us with a grim smile, then guided us into the living room and told us to sit. I couldn't though. Every time I stilled, my nerves started fluttering again. So instead, I'd taken to pacing the room like a caged lion, snarling at anyone who looked my way. Thankfully, everyone quickly caught on and let me be. Even Sam. He'd tried to reassure me once, but I'd shaken off his embrace and returned to pacing. Comfort was the last thing I needed right now. I needed to get out of my own head and focus on the upcoming fight.

Sounded easy enough.

One by one, the pack trickled in.

Olivia arrived about ten minutes early, and she gave me a tentative wave when she first spotted me. Not wanting to scare my new sister, I'd waved back and given her a reassuring nod. After skirting around the room, she'd finally stepped up next to Sam, and they'd begun conversing. About what, I couldn't tell. I didn't feel like listening in. I didn't need to hear Sam comforting her.

Bryn was the next to enter. The entire room

went silent as she stormed inside, looking as fierce as a boxer. Oh, that didn't help my confidence one bit. She strode toward the pack as though she *knew* she'd be made their new leader tonight. I had a feeling some even wanted that. They'd known Bryn longer, and she'd been Reggie's partner. Girlfriend. Piece of ass. I don't know, I'd never asked what official term they'd used. Regardless, I had a feeling a few pack members felt she'd make a better alpha.

I didn't know Bryn well, but I wasn't convinced she truly cared about the pack. This was more about her vendetta than anything else. Someone who cared would put aside revenge and focus on the needs of her pack. And right now, that consisted of finding Corbin.

Cole strode over to me and gave me a light pat on the shoulder. Before I could shrug him off, he leaned down and said, "Make it fast. Make it brutal. And make it count. They'll respect that." And then he left.

I contemplated his words. I understood exactly what he meant. Show no hesitation, because if I did, the other wolves would capitalize on that. They'd wonder if they could take me if I gave Bryn even an inch. I had to make a show out of this and utterly destroy her. The thought didn't sit well with me. I hated the idea of hurting someone just to make a point.

My mom was right—werewolf politics sucked.

At eight p.m., Cole's alarm sounded, and the entire pack snapped to attention. The majority of the pack braved a quick glance my way before shooting Bryn an uneasy look. That told me everything I needed to know. Many did not, in fact, want her as their alpha. I used that information to bolster my confidence, then moved to the front of the room.

"Welcome," I said, my voice carrying through the same mike as last time. I eyed those surrounding me, knowing more of the pack filled the kitchen and hallway. "As you know, it's the night of the full moon, and tonight—"

"I challenge you, alpha," Bryn's voice rang through the room.

I sighed and shot her a dark glare. Yes, she'd needed to formally challenge me, but she could have at least waited until I'd finished speaking.

"Thank you, Bryn," I snapped before turning back toward the crowd. "Before we engage in tonight's challenge, I would like to take a moment to update everyone on the developing situation regarding Corbin."

A ripple of anxiety spread through the crowd.

"I'm sure most of you have heard, but Corbin has abducted another human-born. Lincoln went missing last night. Unfortunately, amidst the attack, we lost Lee. So tonight, after Bryn's and my fight, the pack will mourn the loss of two members. The loser of the fight"—I inclined my head toward Bryn—"and our lost member. May both find the light and run forever beneath the full moon."

The sound of soft cries rose to my ears, and I watched as a few members ducked their heads and swiped at their faces. It brought a lump to my own throat to see them mourn one of their pack members. I hated that I hadn't been able to put a stop to all this before it'd reached this point.

"Has Corbin been located yet, alpha?" someone asked from the crowd.

My eyes scanned their faces. I couldn't tell who'd voiced the question, but I appreciated their use of the word alpha—as though they'd done it to show who they supported in this fight.

"We've been unable to track Corbin down. But I remain hopeful that we'll find something to point us in his direction. I only ask that you be patient and remain vigilant. It's important now more than ever that we take care of each other. Remain partnered up, gather in larger groups. Go nowhere alone. And keep your senses primed. If anyone senses anything at all, contact me or Cole immediately. I promise you, we will put a stop to this."

The pack nodded their agreement, though their grim expressions didn't ease the ache in my chest.

When no one else spoke, my heart gave my ribs a solid kick, and I nodded to Cole. "Very well. Then it's time for tonight's main event."

Cole approached my side. "The fight will take place upstairs in my boxing ring. The room cannot hold every single member, so attendance will be decided by dominance. Those ranked top ten may proceed upstairs. The rest will remain down here until the fight concludes."

Disappointment flashed in so many faces. I only hoped their disappointment was based on not being able to support me in person as opposed to watching a brutal fight. But considering these were werewolves, I highly suspected it was the latter more than the former.

I stalked toward the stairs with my head held high. The crowd parted for me, and everyone stared as I moved. Some patted my shoulder and offered me well wishes, while others hung back and chatted among themselves.

As the alpha, I took to the stairs first and

ascended with Sam close on my heels. Every inch of me wanted to clutch his hand for support. But I couldn't show any weakness here tonight. Instead, I let our hands brush once, twice, and a third time, as we climbed upstairs.

I strode toward the ring, then slipped inside. The second my feet touched the mat, confidence flooded me. It was like my body knew exactly what it was doing. If I succeeded tonight, I'd be buying Cole a basket of baked goods, and Anna a monthly, flavored blood subscription.

Bryn didn't look as confident when she stepped inside the ring. Instead, she studied it as though orienting herself. Suddenly, I understood Cole's machinations loud and clear. He'd forced me to practice here this entire week. He'd shown me how to dance around the ring, taught me how to get comfortable with my surroundings, how to use the space to my best advantage. He hadn't offered the same to Bryn.

The sneaky bugger.

I was in my element. She wasn't. He'd planned this from the start.

Eyes wide, I shot him a stunned look, to which he merely grinned and winked at me.

I glanced at Sam next and shocked him with a

beaming smile. His gaze leapt between me and Cole, and I saw the moment he understood. His muscles relaxed and he leaned against the wall, adopting an air of complete ease. The others noticed it too, and some confusion spread as whispers among the pack members.

"As this is a dominance challenge for control of the pack, there is only one way this fight can end," Cole said, claiming everyone's attention. "With a death. Either our current alpha's or Bryn's. Either way, our pack will mourn the loss of another member tonight."

More murmurs. I got the feeling no one really wanted this. The pack had suffered so much loss recently. No one seemed eager to celebrate another.

Cole turned to Bryn. "As the challenger, you get to choose what form you fight in."

Her mouth curled into a vicious snarl, so I wasn't surprised when she replied with, "Wolf."

More stunned murmurs.

Bryn seemed entirely too confident in her choice. I was happy to show her the error in her ways. Cole might have taught me how to fight in human form, but I'd been practicing my shifting. Something no one other than my family knew.

Nodding, I danced backward and started

removing my clothes. Nudity wasn't a big issue among shifters, so no one batted an eyelash. I piled my clothes just outside the ring, then placed my phone on top.

When I turned to face Bryn, she also stood stark naked.

"When I say go, you may initiate the change," Cole said. "Other than that, there are no rules."

Cole made eye contact with me, as though to communicate that more clearly to me. I frowned, not entirely clear on what he was suggesting.

"The last one alive is the winner and our official alpha."

I gave another nod.

Bryn seemed so sure of her choice. She strutted backward, grinning at the gathered pack members. I understood her miscalculation. The last time the pack had seen me shift had been before I'd left for New Orleans. I'd been slow and clumsy. It'd taken me ten minutes to shift, whereas most completed the change within two or three. I didn't know where Bryn sat for shifting time, but I did know I'd managed to speed my shift up to one and a half minutes the last time I'd timed it.

Cole glanced at me again, then raised a brow.

I nodded. No more delaying. Time to do this.

"Very well. On my count. Three, two, one..."

I barely heard him say the word "go" before I called to my wolf. Like a beacon, my voice awoke her, and she came running, not only happy, but yearning to shift. It'd been a day or two since our last time, and I could sense her eagerness to stretch her legs.

My body immediately began contorting. And much like the night in the woods with Anna and Vlad, I didn't fight it. This was my wolf's domain. Trying to control her would only slow the process down. So, instead, I let her sweep through me, giving her free rein.

Distantly, I was aware of the pack's gasps as I ripped free of my human form and became the beast within. Barely a minute had passed before I stood on all four legs and shook out my fur.

Bryn, however, was caught in the middle of her shift, her legs still forming and her muzzle half-sprouted. I shot Cole a surprised glance to find him gaping at me. I hadn't told him I'd been practicing and working with my wolf. It was worth it to see the shock. And even more worth it to see the awe sketched in Sam's face. He touched his chest, a gesture to tell me he loved me, then pointed at Bryn and mouthed "finish it."

Finish it.

Right.

God, I hated this. I couldn't just kill someone. I knew this wasn't the same thing. She'd challenged me and forced this upon us. But rushing up to her and ripping out her throat felt an awful lot like cold-blood murder.

Cole clicked his fingers to get my attention, then wildly gestured at Bryn.

I stalked toward Bryn, baring my fangs. Still shifting, she gaped at me, eyes white-rimmed as fear spurred her on. I couldn't imagine how she must be feeling in this moment. She'd chosen wolf form thinking it was my weakest, only to learn she'd been sorely wrong. Then to realize I could rip her throat out in the next instant without batting an eye. The fight would be over in seconds.

No, I wouldn't be that heartless. Sam had told me that only I could decide the type of alpha I wanted to be. Did I want to be the sort who ruthlessly tore out someone's throat when they were vulnerable? Or did I want to be better than that? Maybe the pack needed to see me be fierce. But they also needed to know I could show mercy. And mercy wasn't a weakness, not when applied at the right moment.

Instead of ripping out Bryn's throat, I towered over her and unleashed my alpha stare. I'd seen it in the mirror once or twice and new my eyes lit up like a golden star when I did this. Bryn whined at the sight of them, then dropped to her belly the second she finished shifting.

I bared my teeth, giving her an eyeful of my fangs. I knew the rules said this had to end with a death, but I was the alpha. I made the rules. And I didn't agree with this *to the death* nonsense.

So, I stepped back.

In retrospect, that'd been a mistake.

The second I gave Bryn an inch, she bunched her muscles beneath her and leapt. The sight of her flying toward me, jaws gaping, teeth flashing, was one I'd never forget. Sam yelled and Cole shouted my name.

I wasn't quick enough to dodge her attack. Not completely.

Still stunned she would try something so underhanded, I let my wolf take full control, ducking to the side. Bryn's teeth grazed my fur, but didn't catch. Then, I pivoted and lunged. The instant my teeth closed around her neck, I squeezed and tore out her throat.

Bryn's body fell to the ground with a wet slap,

blood gushing onto the floor. It took a few moments for my brain to catch up, but once it did, I shuddered and stepped back before her blood spread over my paws.

Dead.

Mere seconds had passed.

Holy. Shit.

I had done it. And so quickly, too. I almost didn't believe my own eyes.

Bryn was seventh in the pack, and I'd taken her out with hardly any effort. My wolf had known what to do, ripping out her throat before she could do the same to us.

Holy. Effing. Shit.

My body shook, but I willed it to stop. I couldn't let anyone see how this affected me. Later, I could break down. But right now, I had to hold my head high and show them I was their alpha.

When I lifted my head, I found the entire room had knelt, their eyes downcast, showing their loyalty to me. Alpha of the Mississippi Pack.

I needed to change back. Needed out of this fur. I quickly shifted and stood naked in the ring, staring at my pack. I had no idea what to say—or think. I couldn't believe how fast that had gone down. How easily I'd killed her.

But before anyone could speak, a shrill ring invaded the silence.

I whirled around and stared at my phone, surprised to see my mother's number lighting up the screen. She knew not to call. I'd told them I would call when I could. Guess it shouldn't have surprised me that she was incapable of following instructions.

Sighing, I strode across the ring and snatched up my phone. I dragged my finger across the screen, about to ream her out for disturbing the pack, when her sharp scream rang across the line.

"Lucy!" she shrieked, the fear in her voice shaking me to the absolute core.

"Mom? Mom, what's wrong!"

Another scream rent the air, one filled with pain and terror.

"*Mom!*"

Then silence.

"Mom!" I screamed, but there was no answer. No sound at all, in fact. Nothing but empty, silent air. I pulled the phone back from my ear to find the call had disconnected.

Who the hell had disconnected it?

Fear ripped through my nerves like an electrical current, and I whirled around to find Sam standing outside the ring, his face tight with concern. Behind him stood Cole, a frown darkening his usually stoic face. And behind him stood the top echelon of my pack. They whispered among themselves, speculating about the call, but I couldn't focus on that. Couldn't focus on Bryn's dead body sprawled in the middle of the ring. Couldn't focus on anything but the sound of my mother's harrowing shriek right before the call ended.

I didn't hesitate. Didn't pause to ask for help or tell anyone where I was going.

I simply ran.

I bolted down Cole's stairs and shot out of the house like a bullet, naked as the day I was born. But it was the sight of my car blocked into Cole's driveaway that made me want to scream. The entire pack was here, including their vehicles.

My mind whirled with options. The drive between mine and Cole's place was thirty minutes. I pivoted on my heel and faced the sprawling swampland behind Cole's house.

I could run.

If I pushed myself, if I didn't stop, I could maybe make it there in fifteen. It'd be a hard battle, slogging through marshland and mud and whatever else sat between us, but I couldn't wait for people to move their cars. That'd waste too much time.

A rush of people spilled out of the house, Sam at the front.

"Let's go!" he shouted to me, leading me toward the woods. He shifted, his body effortlessly morphing into his giant beast of a wolf.

I nodded, then immediately started shifting. Ten others—the most dominant members of the pack, except for Cole—dashed toward me, already in their wolf forms. A *pack* stood at my side. *My* pack. They'd heard the call and had leaped into action.

I shot a quick glance over my shoulder to find Cole doing his job and handling the rest of the pack. I dipped my head in thanks, then bolted into the trees. I couldn't wait any longer.

The sound of Sam and my pack running at my side bolstered my confidence. They pushed me harder, helping me when I tripped in the muck or fell into deeper water. Their soft growls urged me faster. And they kept my heart from sinking into a deep depression. Kept me from imagining the worst.

My muscles screamed, but I never relented. Every minute was a lesson in patience. My wolf tore at my thoughts, anxious to save our family. I couldn't think of that right now though. I had to focus on the next step, and the next.

When my house finally came into view, I nearly collapsed with exhaustion. Only Sam's nose nudging my backside kept me moving. As a unit, my pack and I tore up the stairs and rushed through the already busted open door.

I wasn't sure what to expect upon our return, but it wasn't this.

I slammed on the brakes and skidded to a stop at the sight of five massive wolves standing in my living room. My eyes narrowed on them, and my lips curled back, flashing my fangs.

But then my gaze dipped.

And my world came to a crashing end.

There, behind the five wolves, lay my parents. Bloody and unmoving.

My breath caught in my throat, and then anger erupted within me like a volcano. Unleashing an enraged growl, I lunged for the five wolves, teeth snapping at their throats. My pack moved with me and attacked in perfect synchronicity. Snarling wolves, gnashing teeth, cracking bones, it all filtered through my head, but I couldn't focus on anything other than my parents.

The next time I blinked, I found another wolf's neck between my teeth. I pressed down until my teeth sliced through fur, flesh, sinew, and bone. When I ripped my head back, a spray of blood came with it. The wolf dropped dead at my feet, and I stared at the gaping hole in their throat, knowing it was a wound they wouldn't recover from.

Before I could rejoice at their death or run to my parents, another wolf slammed into my side. I whipped around to find one of my pack members staggering beneath the weight of their attacker. I leapt to the side, then gripped them by the ruff and ripped them off. I shook my head and sent the enemy wolf sliding across the floor and into the grandfather clock, which came crashing down in a spray of glass.

I didn't hesitate. I stalked over to the wolf and slammed my paw down on its throat.

With a soft whine, they stared up at me, their eyes full of hate. When they snapped at my leg, I full on decked the wolf in the head, slamming it into the nearby wall. Not dead. But not conscious either. We needed one alive to question.

A deafening silence filled the living room. I turned to find four dead wolves scattered across the floor, and my wolves all still standing. A few bled from some minor wounds, but nothing serious. Yipping, I ran to my parents' sides, then immediately shifted. My body took on human form before I crashed down beside them.

"Oh, my god," I whispered, my trembling hands hovering above their battered bodies.

Every inch of them was covered in blood. I

couldn't stop the sob that escaped my throat, couldn't tamp back the panic sluicing up my throat. I turned my head in time to throw up.

"Lucy," Sam whispered. "Lucy, we need to get them to a hospital."

I nodded. My parents weren't werewolves, which meant doctors and hospitals were an option. Except, what the hell would I tell the doctors? They would want to know what happened. And what could I tell them? Wild animals broke into the house and gutted them? They'd call the police. And the police would have *more* questions. Questions I didn't have answers for.

But what else could I do? I couldn't leave them to die. They were my parents!

I pressed my hands against my mother's gaping stomach wound and forced myself to think.

Stomach wounds like this were grave. Corbin's men had practically eviscerated her. My gaze slid to my father and I stared at his mangled body. His wounds looked bad, but of the two, his were less severe. Almost like they'd targeted my mother.

Did I risk moving her? Her heartbeat was so faint as it was. I felt her slipping away with every passing second. What if loading her into a car caused more damage? She wasn't supernatural—she couldn't heal these sorts of wounds. And if I called for an ambulance, would she last the amount of time it'd take for them to arrive?

I bowed my head and sobbed. Fear and uncertainty paralyzed me. No one had ever prepared me for this sort of scenario! And I... I... I *didn't know what to do*.

Think!

Lifting my head, I peered down at my mother and forced my brain into emergency mode. "We need to staunch the bleeding. Jorge, my bathroom has a first aid kit. Sam, there's towels in the kitchen. Everyone else, get these damn wolves out of here. Tie the live one up in one of the bedrooms so we can question him."

I stole another glance around, my eyes processing things faster than my head. Ten naked people surrounded me, the least fun part of being a werewolf. "Everyone find some clothes. And someone fetch something for me too. I c-can't leave my mother." *Wouldn't*, more like. "And someone find me a phone!"

My mother was fading, her pulse weakening. I truly believed it was too late to rush her to a hospital, and I couldn't call an ambulance. The paramedics certainly wouldn't make it in time. Which left me only one plan. But for it to work, I needed Anna. Which meant, I needed a phone. Mine was at Cole's. I hadn't been able to carry it while in wolf form.

Someone appeared with a pile of clothing in their arms and thrust them at me. I removed my hands from my mother's stomach long enough to dress, then scrambled back in place, my clothes already stained.

"Where's that phone?" I demanded.

The wolf shook his head and stepped back.

I growled, frustrating burning through me.

"Lucy?" a tentative voice asked.

My head whipped up and a choked—yet relieved—whimper escaped my lips at the sight of Anna and Vlad hovering in the front door. Anna's eyes were wide, her face pale, even for a vampire.

"What... what happened?"

"Where were you!" I shouted, tears streaming my face.

She flinched at the rage in my tone. "We ran out of blood. We needed more. We were only gone for—"

"Long enough!" I yelled. "Never mind that. Get over here." I turned back to my parents and cried out when my father's eyes fluttered open.

"Lucy..." he rasped.

"Daddy, it's okay. I'm going to fix this."

Sam covered my mother's stomach and my hands with a towel, then dropped to his knees at my father's side and started tending to his wounds. "Some cuts, bruises, broken bones, but otherwise, he seems okay," Sam said.

My mother, though.

I repositioned the towel and pressed, applying as much pressure as I could. She hadn't so much as twitched. And my hands... my hands were pressing things back inside her stomach that never should have seen the light of day.

"Lucy," Anna eased down next to me. "She's dying."

"I know!" I screamed. Even though I knew the truth. A human couldn't survive these sorts of wounds. "Y-You need to change her."

My father's head turned to the side, his eyes wide as he registered my words. He reached out with a mangled arm and gripped my mother's unmoving hand. I nearly broke at the sight of his face, at the utter heartbreak ravaging him. I could practically taste his pain.

"Mom," I whimpered.

I felt like a child again, one who wanted nothing more than her mother's love and comfort. I wanted her to open her eyes and assure me everything would be fine. That she would never leave me. I wanted her to wrap her arms around me and hum, like she'd used to do whenever I was hurt or sick.

I shook my head and banished those thoughts. My head rose and I stared at Anna. "Change her."

"What? Lucy—"

"We don't have time to argue about this, damn it! Just save her!"

She met my gaze, then finally nodded. "If that's what you want," Anna murmured, then turned her attention to my father. "But only if you think she'd be okay with that? I'd hate to force this life on her."

"Dad..." I shot my father another look, and my heart trembled at the sight of the hope there.

"You can fix her?" he rasped, his fingers tightening around hers.

Vlad stepped forward and lowered onto a single knee, careful not to kneel in my mother's blood. "We can. But only with your permission."

Vlad hadn't asked my permission when he'd taken Anna from me, but now didn't seem the right moment to point that out. Anna was his mate. And he'd known it long before they'd even met. I couldn't hold that against him.

"Daddy. Say yes," I urged.

My father spared me one more glance before closing his eyes and whispering, "Yes."

"I'll do it," Anna said. "She's like a mother to me."

Vlad leaned back, then turned to Sam. "Barbara has already bled out, so Anna won't take any blood from her. But we need to ensure that Barbara drinks from Anna. In the meantime, use whatever you have in that first-aid kit to wrap her stomach. So long as Barbara drinks, it'll heal."

"Lucy, you need to move back," Anna said.

I scrambled away, slipping in my mother's blood, but slowly found my way to my father's side. I lifted his head and rested it in my lap, all the while listening to his heartbeat. With every passing moment, it seemed to grow stronger. He would be fine, thank the lord. But my mother was a whole other problem.

Lifting her wrist to her mouth, Anna tore into her flesh like an apple. It wasn't a pretty sight, but I understood her goal. She needed to get as much blood into my mother as fast as possible. They couldn't risk being dainty with two little puncture wounds.

Anna tipped my mother's head back, then pressed her bleeding wrist to my mother's mouth. I watched as the blood spilled past her lips, and only hoped some made it down her throat. Meanwhile, Sam wrapped my mother's stomach tight with gauze. The blood immediately seeped through, but I tried not to focus on that.

"Come on, Barbara," Anna said. "Come on, come on, come on. We can't lose you. Not yet."

I gripped my father's hand hard, probably harder than I should have, but he didn't complain. He squeezed back, clearly just as desperate.

"Come on, Mom," I repeated. "Please."

It was the slightest movement, but Anna exhaled in relief when my mom's lips finally closed around her wrist.

"There we go," Anna whispered. "Good job, Barbara."

Relief had my shoulders slumping and my head dropping forward. I reached out and touched Anna's shoulder, equally grateful and angry with her. Part of me knew this was *all* my fault. I'd never considered that my parents would be in danger. Corbin was watching the *pack*, not my family. I truly believed he'd follow us to Cole's and leave my parents be.

But I'd also forgotten to order more blood, even though I knew we were housing *two* vampires now. I'd made a mental note of it, but somehow, it'd slipped my mind. It wasn't Anna and Vlad's fault they'd had to go out in search of more. No, that responsibility rested with me. I couldn't blame them for leaving. They *had* to feed themselves. But I *did* blame them for not being here when my parents were attacked. At the same time, I was grateful to Anna for having found a way to save my mother's life. My head was a jumble of emotions I couldn't sort out. Not right now. Not with my mother sprawled on the floor.

The minutes passed in tense silence, until finally, Anna pulled her wrist back from my mother's mouth and stood, instantly swaying. Vlad shot to his feet and braced Anna before she fell.

"It's alright," Anna whispered, clutching her arm to her chest. "I just gave her more than I should have. I'll be fine, though."

I nodded, then stared at the surrounding scene. "Um," my hollow voice wavered, "my mom needs to be moved. Sam, can you take her to my parents' room?"

"Of course," he murmured before gently scooping her up and heading for their bedroom. Vlad and Anna followed in their wake.

I blew out a shaky breath, then faced my pack. "Someone needs to stay outside to make sure no one stumbles across the dead. And I want at least two others guarding the remaining wolf until I can question them."

As for my father, he needed medical attention. "Do we have a doctor in the pack?" I asked Jorge.

He nodded, his face still grim. "Her name is Meredith."

"Can you, uh..." I blinked and tried to focus. "Um. Can you call her? Get her here?"

"Of course, alpha," Jorge murmured.

He jumped to his feet and vanished somewhere in the house. I had no idea where. I didn't even know where he'd find this magical phone, but I also didn't question it.

"Should we move him?" I asked Sam when he returned to my side.

"Best not to. We could injure him further."

I nodded. Sniffling, I stared down at my father, who'd closed his eyes again. I didn't panic, though. I could hear his heartbeat thudding heavily in his chest. The sound was like music to my ears.

A few moments later, his lashes fluttered and he opened his eyes, pinning me with a severe stare. "You need to put a stop to this, Lucy. Those werewolves came here looking for you."

I shuddered.

"You can't let this happen again."

No, I couldn't.

Soon, the dead wolves in the back would revert back into human form and I would know if one of them was Corbin. If not, I had a score to settle.

CHAPTER
TWENTY-ONE

THE NEXT HOUR PASSED IN A BLUR. MEREDITH, the pack doctor, came and assessed my father. Other than a broken back and arm, he would be fine. She gave us a believable cover story, one that would explain his injuries without involving the authorities, then agreed to take him to the hospital for us, where they could care for him properly. Before Meredith and my father left, she asked to check on my mother, but admitted there was nothing she could do for her. My mother was on the path to becoming a vampire now. No doctor could help her with that.

Cole arrived just as Meredith and my father left, his eyes on me as Meredith backed out of my driveway. "You okay?"

"Yeah. No. I don't know."

Cole searched my face. "The rest of the pack is still at my place, continuing with the meeting. We buried Bryn and Lee and they're now celebrating their lives."

At least something had gone right tonight. I'd promised the pack a chance to grieve and I was glad they'd been given the chance to do so.

"What happened here?"

"Corbin again. His men attacked. My parents—" My voice fractured. I shook my head, unable to speak of what I'd seen when we'd first found them. Instead, I cleared my throat. "We have a wolf in one of the bedrooms ready to be questioned. I need to handle the mess in the yard first. Meet me inside in a few minutes."

I popped open the fence gate and strode into the backyard before he could answer.

Now that the adrenaline and anger had worn off, I was exhausted. But sadly, now wasn't the time for a break. Instead, I came to a stop on the back deck, and stared at the ten pack members who had stayed by my side the entire time. A grateful smile came to my lips, and I nodded my thanks to each as I strode into the yard and inspected the corpses.

They'd all turned back into human form, and I was dismayed to see none were Corbin. So, he'd sent his lackeys to do his dirty work then. To attack my *family*. My father had said they'd come for me. But when they'd discovered I wasn't here, they'd attacked my parents.

They were alive. I needed to keep reminding myself of that.

But Corbin wouldn't be. Not for much longer.

He needed to die. Now.

And luckily, this time we had someone to question. I thought of the wolf I'd ordered my people to tie up and grinned. Finally, a bit of luck had found us. I didn't care what it took. We'd make that wolf talk, and we'd finally get answers.

"Alpha," a voice came from behind me. "We cracked the encryption."

I turned to find Jorge speaking to another wolf. George, if I remembered correctly. He hadn't been here ten minutes ago. The two shared a few words, then George slipped inside and Jorge strolled toward me.

"I'm sorry, what did you say?" I asked.

"We cracked the encryption. George just arrived to pass that information along. I left him in charge of it yesterday. He's better at breaking codes than I am."

"Okay," I said.

"Thankfully, the encryption wasn't as complex

as it could have been. So we got lucky there. But it's exactly as we feared," he continued. "A recruitment post for those who may feel out of place in their own packs, or those who believe in a superior world."

"Superior?" I repeated.

"A world dedicated to werewolves, from the looks of it. To changing all the human-born, and ridding the world of pure humans."

I shuddered at the thought. Corbin really had a crusade here.

"Can you track the forum back to the owner? Maybe it'll tell us where Corbin is located."

"I can try."

I patted his shoulder and offered my thanks before returning to the other pack members. "We need to take care of the bodies. I assume we can't hand them over to the authorities. Any suggestions?"

"We have our connections," Dominic offered. "We have an in with one of the local crematoriums that often handles these matters for us. Though, we've never had to send them so many at once."

I winced at the dark tone in his voice, but nodded. At least that was better than strapping lead weights to a body and tossing it in a swamp somewhere. I shuddered at the thought.

"Can I leave you in charge of that?" I asked Dominic.

He blinked, as though stunned I'd ask. I probably should have just ordered him to do it, but I wasn't feeling very commander-y right now.

"Uh, sure," Dominic said. "I'll reach out to them immediately. We'll need to locate a van to transport the bodies. But I can take care of that too."

"Thanks." I eyed the other pack members. "In the meantime, I need to question our prisoner. I don't mind if you'd like to stay, but if you'd like to leave, feel free to do so. Just be aware that if I get Corbin's location, I'll be rounding up the pack again to help me put an end to all this."

I left them to make up their own minds, then headed back inside.

Sam and Cole stood in the hallway, and I listened for a moment as Sam gave Cole a rundown of everything that'd happened. I wasn't really in the mood to hear the play by play, so instead, I strode toward my parents' bedroom.

My mother lay on the bed, completely still and so pale. Anna had thankfully cleaned her up and dressed her, but it still hurt me to see her like this. I remembered when Anna had gone through the process. It didn't frighten me quite so much this time, but I still felt a thrum of fear in my blood. That my mother wouldn't wake. That her wounds were too severe. That she was too old to make this change.

Anna and Vlad stood next to the bed, talking quietly.

"How is she?" I asked.

Vlad eyed me, then nodded. "She's progressing nicely. I have no doubts she'll wake in three nights' time."

Relief rounded my shoulders.

"Lucy, I am so sorry," Anna said. She rose to her feet and approached me. I could tell she'd been crying, which wasn't a good look for her. A good look for any vampire, really. The blood tears weren't their most attractive feature. "We never should have left."

I raked a hand down my face, unsure of what to say. It was my fault. Truly. I knew they would run out of blood, knew we had another mouth to feed. But I'd been so caught up in everything, I'd forgotten to adjust the order. How something so simple could result in something so disastrous baffled me. Wrecked me.

My eyes closed and I drew in a deep breath. Anna loved my parents and would never knowingly put them in danger. I knew that.

"It's okay," I croaked. "It wasn't your fault. It was mine."

She shook her head, her blonde hair bouncing around her shoulders. "No, Luce, don't say that."

I shrugged off her words. "I didn't think Corbin would come after my parents. They're human. They have nothing to do with this." I gave a rough laugh. "I won't make that mistake again."

"Lucy—" Anna whispered.

I cleared my throat. "Could you guys give me a few minutes alone with her?"

"Of course." Anna grasped Vlad's hand and led him to the door.

Before they left, Vlad turned to face me. "Your mother will require a coffin by sunrise. This room isn't equipped to keep her safe."

Great. I pinched the bridge of my nose. "Do you have one she could use?" It wasn't like I had coffins just laying around.

"Not nearby. But I can arrange to have one delivered in time."

"Thank you."

"Of course, Lucy."

When they finally left, I blew out a heavy breath and sank onto the bed beside my mom. "What a night."

I slipped my hand into hers and squeezed, hoping she'd squeeze back. But I knew better. I'd done the same thing with Anna during her transition, and she hadn't so much as twitched. For the first three nights, a new vampire was in essence, dead. They didn't so much as blink. Their hearts stopped and their lungs emptied. They were eternally frozen in that moment.

I touched my mom's curly hair and grimaced. She was currently between dye jobs, meaning she'd forever be graced with silver in her hair. I couldn't wait to hear her complain about that. She hated her grays. Not to mention her fine lines and wrinkles. There'd be no escaping them now. She would forever be sixty-three years old. And I had no idea how she'd feel about that.

Leaning down, I brushed a light kiss across her cheek, and fought not to grimace at the feel of her unnaturally cool skin. There was no point complaining about it—this change couldn't be undone. And I'd rather grieve her human life than grieve her completely. At least now, I'd hear her scolding voice again, and that was all that mattered.

I spent a few more minutes with her before finally rising from the bed and heading for the door.

With my hand on the doorknob, I paused and glanced back at her.

"For what it's worth, Mom, I'm sorry," I whispered before letting myself out.

Sam leaned against the nearest wall, arms crossed over his chest. I immediately went to him, sighing when he tucked me into his chest.

"I am so sorry," he murmured, brushing a light kiss against the top of my head.

"It's not your fault."

"It's not yours either," he cautioned, going right for the heart of the matter, having clearly heard our conversation in the room. I didn't scold him for eavesdropping. I would have done the same.

I tipped my head back and stared at him. "I know that."

"Do you?"

Truthfully, I was struggling with that bit. And I didn't expect that to change any time soon. But I could place equal blame on someone else. "It's Corbin's fault."

"Yes, it is. So how about we go question that wolf of his and finish this?"

Exactly what my father asked me to do.

I rose upward and brushed my mouth against

Sam's, drinking in the moment. Sam kissed me again, and again, before finally pulling back.

"I love you," I said.

He blinked. "I love you too."

"Just thought I should say it, you know? In case—"

"Don't 'in case' me," he said gruffly. "We're merely questioning our enemy. As Anna would say, easy peasy."

Except nothing in my life ever seemed to go "easy peasy." Not anymore.

I STARED AT THE DICKMONKEY WITH THE sternest glare I could muster and crossed my arms over my chest. No one was laughing, so I must have struck an intimidating pose. Corbin's lackey sat in a wobbly chair, dressed in a pair of old sweatpants that I assumed were Sam's, his hands pulled tight behind his back and restrained with a zip tie and duct tape. Honestly, a werewolf could have busted out of that in seconds. The real restraints were the many werewolves surrounding him. Three stood by the door and two hovered at my side. Even if the asswaffle intended to escape, he wouldn't get far.

"Name," I demanded.

His eyes slitted, and he glared at me. "Brandon."

"Nice to meet you, Brandon." The false sincerity in my voice came through loud and clear. "I'd really like to make this easy on everyone. So how about you tell me where Corbin is and where he's keeping Laini and Lincoln?"

He didn't respond. Instead, he leaned over and spat on the floor.

I lifted a brow. "Wow. That was disgusting. Didn't your mother teach you any manners?"

Cole stalked over and cuffed Brandon upside the head hard enough to snap his head forward. "Do that again and you'll be wiping your spit off the floor with your face."

"Yeah, what he said." I gestured to Cole with my chin. "So, let's try this again. Where are my people?"

"Fuck you."

I rolled my eyes and uncrossed my arms. "See, here's the thing. These interrogations always start like this. Some dillweed—*you*—tries to be all strong and secretive. Until me and my people come in and rough you up. We break bones, pull out nails, yank out teeth, burn you, all that good stuff, until *finally* you talk. I mean..." I stalked toward Brandon, then ran a finger down his arm, watching as goosebumps puckered his skin. "Wouldn't it just be easier to tell us what we want to know before we have to resort to such nastiness? I don't mind torturing you, but I really don't think you'll enjoy the experience."

Brandon trembled in the chair.

I circled behind him, letting my hand trail upward over his shoulder and to his throat. I placed my fingers against his neck and slowly willed my claws to extend. When they did, I dug the pointy ends into his flesh and leaned down so I could whisper in his ear. "Let me remind you that you and your people tried to murder my family tonight. I've killed four of your pack members already, but I think it's fair to say that I'm still a wee bit upset about what you did." I applied pressure, my claws puncturing his throat. "So, how about we make a deal. You tell me what I want to know, and I let you go. But if you don't..." My hand shot down, my claws narrowly missing his precious family jewels by a millimeter. "I'll start by skinning your testicles. How does that sound?"

I swear, every male in the proximity sucked in a sharp breath.

I lifted my eyes and met Sam's gaze, who looked properly stunned by my actions here. I wouldn't actually torture poor Brandon—that wasn't really my cup of tea—but he didn't need to know that. I just needed to convince him that I would.

"Oh my god," Brandon blubbered, his wide, terrified eyes staring down at my hand, which rested uncomfortably close to his balls. "Corbin has Laini... And Lincoln. He's changed them both. They're wolves now. Please, please, don't hurt me."

I ignored the pain that came with Brandon's revelation and instead retracted my claws and straightened. "Good boy. Now tell me *where* Corbin has them."

"A w-warehouse," he stammered. "But I don't know where it is. We've never been allowed to go. He keeps it secret so you can't find them. We always meet at different locations as a precaution. Laini and Lincoln are okay, though, I swear. Corbin hasn't hurt them, other than what was needed to change them. He's trying to get them to join his pack, to help him usher in a new era."

I trailed a clawed finger across the back of his neck. "How many of you are there?"

"I-I don't know. Twenty maybe? Well, sixteen now."

Decent sized, but not something we couldn't handle.

"There's another alpha, too," Brandon

continued, happily spewing all the information he could think of. Guess the tough-guy act had been exactly that. "A w-woman. She controls Corbin. Tells him where to go, who to grab, and when."

My head lifted and I met Sam's gaze, the both of us stunned by this new revelation. "Corbin isn't the true alpha?"

"No." Brandon whimpered when my clawed hand closed around his thigh. "Oh god. I don't know. No, he's not the alpha. He's her second."

"Who is she?"

"I don't know," he wailed when my hand tightened, my claws slicing into his flesh. "We haven't met her yet. She doesn't come to the meetings. We only know about her because she calls Corbin and gives him orders. Orders that he takes."

I frowned and shook my head. This went against everything we knew about Corbin. He'd always acted as though he were the one in charge. The one with all the master schemes.

"I-I think they're lovers or something," Brandon continued.

I finger-walked my hand up Brandon's leg, nearing the junction of his thighs. He practically burst into tears. I didn't enjoy tormenting him. But then I remembered he'd been part of the attack on my parents, and suddenly I didn't feel so guilty anymore.

"Give me a name, Brandon," I said.

"I swear, I don't know it! I swear. Oh god, I swear."

An acrid stench filled the air and my gaze dropped in time to watch the guy wet himself. Huh. Good to know I could terrify someone to that point. Not that I was proud of it—okay, maybe a little. These people wanted to slaughter people and turn all human-borns into wolves. With or without their consent. A process that could kill them. He'd laid siege to my house and attacked my parents, nearly killing them. He didn't deserve sympathy from me.

It concerned me that Brandon didn't know this other alpha's name. Did Corbin trust his people so little? Rightfully so, I supposed, considering how fast Brandon had spilled the beans. I needed more information, though, if we were going to put a stop to all this.

"How can you be part of a pack and not know your alpha's name?"

Brandon shut his eyes and whimpered. "Corbin keeps it that way. For her safety, he says. He told us we'll meet her when the time is right. But in the meantime, we're to take his word as hers."

I shook my head, marveling at his stupidity.

"Which pack do you hail from?"

"Alabama," he said. "A friend showed me the recruitment post, and I left. My alpha doesn't know where I went or why."

"Fine. So this is what's going to happen." I sidestepped the pool of urine on the ground and curled my fingers around his upper thigh. "You're going to call Corbin and tell him you need to meet with him at a place of my choosing. Then you're going to stay with my people until this matter is resolved. Once it is, I'm going to hand you back over to your alpha. He'll be made aware of everything you've done, and he can handle your punishment."

Brandon's eyes grew alarmingly wide. "No. No, please."

"Would you rather I kill you right now?" I asked.

He shook in his chair. "Please, no."

"This is real life, Brandon. We all have to deal with the consequences of our actions. These are yours."

Crocodile tears rolled down his face, and for a moment, I almost felt sorry for the guy. I quickly shook the emotion off, then straightened and strode back to Sam and Cole. The two stared at me with what looked like equal parts awe and surprise.

"What?" I snapped, hating how dirty I felt.

"Nothing. Nothing." Cole held up his hands as though afraid to push me farther.

Sam, however, just chuckled and pressed a kiss against my cheek. "You're going to be an amazing alpha."

I rolled my eyes. "Someone get Brandon out of that chair. And for goodness' sake, get him some clean clothes. Then get him to make the call. Once we have a location, we can head out."

Cole gestured to Dominic to do as I asked, then followed me and Sam out of the bedroom. I wanted to discuss this with them somewhere we wouldn't be overheard by Brandon.

I strode to the living room and stared at the bloodstained floor. My eyes closed, and I counted to five as I reminded myself my mother would be fine. Undead, but fine.

"Another alpha?" Cole asked as he approached from behind.

I turned, about to respond, when someone stumbled through my already broken front door. I gasped when I spotted Olivia, bruised and beaten to hell.

"Jesus!" I shouted. "Olivia, my god. Are you okay?"

She staggered to a stop in front of me and grabbed my hand. "They took her. They took her. They took her."

"Who? Took who?"

"Scotia," Olivia wheezed. "We'd just gotten back to her place and were settling down to watch a movie when they broke in. Attacked us. Took her."

Corbin.

The man was relentless.

"Lucy, I followed them," Olivia panted. "I think they thought I was dead or something, but I followed them. I know where they are. Scotia, Lincoln, and Laini."

Oh thank fuck.

Relief had me pulling Olivia in for a tight hug.

Finally. *Finally*. A break.

And now, it was time to end this.

CHAPTER
TWENTY-TWO

I STOOD ON THE EDGE OF THE PROPERTY AND eyed the warehouse in the near distance, my pack spread out behind me.

Olivia assured me this was where they'd brought our people. I peered into the darkness and studied the building. The ten wolves at my back were eager to move, to lay siege on this place and tear it down to the ground, but I held them back. We had to be smarter about this. At this moment in time, Corbin had no idea we were here. Giving away our position due to impatience was folly. We needed to be cautious.

Especially considering how quiet it was. It made me nervous. If this was the right place, why couldn't I see anyone? Why did it look so abandoned? I'd expected to find Corbin's people guarding the perimeter. Brandon claimed no one knew of this location—but I honestly hadn't believed him. If they hadn't known the location, how would they know to bring Scotia here?

Everything about this smelled off.

Even the grounds were eerily silent. No grasshoppers or birds chirping nearby, no traffic, no reeds swaying in the breeze. Nothing. I couldn't remember a time when the night had ever felt so unnaturally still.

I leaned over to Olivia and whispered, "Are you sure this is the right place?"

Her bright green eyes found me in the dark, and she nodded. "This is where I followed them to. Watched when they shoved Scotia inside. Heard her screams when..." Her voice trailed off, a broken whisper of what it'd been seconds ago.

My hands fisted at my sides. *When Corbin hurt her*, Olivia had intended to say.

Sam's fingers brushed mine, and I glanced his way. Unease narrowed his eyes and tightened his jaw. I nodded. I felt it too. There was just something off about this. I could practically taste it.

"We go slow," I murmured to everyone. "Split up. Try not to announce our presence here. Our main priority is Corbin. Take him down, but keep him alive. I need to question him. If our source is correct, Laini and Lincoln have already been turned. But Scotia may be transitioning." If she survived, that was. "We need the name of Corbin's alpha, so be careful with him." It still blew my mind to realize I'd fallen for all his lies. Believed him when he claimed he was building this pack for himself. All to keep his true alpha a secret.

"Sam and I will take the front," I said. "Cole and Dominic take the back. Everyone else, pair off and keep an eye on the perimeter. Olivia, I want you to stay behind with Jorge."

"What?" she hissed, rage darkening her face.

"You're hurt."

"But not useless," she quietly snapped. "Don't keep me out of this. These are the bastards that did this to me. They took Scotia. I want to help."

A smile pulled at my lips. Yeah, we were definitely related. I could totally hear myself saying something similar. "You are helping. You and Jorge can keep watch from here, and take out any stragglers that manage to escape once the fun starts."

I didn't allow her to argue further. Instead, I turned back toward the building. Only one light shone, and it came from the upstairs. Was that the room where he was holding our people? Or had he locked them up in a dark room somewhere? Guess I wouldn't know till we entered.

With a silent signal, I gestured the pack forward. Together, we crept through the tall, unkempt grass, our heads low so as not to be spotted. I focused on my breathing, keeping it slow and quiet, but my nerves jangled with every step. We were *so* close to finishing this.

I kept waiting for someone to call out, to alert others to our presence, but the night remained silent. So silent, I could hear my pack mates moving through the grass. Eventually, they split off from me and Sam, and we pressed forward, aiming for the front door.

It hung open a few inches, compliments of a broken hinge.

I paused and eyed it, concern deepening my frown.

Who kidnapped people and kept them in a warehouse with a faulty door and no guards?

"This doesn't add up," I whispered.

Sam followed my gaze, his own frown forming when he spotted the door. Unless Corbin had restrained our pack members, they could have just walked right out the front door. That didn't sound like a kidnapping to me. But we'd seen the state of Laini's car. Lee had died during Lincoln's abduction. And had Olivia been human, she wouldn't have survived the beaten they'd given her. That made me think my people hadn't gone willingly.

So why the lack of security?

"What do you think?" I asked Sam.

Light flared in his eyes as his wolf rose to the surface. Clearly, he was equally concerned. "Something's not right."

I nodded, then stared at the front door. "We've come this far. Let's at least check the place out."

I reached for the door, but paused before my fingers connected and drew a deep breath. All I could smell was the overpowering scent of swampland and the coming rain. I couldn't pick up on anything else, but that didn't surprise me. The acrid stench of marshland was clogging my nose. Because of it, we had no way of knowing what was inside.

Guess there was only one way to find out.

I gripped the door handle and slowly edged it open. The creak of the ancient hinges made me wince. Nothing like announcing our presence to the *entire* world to make a girl jumpy.

Sam and I quickly stepped into the darkness, but

the second we did, lights flashed on, momentarily blinding us. I swore out loud and lifted my arm, shielding my eyes from the painful glare. Sam wasn't quite as distracted as I was, and I grunted when his arm swept around my waist and shoved me behind him.

Finally, my vision cleared, and I stared at the developing scene.

Surrounded by at least twenty werewolves—none of them mine—and Corbin.

A trap. Yup, that seemed about right.

Corbin stalked toward me, his knees and neck completely healed. Boy, did that piss me off.

"Welcome, Lucy." Corbin grinned at me, his teeth flashing as he descended a rotting staircase. "I was wondering how long we'd have to wait for your arrival."

I bared my own teeth and tried to step out from behind Sam, but he wasn't having it.

Before I could retort, a scuffle broke out near the back of the warehouse. I didn't bother to look. I knew Corbin's men had overwhelmed Cole and Dominic. We were outnumbered two to one.

The crowd parted, and four of Corbin's men shoved Cole and Dominic forward. They stumbled toward us, their faces grim.

Corbin had used his surroundings to mask their scent and lay their trap. And we'd walked right into it. When this whole thing was done, I needed to have a talk with myself about trusting my instincts. They'd been telling me something was off, and I'd completely ignored them.

"I know you have more outside," Corbin said. "Call them in."

Laughter slipped past my lips. "Yeah, no. That won't be happening."

Corbin studied me with a cocky grin, then lifted his hand. The sight of a gun made my breath catch. First, he'd stabbed me with a silver blade, and now he planned to shoot me? I didn't know much about bullets and werewolves, but I had to imagine there'd be no healing a bullet to the brain or heart. Not even werewolves could regenerate that kind of damage.

"Call them inside," he repeated.

"Why? So you can shoot them?"

Corbin sighed, then took four steps closer and pointed the gun right at Sam's head. "Call. Them. Inside."

The sight of the gun aimed at Sam had my knees trembling.

Out of options, I called out to the pack, knowing the sound would carry through the dead night. It didn't take long for the front door to open and my last remaining wolves—all except Olivia and Jorge—to filter inside. I could only hope Jorge and Olivia had heard, and had either gone back for help or were coming up with some plan to miraculously save us.

"Is that everyone?" Corbin demanded.

"Yes," I bit out through gritted teeth. A lie, but apparently he couldn't tell.

"Good." He gestured with his gun. "Line up against the wall."

Oh, I didn't like the sound of that. Nor did I particularly enjoy the sight of a few of Corbin's men drawing their own guns. We hadn't come unarmed, but we'd literally brought silver knives to a gun fight. My fingers inched to pull the blade and bury it so deep in Corbin's chest, he'd be spitting silver.

My pack did as he told us, but we faced forward. He could at least look us in the eyes before killing us.

"Where's Brandon?" Corbin demanded, stalking toward me. He didn't stop until he stood half a foot away, his gun too close for comfort.

"Where are Laini, Lincoln, and Scotia?"

He waved his gun in the air. "They're around."

"So's Brandon."

Corbin eyed me, anger flashing in his eyes. "I want my pack mate back."

"Ditto," I retorted.

Corbin growled, and lashed out, the butt of his gun striking my cheek. I heard the crack before I felt the pain, and my eyes instantly watered as my head snapped to the side.

Sam unleashed a hair-raising snarl and lunged at Corbin, only to be restrained at the last moment by three of Corbin's men. Sam thrashed in their grasp, his eyes burnished gold as he stared Corbin down.

"Touch her again, and I'll rip you limb from limb," Sam threatened, his voice guttural with his wolf.

Corbin completely ignored him and kept his focus on me. "I'm only going to ask you once more."

I worked out my jaw but refrained from touching my cheek. I had a feeling my body wouldn't enjoy that too much. "You can ask me as many times as you want. Until you return my pack members, I'm not returning yours."

"They're not even your pack members anymore," Corbin snapped. "They're *mine*."

My eyes narrowed, and even that slight movement hurt.

"They *chose* to be turned. I gave them the option, and they said yes. That makes them mine."

I fought back the urge to accuse him of lying. It

truly didn't matter whether or not he was telling the truth. "Funny, considering your pack doesn't even belong to you."

Corbin froze, anger reddening his face.

"Yeah, Brandon told me everything," I crowed. Probably not the best thing to do when someone held a gun to you, but I couldn't help myself. I loathed the man and loved being able to rub something in his face.

"Who is she?" I needled. "Brandon told me you've grown close to her too. Tell me something Corbin. Couldn't hold the pack yourself, so you started fucking her? Made yourself an alpha by association?"

His face mottled. I had two seconds to scold myself for letting my mouth run amok before Corbin sucker punched me in the gut, then backhanded me across the same cheek as before. Stars erupted behind my eyes and for a moment, I couldn't hear anything except the ringing in my ears.

Groaning, I held my hand to my cheek and leaned my head back against the wall, my eyes closed. How was it men always knew the exact place to strike a woman to cause the most pain?

When the world finally returned to normal, I found Sam kneeling in front of me, fury burning in his eyes. Corbin stood behind Sam, and had the gun pressed to the back of his head.

Every inch of me turned to solid ice.

"That's better," Corbin said. "A little respect, Lucy."

I bit back a snide retort about him having to earn respect. The comment wasn't worth a bullet in Sam's head.

"Now, I'm only going to ask once more—"

Yeah, he'd said that already.

"Where's Brandon?"

"At my house," I bit out, my gaze locked with Sam's.

A tic formed at his temple as his jaw tightened, but he didn't speak or move. Not with the three wolves holding him down and the gun held against him.

"Thank you," Corbin said.

My heart thundered in my head, my focus flicking to Corbin's hand. His finger rested against the trigger a little too casually for my liking. I needed to take back control of this situation, but honestly, I had no idea how. The odds weren't in our favor, not with Corbin's armed men holding my pack hostage. But I couldn't stand here and watch as they executed my pack one by one. I needed to give Olivia and Jorge time to do something.

"Did my people really agree to let you turn them?" I asked, hoping to get Corbin talking.

"Two out of three," he said, "but that's not a bad ratio."

That lined up with what Brandon had said—that Laini and Lincoln had agreed. But what about Scotia? Had he forced the change on her?

"So this entire time, you've been doing the dirty work for another alpha?"

Corbin's gaze slitted, but after a moment, he shrugged. "It isn't dirty if you enjoy the work."

Okay, gross.

I studied the three wolves holding Sam and recognized two. I'd fought them in the park. That bolstered my confidence a bit. If I'd been able to handle them all by myself, surely Sam and I could take the three out together. My pack would have to fend for themselves and take down the rest of Corbin's men. Better that than let them shoot us.

Maybe I could draw Corbin away from Sam somehow. Get the gun pointed at me. Without the gun in play, Sam could defend himself. And that was all that mattered.

"Who is she?" I asked. "This mystery woman?"

Corbin waved his free hand. "Don't worry about her. She's none of your concern."

"Did she come with you from England?" I already knew the answer, but I was just trying to get him talking long enough for me to come up with a plan.

"No."

Okay, one-worded answers certainly weren't going to help us here.

"And she wants the Mississippi Pack? Why?"

"Why all these questions?" Corbin replied. "It doesn't matter. You won't be around long enough to need to know."

"Then tell me now," I said. "For curiosity's sake."

He scoffed and shook his head. "You astound me. Here I am, holding a gun to your mate's head, and you want to play Twenty Questions."

"Just trying to understand you better," I said.

"You don't need to understand me better. Now shut up."

Before I could reply, Corbin fished a phone out of his pocket and dialed a number. I eyed the gun, watched it waver and dip downward. Watched Corbin's focus on it slip as he lifted the phone to his ear. Calling his alpha, most likely. But maybe this was the advantage we needed.

I turned my gaze on Sam and gave an almost imperceptible nod. Then I slowly glanced at the rest of my pack. Every last set of eyes were on me, their faces grim. They knew our chances, and from the determined looks on their faces, they didn't care. Each steadied themselves, a silent indication that they were ready to make a move.

Corbin shifted his weight slightly, to keep the phone out of sight. But it was the perfect distraction I needed.

Slowly reaching behind me, I drew my blade with one hand, while I willed my other to grow into claws, ignoring the burn of the shift. I caught Sam's gaze once more, and silently mouthed, "I love you."

Then I lunged at Sam's guards.

CHAPTER
TWENTY-THREE

CHAOS ERUPTED WITHIN THE WAREHOUSE. FOR A moment, a barrage of snarls and shouts rang through my ears, distracting me, but my focus narrowed back on my target the instant we collided. It was the one whose nose I'd broken in the park, and we pitched to the ground with me landing on top. His grunt vibrated through me, even as I struggled to gain the upper hand.

I jammed a knee in his gut and punched him as hard as I could. The hit landed awkwardly, and I felt my third knuckle pop out of place. But now wasn't the time for worrying about miniscule injuries. What was a dislocated knuckle compared to death if I let this wolf get the upper hand? Without even the slightest hesitation, I drove the silver blade hilt-deep into his chest. Blood seeped through his shirt, and the werewolf fell dead beneath me, his mouth gaping over. I'd never stabbed anyone before, and for a moment, I stared into his unseeing face, my pulse thundering in my ears.

Before Corbin, I'd never believed I was the kind of person who could kill someone. But since turning into a werewolf, I'd killed more than my share. The first—one of Corbin's men back in New Orleans—had nearly destroyed me. The guilt I'd felt had overwhelmed me, left me shaking in shock. Now, I hardly felt anything. Yeah, it sucked killing people. But better them than us.

I wrenched out the blade, then leaped to my feet and tackled one of the two remaining wolves grappling with Sam. They were battling for control, meaning their attention wasn't on me. Again, we went down in a lump. Cole had always cautioned me to keep my feet in a fight, but if there was one thing I'd learned, it was that fights were unpredictable at best. I couldn't control it any more than anyone else could. All I could do was adapt.

I rode the wolf to the ground, then drove my blade upward, spearing the wolf beneath the chin.

The blade cut through like butter, ending his life with hardly a final breath.

Hands gripped my waist, and I came up swinging, only to hold back at the sight of Sam. He lifted me to my feet, then tucked me behind him. A small growl slipped past my lips, until I realized Sam wasn't protecting me because he didn't think I could handle myself. He was protecting me because he *loved* me. Two very different reasons, the latter of which I completely understood. I didn't want him anywhere near this mess either. Especially considering this was *my* mess. If Sam had stayed in New Orleans, he'd be safe right now.

However, I couldn't hide behind Sam and do nothing. Not when my pack was here, fighting for their damn lives.

At the sound of a loud gunshot, I jumped and gripped Sam's arm. A thump quickly followed, and I whirled around in search of the victim. I only hoped it was one of theirs. But too many bodies littered the ground for me to know who'd just fallen.

I had to put a stop to all this. Now.

Shoving past Sam, I bolted into the fray in search of Corbin, only to find him attempting to flee. He moved toward the back of the warehouse, two of his men flanking him, and his gun in hand.

Oh hell no. He wasn't getting away this time. The man was slipperier than an eel, but this time, I'd rip him to pieces. After I got my answers, of course.

My eyes quickly shunted to the side, where I found my pack struggling to take down Corbin's. The guns gave my pack a drastic disadvantage. Cursing, I reached for the nearest asshole, latched on to his arm, and snapped it in two. His gun fell to the ground with a clatter.

A quick kick to the closest knee had the werewolf dropping to the ground with a sharp cry. I scrambled to pick up the gun, then fired a single bullet into his head. We were so close, I'd barely needed to aim, which was good, because I had zero knowledge of how to shoot a gun.

The werewolf collapsed in a bloody heap, and I stared at the gun, almost offended by it.

"Let me," Sam said, his hand scooping the weapon from my hand.

I relinquished it willingly, hating how it felt between my fingers. The unfamiliar weight, the uncomfortable kick back.

Sam took aim and as quickly as a professional sharpshooter, he took out two of Corbin's men. The second Corbin's remaining pack mates figured out that our side had turned the tide, they started to break apart, unable to maintain control.

A few of Corbin's people whirled and returned fire, but their clear lack of training failed them, and my pack took them out. I watched as one by one, they fell dead in the middle of the room.

Relief scoured through me at the sight of my pack mates. Two lay on the ground, bleeding but not dead. The rest remained standing. Unlike Corbin's people who littered the ground. I couldn't focus on that though, couldn't let it distract me from the main goal.

Without a word, I bolted into action and took chase after Corbin and his two remaining men. Footsteps rushed behind me, and a quick inhalation told me it was Sam.

"Corbin!" I shouted just as he slipped out the door.

I reached the exit, then leapt back into the warehouse when I caught sight of Corbin lifting his gun. Two shots rang out in quick succession, both hitting the warehouse wall.

Cursing, I gripped my blade's hilt and considered my choices.

No matter what, I couldn't let them escape.

Which meant bolting out in the open with the possibly of Corbin shooting us.

Sucking in a deep breath, I dropped low to the ground and exploded out the back door. Corbin and his men were already to the grass, vanishing in the tall reeds. He half-turned and fired off a few errant shots, but none hit us. Thank god.

I raced forward and called on every ounce of strength I possessed. This ended tonight. I wasn't going through all this again. Corbin died. Here. Now.

My feet ate up the distance between us, and at the first chance, I lunged and took Corbin out at the knees, his gun tumbling into the grass. He was quicker than his pack mates, though. And before I could even gather my wits, he'd shoved me off him and jumped to his feet. He delt a swift kick to my ribs, but I blocked the pain from my mind as I rolled out of reach for the second kick I knew was coming.

Out of the corner of my eye, I saw Sam engage the other two wolves, leaving it down to me and Corbin. Just the way I wanted it.

I leapt to my feet and lowered my arms in time to block another kick, then gripped my blade and swiped at his throat. The edge grazed his flesh, not nearly as deep as I would have liked, but enough to spill his blood. And silver wounds wouldn't heal as quickly.

Corbin choked on a breath and staggered backward, his hands cupping his neck. I didn't give him time to recuperate, unleashing a series of attacks that Cole had taught me. I lost myself in the flurry of movements, letting my body lead the way. My strikes were fluid and powerful, the blade cutting him again and again. If I had to slowly bleed him out, I could do that.

Frustration welled within me every time he blocked an attack. With every hit, I took an ounce of his flesh and blood, but it didn't seem to be enough to slow him. Cole's final lesson had taught me well, taught me how to read his body language, and most importantly, taught me how to remain focused. No matter how badly I wanted to check on Sam and see how he fared, I couldn't break contact with Corbin, couldn't look away. Doing so would give Corbin the exact moment he needed.

Crying out, I attempted every move Cole had taught me. I needed to take Corbin down, so I could restrain and question him. I needed answers regarding this new alpha. Needed her identity. But he was too quick, too strong.

A pained grunt cut through my rage-induced

haze, and I watched as Sam fell. Corbin's men descended on him, kicking and hammering at every inch of his body.

"Sam!" I shouted, thoroughly distracted now.

The word had barely left my mouth when *slam*! Something hard connected with my already abused cheek. The world spun as I toppled helplessly to the ground. Shit. Shit. Shit. I couldn't see, couldn't think. But I could hear. And I heard the telltale click of a gun being cocked.

Triple shit.

I couldn't die here. Couldn't leave Sam. Couldn't let Corbin kill me.

I lashed out, thrusting my arm forward, my blade an extension of my arm. I felt it slide through him, heard the telltale hiss of pain, and heard him stagger backward.

I blinked and shook my head, if only to clear the dust from my vision.

When I could finally see, I found Corbin kneeling in the grass and clutching at the blade I'd buried four inches deep in his belly. But it was the sight of his gun lying next to him in the grass that sent fear coursing through me. I scrambled across the grass, crying out when my fingers closed around the chilled weapon.

I snatched up the gun, then whirled on my knees. Corbin's wolves stood in front me. I pulled the trigger twice, my body absorbing the recoil with each shot. The two toppled to their knees, their hands gripping their chests. With matching shocked expressions, they both collapsed into the grass. I stole a quick glance at Sam only to find him gathering himself, then whirled back around on my knees to aim the gun at Corbin. He held my blade in his hands, blood flowing freely from his stomach and staining his hands.

He lifted his head and stared at me, just as surprised as me that we'd won.

"Give me her name," I growled.

He leaned over and spat a mouthful of blood onto the ground. "Fuck. You."

I studied him and wondered if I could terrorize him into giving me the information as I had Brandon. But a thought occurred to me. Every second I let him live was another chance he had in escaping, in causing more chaos, in hurting another person I loved. And I couldn't allow that.

So even though the old Lucy had loathed violence, and would never have imagined herself killing someone in cold blood, the new Lucy didn't share those qualms. Not with these people. Not after everything they'd done. Not only had Corbin nearly killed me, but he'd also nearly killed my parents. No, he *had* killed one of them. My mother would rise as a vampire. The undead. I also couldn't forget that he'd killed Sam's little sister. And that was the only motivation I needed. I absolutely refused to give him a second chance to start this madness up again.

I didn't have his alpha's name, but I had a feeling I'd be able to figure it out with time. Letting Corbin live just so I could learn a name seemed stupid. The risk wasn't worth it. In my opinion, a dead Corbin was the best option.

So, locking eyes with him, I said, "Goodbye, Corbin."

His briefly widened before I pulled the trigger.

I made sure to watch as the bullet ended his life. Watch as Corbin's eyes went from shocked and frightened to unseeing. Watched as every last bit of life drained away from his body.

And only then did I release the gun. It fell to the ground with a soft thud, the grass absorbing the sound.

Wow. Corbin was dead.

And I...

Felt nothing.

What did that say about me? About the person I'd become? That I could so coldly kill someone.

Honestly, I didn't want to think about that right now.

Instead, I just wanted to focus on the win. Corbin was dead. And Sam, my pack, and I were all alive. That was a pretty damn fine win in my books.

"Are you okay?" came Sam's rough voice as he picked up the gun and checked the chamber and magazine. Only one bullet left. To think how close we'd come to losing.

"I'm okay, I think. You?" I faced Sam, kneeling in the grass in front of him. His face was one giant bruise, and he was clutching his ribs, but otherwise, he seemed alright. Thank goodness for that. A good sleep would take care of most of that.

Sam lifted his hand and touched my cheek, his face breaking when I winced.

"I'll be okay," I said. "But you didn't answer me. How are you?"

"Fine," he said gruffly. "Nothing I can't handle. I've had worse than this."

"You have?" I asked, raising a brow.

"Well, I can't think of when right now, but I'm pretty sure I have."

Considering Sam's siblings were all sisters, I

highly doubted it. It wasn't like he had a bunch of brothers to roughhouse with. And his parents were the best kind of parents, the kind that never harmed their children intentionally. So unless he had some friends out there that he enjoyed engaging in a fight club with, I highly doubted he'd ever had worse than this.

Sam's focus dropped to Corbin. "I can't believe he's dead."

A faint thread of guilt wove through me, one I snipped and tossed aside as quickly as possible. Corbin didn't deserve my guilt. He'd caused so much pain.

"We should get back inside," I said. "Check on the rest of the pack."

Sam nodded, then slowly pushed to his feet, helping me up as he went. I didn't hurt too badly for once. Guess Anna's and Cole's lessons had really paid off. And speaking of Anna... I knew I should call her. Let her know we were fine and would be heading home soon. She and Vlad had wanted to accompany us, but honestly, I'd just wanted them to stay with my mother. She was vulnerable right now. Unable to defend herself. My father, at least, was in the hospital, which I hoped would keep him safe. But my mother...

No. I needed them to stay with her, in case Corbin had something tragic planned for her.

I reached into my back pocket for my phone, but paused at the sound of approaching footsteps. I lifted my head, relaxing at the sight of Olivia. She stared at me, then her gaze dropped to the ground where Corbin lay. Something flickered in her eyes, a darkness I'd never seen before. It made me wonder if he'd been part of the attack on her house, if he'd hurt her. Her expression was terrifying. Enraged. And it gave me chills.

"Olivia?"

Her gaze flicked back to mine. "He's dead."

I nodded. "Are you okay?"

She didn't respond. She merely stood there, staring at me. Almost as though she couldn't comprehend that Corbin was dead.

"Olivia?" I repeated, braving a step toward her. I peered past her. "Where's Jorge?"

Something was going on in that head of hers. Corbin must have really done a number on her. But before I could figure it out, Olivia lifted her hand and aimed something at me, something that glinted in the moonlight. I barely had a chance to scream her name, barely felt the wind rustle near my head as someone shoved me aside just as her gun boomed. A second explosion came next, one closer to me. Then a scream. An enraged cry. Footsteps rushing toward us. People shouting.

But I couldn't focus on it. Couldn't focus on anything other than the sight of Sam sprawled on the ground, blood spreading across his chest.

CHAPTER
TWENTY-FOUR

"Sam..." I whispered, crawling on my hands and knees toward him. The gun hung loosely in his hand, now empty of bullets. I knocked it aside and latched onto his hand. "Sam?"

He didn't so much as twitch at the sound of his name.

"Sam!" I screamed. I pressed my hands against his chest and pushed with all my strength. Fear suffocated my heart as I leaned over him, whispering his name over and over again. This was the second time tonight I'd held a loved one's life in my hands. But this time, I didn't even know what happened.

Someone dropped to my side, their scent familiar. Cole.

"I-I don't know what happened. One moment

Olivia was here, and the next... Oh my god. Oh my god, Sam!"

"Lucy," Cole said, his voice low but urgent. "We need to get Sam back to the house so we can remove the bullet. Now."

I knelt there trembling, my hands shaking as I pressed them to his wound. I couldn't move. Couldn't think.

"Sam... Sam..."

"Lucy!" Cole shouted, his voice startling me out of my shock.

I lifted dead eyes. "Olivia did this."

He nodded, his expression gentle, as though speaking to a toddler.

"She meant to shoot me, I think... and Sam..."

"Pushed you out of the way," Cole said. "We saw. But Lucy, we can't sit here talking. We need to move."

I felt a shiver of emotion run through me. Why... why on earth would Olivia want me dead? I replayed the last few minutes. Recalled the look on her face when she'd spotted Corbin dead on the ground. The darkness in her eyes, the rage... something I felt festering within me now.

"Oh my god," I breathed, my words barely audible. "She's the alpha. And Corbin's lover. The look on her face. My god, *she's* the one responsible for all this!"

Cole's eyes widened. "Your sister?"

Why hadn't I seen it? How blind had I been to let this slip past me? How stupid was I?

"Lucy, we can discuss this later," Cole urged. "Right now, you need to let us take care of Sam. The longer we wait, the less chance he has of surviving."

His words distantly registered in my head, but the thought of removing my hands, of letting that blood run free again terrified me.

Cole's hands took mine and he lifted.

Sam's blood gushed and I cried out, wanting to throw myself on top of him. But I didn't. I restrained myself. I had to be strong. Had to let the pack help us. They knew what to do.

"Now!" Cole shouted.

The pack bolted into action. Three of them worked as one to lift Sam and get him to the car. They strained beneath his enormous size. I merely ran after them, all the while staring at my bloody hands.

"Where is she?" I demanded.

Cole didn't ask who I meant. Instead, he grabbed my phone and shot a quick text to Anna, warning her about our situation before saying, "Sam got a shot off as he fell. Got her in the shoulder. She ran."

Escaped, so she could try to kill us another day. I still couldn't believe it. My own sister. Why was I so surprised? It wasn't like I knew her. We'd only spoken twice for crying out loud. And I'd believed every word she'd fed me, believing the worst in Reggie, because that was who I'd known him to be.

But Olivia? I'd fallen for those gentle green eyes and shy smile.

If Corbin was her lover, I had to assume everything else she'd told us was a lie as well. No fiancé, no home in the city... Hell, she'd probably handed Scotia over to Corbin, then had him rough her up to look the part. Had she been planning this since Reggie turned her? I'd fallen for all of it. Even let her lead me and the most dominant members of my pack right into this trap.

"Meredith is enroute to your house," Cole continued. "She'll be there waiting for us."

I nodded, grateful for the pack doctor.

"What about Jorge?" I asked. I'd left him with Olivia. He had to be here somewhere. But I couldn't see him among the throng of pack members.

Cole shot me a look, then shook his head, telling

me everything I needed to know. She'd killed him. But I couldn't focus on that now.

My people loaded Sam into the car, and I crawled into the back with him, once again pressing my hands against his chest. It was a forty-minute drive back to my place. But at this time of night, we could make it in twenty if we broke every law in the book. Which we would. I didn't care if the police tried to pull us over. Saving Sam's life mattered more.

"Go!" I ordered the second Cole hopped behind the wheel.

He tore out, the wheels screeching against the road the second they connected. I stared at Sam's face and counted every single strained breath. They were slowing. Oh Christ, they were slowing. He was dying right beside me.

"Cole!" I shouted. "Faster."

I felt the car lurch when Cole pressed the gas pedal against the floor of the car. We had to make it. We *had* to. Because I wouldn't accept anything else. Suddenly, I knew how Sam must have felt when Corbin stabbed me. The anxiety, the utter fear, the impending grief. My brain kept telling me he was dead, but then I'd feel his chest struggle to rise, and my heart would tell my brain to shut up.

Finally—*finally*—we slammed on the brakes in front of my house.

Cole had barely parked the car before the back doors were ripped open and my people stared in at us. Gentle hands lifted Sam out, then as a team, they rushed him inside. I raced after them, my heart hammering in my chest.

We dashed inside only to find the house already set up.

Vlad had dragged the kitchen table into the living room to give us more room to work. They laid Sam down on top, then immediately set to action.

Someone shoved me aside, and I unleashed a threatening growl, one that had every last werewolf lifting their head in reverence.

"It's Meredith," Cole said.

Right. The doctor. I gave a jerky nod and stepped aside. If anyone could save him, it would be her. I had to trust that.

"Lucy?" came Anna's soft voice.

I lifted my head, and at the sight of her worried face, I nearly broke down into tears. But I held myself together. For Sam.

She must have caught the gist of my emotions, because after a few seconds, she nodded, then walked over and took my hand. Together, we stood there silently and watched as Meredith worked on Sam.

Every second was pure agony for me, but I was so grateful Sam hadn't woken for any of it. Werewolves metabolized drugs too quickly for anesthesia to work. If he'd been awake, he would have felt every cut, every inch of her rooting around inside his chest.

After what felt like an eternity, something metal clinked into a nearby bowl, and Meredith sagged with relief.

"I got it," she said to the entire room. "Now he just needs to heal."

"Will he, though?" I pressed.

"The bullet wasn't silver, so he should. We'll know more soon, once his body starts regenerating."

Relief had me gripping Anna's hand so hard she sucked in a sharp breath. I shot her an apologetic wince, then let go. She could handle it, but I really didn't want to break her hand. Instead, I stood there and counted Sam's breaths and heartbeats while Meredith bandaged his chest.

"Come sit," Anna urged me. "Take a second to breathe. Sam's okay."

I released a harsh breath, then slumped into a

nearby chair. I couldn't believe how close I'd come to losing him.

"He's okay," Anna repeated, crouching next to me. "But are you okay?"

I waved a flippant hand. "All surface bruising. Nothing serious. I'll be fine."

She cupped the back of my head. "Good. Can you tell us what happened?"

I sat up and stared at my pack, who all watched with a keen eye. Half hadn't come with us to the warehouse, so they were as oblivious as Anna.

"It was a trap," I said. "Set up by Olivia, I think."

"Olivia," Anna repeated. "Your sister?"

Ugh, the betrayal stung. "I think she's the alpha Brandon was telling us about. She certainly was in love with Corbin. The look on her face when she realized I'd killed him—"

"Corbin's dead?" Anna asked.

"Yeah. Yeah, he's dead."

The pack released a collective breath.

"We killed quite a few of his pack members, but I'm not sure if it was all of them."

"But Olivia survived?" she asked.

"Yeah." Memories flashed through my mind. "She saw Corbin and tried to kill me. Sam..." My voice broke. "Sam pushed me out of the way. She shot him instead."

"He got her, though" Cole announced. "So she's injured too."

I waved another hand. "Not silver. So she'll be back on her feet in no time." I just couldn't believe it. Olivia. All this time.

"Do you think she lied about being your sister?" Anna asked.

I shook my head. "No, she has Reggie's eyes. The same eyes I have. She's my sister. But she's..."

"Insane," Anna finished.

I winced. "Look, I don't want to think about this right now. I just want to get Sam tucked into bed and check on my parents. Olivia can wait until tomorrow."

Anna slung an arm around me and squeezed. "Why don't you take a quick shower. I'll get Sam settled into bed."

I shook my head, refusing to leave his side, but Anna wouldn't hear of it.

"I'll sit with him while you clean yourself up. Just take a moment to relax, okay? It's been a tough night."

I glanced down at myself and saw what Anna meant. I was covered in blood. Mine, Sam's,

Corbin's, and everyone else's. I looked like a monster. Grateful for her assistance, I patted her hand, then rose to my feet. "Go home," I told the pack. "Get some sleep. Hug your loved ones. Corbin is dead, so we won tonight."

"But what about Laini, Lincoln, and Scotia?" someone asked.

Right. I hadn't broken that news to them. "From the sounds of it, Laini and Lincoln willingly joined Corbin's pack. I don't know about Scotia. All I can say is she wasn't at the warehouse. None of them were."

Disappointment flashed in a few of their eyes, and I couldn't help but wonder if it was disappointment with me, or their pack mates for choosing to join Corbin's cause. Honestly, I wasn't sure I wanted to find out.

"Go home," I repeated. "Cole and I will reach out when we learn anything new. In the meantime, get some rest."

It didn't take long for my house to empty of werewolves, and I found myself breathing a little easier. Even Cole left. All that remained were me, Sam, Vlad, Anna, and my parents. True to her word, Anna was sitting with Sam, monitoring his vitals while I showered.

The room filled with steam as I scrubbed my skin raw. Once clean, I shut off the taps, dried off, then jumped into the nearest set of pajamas. I just wanted to get back to Sam. I needed to hear his heartbeat and feel him breathe. Just to reassure myself.

I entered my bedroom to find Anna still sitting in a chair next to the bed, her head tipped back and eyes closed. Her mouth curved though, so I knew she'd heard my approach.

"He's doing really well," she told me. "His heartbeat is getting stronger with every passing minute."

I closed my eyes and thanked the universe. His was a death I knew I couldn't handle. Alpha or not, I wasn't strong enough to survive that.

"You can go," I said. "I'll stay with him."

Anna opened her eyes. "You sure? I can stay with you."

"Thanks, but I've got it covered."

She nodded, then pushed to her feet with a grace I lacked. Before leaving, she paused at the door, her hand pressed on the frame. "I'm so glad you guys are alright." Then she slipped out.

I climbed into bed, and snuggled up against Sam. I intended to stay awake, to keep counting his heartbeats, but my exhaustion was stronger than my will, and I dropped into a dreamless sleep.

MOVEMENT STIRRED AGAINST MY SIDE.

I jerked awake and practically shot up in bed. Sam laid beside me, his eyes lazing open and a gentle smile curling his lips. At the sight of his beautiful face, something within me broke and a flood of tears cascaded down my cheeks. I didn't even attempt to stop them. They just kept coming.

Sam rose up on an elbow and brushed the tears from my face. "Shh."

My gaze dipped to his chest, the white gauze stark against his tanned skin. Spots of red bled through, but nothing serious.

"Don't. Ever. Do. That. Again," I growled, gesturing to his wound.

He gave a quiet chuckle, and it was a sound that soothed the raging beast within. But he didn't promise that he wouldn't take a bullet for me again, and when I attempted to press the matter further, he merely wrapped his arms around me and pulled me down into a deep snuggle.

I went without complaint, just happy to be in his

arms right now. Last night could have ended very differently—with me burying him instead of cuddling him. And ugh, wasn't that a dark thought. *Happy thoughts*, I told myself. Sam was alive. I was alive. Corbin was dead. All things to celebrate. Right now, nothing else mattered. Not even Olivia. I wouldn't let her steal this moment from us.

I tilted my head back and examined Sam. "You *are* okay, right?"

"Fit as a fiddle," he murmured, though his voice betrayed his exhaustion.

Shadows bruised his skin, and his mouth fell into a slack line. Not surprising, considering everything he'd been through. I snuggled closer, then rested a hand on his chest, reveling in the feel of his heartbeat against my palm.

Olivia had come so close to destroying everything that mattered to me. I wanted to know why. Surely, this couldn't be about some silly crusade. I didn't know the first thing about Olivia, but I hadn't picked up any genocidal vibes like that. Then again, I never would have imagined she'd betray us either. So what did I know?

"I can hear you thinking down there," Sam rumbled, his arms tightening around me. "Get some more sleep. Worry about everything else later."

I wasn't sure I could just turn my mind off like that. He was right, of course. These thoughts could wait for another day. Today should be about celebrating Sam and everything we'd accomplished. But the thoughts persisted, like little gnats gnawing at the outer edges of my brain. I wanted answers. I wanted reasons. Wanted to understand what had happened to Olivia to turn her into this?

"Lucy..." Sam grumbled.

Guess my thoughts were pretty loud. Which said a lot considering Sam and I couldn't read each other's minds like Anna could with animals.

"Sorry," I whispered. "It's just... you nearly died because of me."

Sam sighed, then rolled onto his side to face me, his head resting on a pillow. "No. I nearly died because of Olivia. There's a difference."

"Yeah, but Olivia is my sister."

"I never hold myself accountable for the actions of my sisters. Nor should you. They're their own people. We can't control what they do."

A fair point. Except, I still felt responsible. I should have seen the signs, should have delved deeper into her background, picked apart the story she'd told me.

"Lucy," Sam said again.

I met his gaze, then forced myself to smile. "Okay. Shutting my brain off now."

"Good." His gruff voice made me laugh.

Sam rolled onto his back and pulled me up against him. His contented purr helped me relax and push my dark thoughts to the farthest recesses of my mind.

It didn't take long for sleep to claim us again.

CHAPTER
TWENTY-FIVE

Sam and I slept deeply and contently. I woke first the next morning and left Sam to rest. The house was so quiet with the vampires all snoozing in their coffins and my father in the hospital. I took the time to call Cole and get an update, but he had no new information for me. Afterward, I prepared a meal high in protein, then woke Sam and helped him eat. The food brought a little color back to his cheeks, but the moment he swallowed the last bite, he fell back into a restful sleep.

As for me, I did the dishes, then stood in the living room, staring at the bloodstained floor. I so didn't want to deal with that right now. So instead, I crawled back into bed with Sam. For a moment, I wasn't sure I'd be able to sleep, seeing as how it was mid-day, but the moment Sam slung an arm around my waist, I closed my eyes and drifted off.

When my eyes finally opened, light filled the room. I squinted at the clock to find it was nine in the morning. The *next* morning. Damn. We'd slept all afternoon and night. Our poor bodies must have been so exhausted.

I slipped out of bed, but paused when I entered the living room. Someone had taken the time last night to clean the place from top to bottom. Not a drop of blood remained. I had a feeling Vlad had hired a professional company, and made a mental note to thank him.

I stepped into the kitchen and prepared another protein-rich meal for Sam and me. One he devoured within minutes before falling back into another deep sleep. I phoned Meredith to ask if that was normal, and she assured me it was. Relieved, I showered, then crawled back under the blankets, this time with a book. I managed to read three pages before I fell asleep with the book resting on my chest.

I wasn't sure how long we slept that time, but the sun was certainly shining again when I woke with Sam's mouth between my legs. It could have been days, for all I knew. My stomach certainly felt as though I'd starved it. While that might have concerned me, the feel of Sam's hot, wet mouth at the apex of my thighs had me focusing entirely on him.

"Feeling better then, I presume?" I managed to whisper around a sharp breath.

"I was hungry," he teased, his lusty eyes peering up at me from between my legs.

I choked out a laugh, one that ended on a whisper of a moan. The man was a wizard with that tongue of his. And he knew exactly how to read my body. It wasn't long before my hands were fisting the sheets and I was crying out his name. Thankfully, the entire house was currently *dead* to the world, so for once, I didn't need to muffle my cries.

Still resting between my legs, Sam watched me as I orgasmed. Pure male satisfaction shone in that burning golden stare of his. I felt a bit like prey, captured by the big bad wolf, and I loved it.

"My, my, what a wicked tongue you have," I teased. Those weren't the exact words from Little Red Riding Hood, but hey, a girl was allowed to improvise.

"The better to taste you with, my dear," Sam replied before returning to his task at hand.

Hardly a breath passed before a second climax

swept through me, a bit weaker than the first, but pleasurable, nonetheless.

I rode the high and was enjoying all the colors in the rainbow, when Sam pulled me out of bed. Giggling, I followed as he led me into the en suite bathroom.

He sat me on the counter, then strode to the shower and turned the taps. Oh, goody! Shower sex time. One of my favorites. But first...

I reached for my toothbrush and quickly scrubbed out my mouth. No morning breath for me, thank you. Sam tested the water, then returned to the sink and did the same, rinsing out his mouth. The thought of minty fresh breath had me clenching my legs to hide my arousal. Not that it mattered. Sam could smell it, as evidenced by the manly smile tugging at the corner of his mouth.

"How are you feeling?" I asked, needing to know before we engaged in any rowdy activities that kicked his heart into overdrive.

"Like I could devour you," he said, leaning down to steal a kiss.

I leaned into his touch, my tongue happily tangling with his. But I stepped back before he could lead me into the shower. "Be serious, Sam. Please. I need to know."

"I feel fine, Luce. I promise. If it starts to feel like it's too much, I'll tell you."

"Swear?"

"Absolutely."

Smiling, I let him take my hand and lead me under the spray, though we were careful not to get his bandage wet. It needed to be changed regardless, but it seemed best to keep his top half as dry as possible.

Sam turned me and slowly started shampooing my hair. I moaned at the feel of his fingers massaging my scalp, and nearly melted into a puddle of goo at his feet. The conditioner came next. Then slowly, he washed my body, teasing me with gentle touches along the way. I returned the favor, my fingers stuttering to a stop over his chest, and my heart giving an unpleasant thump. It still frightened me to think how close I'd come to losing him yesterday.

"Shh," he murmured, his brow pressed against mine.

I needed to banish these thoughts. So, I looped my arms around his neck and kissed him, deeply, passionately, and a bit desperately. My mouth parted and our tongues came together in a sensual dance that had my knees going weak.

God, I loved this man with every fiber of my being.

The way he made me feel was indescribable. I'd hidden from him for so long, and we'd gone through things most couples wouldn't even understand. Things that had nearly separated us forever. But here we stood. Together. Stronger than ever. I had a feeling nothing would ever tear us apart. Sam was the other half of my soul, the piece that had always felt missing. And I would do anything to protect him. As he would me.

I lost myself in him then. Lost myself to the emotions and sensations he evoked in me. His every touch sparked a hungry flame that only he could sate. And when he slid within me, it felt as though the world had finally returned to normal.

Sam took his time, lavishing so much attention on me that my body felt pleasantly boneless. I relished the feel of him inside me. Savored the feel of his cock swelling and thickening seconds before he succumbed to his own orgasm. He gave a soft grunt as he poured everything he was into me, and I smiled, utterly content for the first time in days. Months even.

"Sam," I whispered, pushing his mop of wet hair back from his face.

His eyes opened, hazed with lust and pleasure, and he stared at me.

"I love you."

The smile he gave me made my heart skip a beat.

"And I love you."

I kissed the tip of his nose. "I know."

Laughing, Sam lowered me back onto my feet. We needed to wash up again, but thankfully, we were already in the shower. Once clean and dried, I changed Sam's bandage, then let him chase me back into bed. But sleep didn't come this time. Instead, Sam and I came—pun intended—again and again.

And I wouldn't have had it any other way.

One Month Later

I stumbled into my house, arms laden with grocery bags. "Hello?"

"Coming!" Anna shouted back. I knew she'd be awake, but thankfully, my mother and Vlad were still dead to the world. One upside to my mother being a vampire—she couldn't hound me every second of the day anymore.

I only wished she'd taken to the lifestyle better.

There'd been a slight... adjustment period. When she'd first woken, she'd sobbed for a week. Next came the anger—at both me and my father—for allowing this to happen to her. In a rather painful argument, she'd told us she'd rather we'd let her die. My father and I had lost it on her. Since then, she'd been a bit more sensitive about the things she said. But she hadn't gone home to my father yet, and she refused to let him come here. It would take time, I told him, for her to adjust. But I knew my father was going out of his mind. If my mother didn't cave soon, I had every intention of loading her coffin into a van while she slept and driving her back to Perish myself. She couldn't hide here forever.

"Damn girl." Anna whistled under her breath. "That's a lot of groceries. You do know it's only you and Sam who eat, right?"

I stared at the mountain of groceries and shrugged. "Truthfully, I went shopping on an empty belly. And I'm hungry. What can I say, we werewolves have high metabolisms. And I swear, Cole is here more than his house now."

Anna barked out her own laugh. "Isn't that the truth. He was here an hour or so ago, and he and Sam decided to do a loop around the neighborhood. You know, for safety measures."

I rolled my eyes. I wasn't sure what had caused it, but a couple weeks ago, Sam suddenly went into overprotective mode. He started doing these rounds —as he called them—to ensure everything was safe and quiet in the area. I questioned it at first, then decided it wasn't something I wanted to fight about. If him walking the neighborhood made him feel better, so be it.

Eventually, Cole had joined, claiming he saw the logic in Sam's decision.

Werewolves were a weird breed. And Sam and Cole were both feeling a bit at a loss. In the month since I'd killed Corbin, we'd heard nothing from Olivia or any of her remaining pack members. Perhaps they were just laying low, but I wasn't so sure about that. Considering Corbin and Olivia had loved each other, and I'd killed Corbin, I had a feeling she was out for blood.

Perhaps that was the reason behind Sam's sudden overprotectiveness. I couldn't go anywhere without him right now. The only reason I'd managed to do groceries by myself today was because I'd left while he was distracted. I'd received a few texts while out, cautioning me to be careful, and scolding me for going out without telling him. I'd merely rolled my eyes and pocketed my phone.

As I said, werewolves were a weird breed. If he kept this up, though, I'd have to show him just how capable of protecting myself I was.

Anna picked through the bags, and gave a quiet cheer when she found the bottle of fresh blood I'd grabbed her.

"Mm, thank you!" She leaned over and planted a kiss on my cheek, then pulled back with a confused frown.

"What's wrong?" I asked.

She leaned back in and sniffed my neck.

"Whoa!" I playfully shoved her away. "Your blood comes from the bottle, not my neck."

Anna caught her balance, but a perplexing frown lined her face. "You smell weird."

Laughter erupted from me. "Sorry? I'll go shower if it offends you so badly."

"Not offended. Just curious. Your scent doesn't usually change. I mean, sure, when you're a bit rank, I can smell it. And when you've had sex—"

"Oh my god, Anna." I waved her away. "I probably just stepped in something at the grocery store." I couldn't smell anything, but sometimes Anna's nose picked up things mine didn't. I could smell a wad of gum on the sidewalk three blocks away, but I couldn't smell the different flavors of blood like she could.

I started putting the groceries away. When I reached for a top shelf, a slight cramp twinged in my side, and I winced. I rubbed the offending spot, and the cramp slowly dissipated. Weird, I'd never felt anything like that before.

"What's wrong?" Anna asked.

"Nothing," I assured her, shaking my head. Everyone was a bit on edge still, thanks to Olivia. We were all coping, but sometimes I'd had to retreat into the bedroom for a few moments of peace and quiet.

My phone pinged, and I glanced down to find a text from Sam asking if I'd returned home yet.

With an eye-rolling emoji, I sent back yes, then continued unloading groceries. I'd bought enough stuff to feed the entire pack if necessary, which it might be considering how often many stopped by now. And if not, then I wouldn't need to do groceries for at least another month.

Closing the fridge, I turned around and practically shrieked. Anna stood an inch away from me, her eyes boring into mine and her face deathly serious. I clapped a hand to my chest and tried to side-step her. But every move I made, she countered.

"Okay, girl, you're freaking me out," I said, my

heart now racing a mile a minute.

Anna didn't respond. Instead, she reached for my hand and lifted it to her nose, inhaling deeply.

What. The. Hell.

"Anna?" I whispered, my voice meek. "What's wrong? You're scaring me."

She'd gone into full vampire mode, and my skin was practically crawling. Right now, she didn't look a thing like my friend, and instead looked for all the world like a monster about to devour me.

"Anna?" I whispered again.

Her eyes, a shade darker than normal, lifted to mine. "Trust me."

Those two words loosened something in my chest. "Care to tell me what's going on?"

"I'm going to bite you," she said.

"What? No, you're not!"

"Lucy." She blinked, and the monster faded until all that remained was Anna.

I breathed a little easier.

"Trust me," she said.

"Why... why do you need to bite me?"

"I'll let you know after, if my suspicions are correct."

"Suspicions?" I repeated. What the hell was going on?

Before I could demand more answers, Anna pressed her teeth into my wrist. She took care not to harm me, and her teeth were so sharp, I barely felt it. Anna had *never* bitten me before. We'd come to that agreement when she'd first changed.

I sucked in a sharp breath at the sensations that darted up my arm. I knew a vampire's bite was pleasurable, but since I'd never experienced it before, I didn't realize *how* pleasurable. And I wasn't too comfy feeling certain things for my best friend that I'd never felt before.

Clearing my throat, I tried to tug my arm back, but Anna held tight. She didn't hurt me, though. Nor did she start feasting on my arm. She took a couple sips, then released my arm and stood back.

I cupped my wrist to my chest. "Care to tell me what that was about?"

"I've had werewolf blood before," she told me. "You can buy it on the streets, similarly to human blood. They donate it just like humans do. There's a little kick in werewolf blood that vampires enjoy."

"Gross!" I told her. "Did you seriously bite me to get a special snack?"

"No. I only mentioned it so you'd know that I know what werewolf blood tastes like."

"Okay..." Was she trying to tell me I wasn't a

werewolf?

"You smell different," she said. "And I couldn't place it, so I wanted to taste your blood. Make sure you hadn't been poisoned or something."

My breath caught. "Oh my god. Has someone poisoned me?" Had Olivia done something that we weren't aware of?

"No. Your blood is clean of toxins."

Relief had me slumped against the counter—a relief so strong that I felt a little dizzy. Damn, Anna must have really frightened me there.

"I did taste something, though," Anna continued. "And if I'm right..."

My head snapped back up and I stared at her, even as the world starting spinning. She'd tasted *something* in my blood? Not a poison, though. Was I sick? Could werewolves get sick?

"If I'm right, you need to go back to the grocery store," Anna said.

"What, why?" All this anticipation was killing me. "Just tell me, for crying out loud. What's wrong with me?"

A flicker of a smile chased across her face, but it was more sympathetic than happy. I didn't quite know what to make of that.

"Lucy, I think you're pregnant."

EPILOGUE

I KNOW I'M SUPPOSED TO SAY SOMETHING HERE. Recap everything that went down but I'm... at a loss.

And why?

Because I'm staring at a stupid plastic stick with two stupid lines stretched across it. The instructions assure me that means I'm definitely pregnant. And I...

I...

I don't know what to think. Or say. Or do.

It explains so much. Especially Sam's sudden overprotectiveness. Anna had been the one to detect the change in my scent and deduce I might be pregnant, but on some subconscious level, Sam must know too, even if he doesn't *know* he knows. So why am I the last one to find out? Shouldn't I have been the first?

I haven't told Sam yet. Haven't even begun to process this yet.

I'm on birth control, for crying out loud. Not that birth control is foolproof. And we haven't exactly been using condoms. But I mean...

Oh my god.

Oh my *god*.

I'm so stupid.

Birth control is a drug.

And werewolves metabolize drugs too quickly to be effective. How many times have I heard that? How many times have I *told* myself that? I've been taking something that's likely far less effective on my kind than humans. I never even gave that a thought. Clearly, Sam hadn't either. But shouldn't he know about this? His sisters are werewolves, for crying out loud. I couldn't imagine his mother would forget to mention such a thing. Then again, most werewolves are born as such and grow up with this knowledge.

What am I going to do?

This isn't the right moment to have a kid. I have priorities. Responsibilities. A pack that depends on me. An alpha werewolf-slash-sister out to kill me. And a vampiric mother who needs help adjusting to her new life. Isn't that enough without throwing a baby into the mix?

Good lord, someone send chocolate.

Not that I can actually eat any...

Oh man. A chocolate-less pregnancy.

Now that's pure evil.

WEDDING THE WOLFMAN SNEAK PEEK

Taking my hands in his, Sam gave them a squeeze before pulling them upward and resting them on his chest. "In a perfect world, I would have taken you out tonight. We would have gone to dinner at a fancy restaurant to celebrate our news, then I would have taken you for a walk in the moonlight. We would have shifted and run free through the woods. And once we'd shifted back, I would have made love to you under the stars."

I shivered. "That sounds wonderful."

"It does. And when we've put all this behind us, when we've handled Olivia, we'll do just that." He lifted one hand from mine and brushed my hair back from my cheek. "I know we didn't have the easiest start to our relationship. We've faced many obstacles, but we're here together. We've survived more challenges than a normal couple. Faced separation and death. Grief and loss. And we've come out of it stronger than ever. I know, as do you, that you're my soulmate."

A smile touched my lips. That was one thing I knew without a doubt.

"I've known since the day we met that we were destined to be together. And I know that we'll be together until our dying days." He dropped a hand into his front pocket and withdrew a box.

At the sight of the black velvet, my heart slammed into my ribs. "Sam—"

"Now, before you start panicking, I want you to know that I've been working on this for a few weeks now."

"Working on what?"

He eased open the lid, and my heart stopped dead at the sight of the most beautiful ring I'd ever seen. My breath whooshed past my lips, and I clapped my hands to my mouth.

"Would you believe I got the call this afternoon that this was ready to be picked up?" he asked, chuckling. "Providence, I say. I'd planned to pick it up tomorrow, but then you told me you're pregnant, and I just couldn't wait any longer."

Speechless, I stared at the gorgeous ring, glimmering up at me from inside its velvet case.

"The band is from my grandmother's wedding ring," Sam said. "And the first gem, this one here"—he pointed at the moonlit black diamond—"is from my great-grandmother's wedding ring. I had the jeweler add an accent diamond for every person we love to symbolize the joining of our two families."

Tears stung my eyes. "Sam..." My voice came out hoarse. "It's beautiful."

It was more than beautiful. It was downright stunning. The entire piece reminded me of the night sky, sparkling with countless stars surrounding the full moon. To think that he'd done this, that he'd been working on this without my knowledge, robbed me of breath.

"My mother gave me the original ring when she first met you," he said, his voice full of warmth. "She said she knew the second she saw us together that we would be eternal. I asked if I could change a few things, and she loved my idea."

Still stricken speechless, I tore my gaze from the ring and stared up at him, tears sliding down my cheeks as I did.

"Lucy, I love you more than anything. You're all I want, all I'll ever want, and all I'll ever need. Fate knew exactly what it was doing when it brought us together. You're the reason my heart beats, the reason I smile, the reason I live. No matter the obstacles we face, no matter what happens in life, I will always love you." He sucked in a deep breath, then stared deeply into my eyes. "Will you marry me?"

ACKNOWLEDGMENTS

Thank you so much to everyone who helped spit shine this book into existence.

I feel like I say this with every book, but this one was certainly challenging. I can't even remember why, my brain is all mushy.

But as always, I need to think my editors and critique group for all the hard work they put into this. So, thank you Missy and Elizabeth. Without you two, this book would look like a pile of poo.

I'd always like to acknowledge my cover artist. She always kills it with these covers.

Thanks, everyone!

ABOUT THE AUTHOR

Kinsley Adams is a thirty-something-year-old author who stopped counting when she turned twenty-five. When she isn't writing uproariously hilarious romantic comedies, she's raising her womb-gremlin with the hopes that he might one day become the world's first Supreme Leader (and yes, *Debbie*, that's a Star Wars joke). You can find her and her books online at kinsleyadams.com.

If you enjoyed this book, please leave a review! Your support and feedback are greatly appreciated. And be sure to sign up for Kinsley's newsletter at kinsleyadams.com/newsletter for updates on new releases, sales, and more!

ALSO BY KINSLEY ADAMS

DATING MONSTER MAIN SERIES

DATING DRACULA

LOVING DRACULA

MARRYING DRACULA

WOOING THE WOLFMAN

MATING THE WOLFMAN

WEDDING THE WOLFMAN

SMITTEN WITH THE VAMPIRE KING

HOOKED ON THE VAMPIRE KING

HITCHED ON THE VAMPIRE KING

DATING MONSTERS SIDE STORIES

WHEN VLAD MET ANNA

MR. & MRS. DRACULA

MONSTERS & CHOCOLATE

www.ingramcontent.com/pod-product-compliance
Lightning Source LLC
Chambersburg PA
CBHW020251030726
47499CB00001B/153